CW00854520

The Lure of the Mask

Harold MacGrath

Contents

Chapter 1 *THE VOICE IN THE FOG*

Out of the unromantic night, out of the somber blurring January fog, came a voice lifted in song, a soprano, rich, full and round, young, yet matured, sweet and mysterious as a night-bird's, haunting and elusive as the murmur of the sea in a shell: a lilt from *La Fille de Madame Angot*, a light opera long since forgotten in New York. Hillard, genuinely astonished, lowered his pipe and listened. To sit dreaming by an open window, even in this unlovely first month of the year, in that grim unhandsome city which boasts of its riches and still accepts with smug content its rows upon rows of ugly architecture, to sit dreaming, then, of red-tiled roofs, of cloud-caressed hills, of terraced vineyards, of cypresses in their dark aloofness, is not out of the natural order of things; but that into this idle and pleasant dream there should enter so divine a voice, living, feeling, pulsing, this was not ordinary at all.

And Hillard was glad that the room was in darkness. He rose eagerly and peered out. But he saw no one. Across the street the arc-lamp burned dimly, like an opal in the matrix, while of architectural outlines not one remained, the fog having kindly obliterated them.

The Voice rose and sank and soared again, drawing nearer and nearer. It was joyous and unrestrained, and there was youth in it, the touch of spring and the breath of flowers. The music was Lecocq's, that is to say, French; but the tongue was of a country which Hillard knew to be the garden of the world. Presently he observed a shadow emerge from the yellow mist, to come within the circle of light, which, faint as it was, limned in against the nothingness beyond the form of a woman. She walked directly under his window.

As the invisible comes suddenly out of the future to assume distinct proportions which either make or mar us, so did this unknown cantatrice come out of the fog that night and enter into Hillard's life, to readjust its ambitions, to divert its aimless course, to give impetus to it, and a directness which hitherto it had not known.

"Ah!"

He leaned over the sill at a perilous angle, the bright coal of his pipe spilling comet-wise to the area-way below. He was only subconscious of having spoken; but this syllable was sufficient to spoil the enchantment. The Voice ceased abruptly, with an odd break. The singer looked up. Possibly her astonishment surpassed even that of her audience. For a few minutes she had forgotten that she was in New York, where romance may be found only in the book-shops; she had forgotten that it was night, a damp and chill forlorn night; she had forgotten the pain in her heart; there had been only a great and irresistible longing to sing.

Though she raised her face, he could distinguish no feature, for the light was behind. However, he was a man who made up his mind quickly. Brunette or blond, beautiful or otherwise, it needed but a moment to find out. Even as this decision was made he was in the upper hall, taking the stairs two at a bound. He ran out into the night, bareheaded. Up the street he saw a flying shadow. Plainly she had anticipated his impulse and the curiosity behind it. Even as he gave chase the shadow melted in the fog, as ice melts in running waters, as flame dissolves in sunshine. She was gone. He cupped his ear with his hand; in vain, there came no sound as of pattering feet; there was nothing but fog and silence.

"Well, if this doesn't beat the Dutch!" he murmured.

He laughed disappointedly. It did not matter that he was three and thirty; he still retained youth enough to feel chagrined at such a trivial defeat. Here had been something like a genuine adventure, and it had slipped like water through his clumsy fingers.

"Deuce take the fog! But for that I'd have caught her."

But reason promptly asked him what he should have done had he caught the singer. Yes, supposing he had, what excuse would he have had to offer? Denial on her part would have been simple, and righteous indignation at being accosted on the street simpler still. He had not seen her face, and doubtless she was aware of this fact. Thus, she would have had all the weapons for defense and he not one for attack. But though reason argued well, it did not dislodge his longing. He would have been perfectly happy to have braved her indignation for a single glance at her face. He walked back, lighting his pipe. Who could she be? What peculiar whimsical freak had sent her singing past his window at one o'clock of the morning? A grand opera singer, returning home from a late supper? But he dismissed this opinion even as he advanced it. He knew something about grand opera singers. They attend late suppers, it is true, but they ride home in luxurious carriages and never risk their golden voices in this careless if romantic fashion. And in New York nobody took the trouble to serenade anybody else, unless paid in advance and armed with a police permit. As for being a comic-opera star, he refused to admit the possibility; and he relegated this well-satisfied constellation to the darks of limbo. He had heard a Voice.

A vast, shadow loomed up in the middle of the street, presently to take upon itself the solid outlines of a policeman who came lumbering over to add or subtract his quota of interest in the affair. Hillard wisely stopped and waited for him, pulling up the collar of his jacket, as he began to note that there was a winter's tang to the fog.

"Hi, what's all this?" the policeman called out roughly.

"To what do you refer?" Hillard counter-questioned, puffing. He slipped his hands into the pockets of his jacket.

"I heard a woman singin', that's what!" explained the guardian of the law.

"So did I."

"Oh, you did, huh?"

"Certainly. It is patent that my ears are as good as yours."

"Huh! See her?"

"For a moment," Hillard admitted.

"Well, we can't have none o' this in the streets. It's disorderly."

"My friend," said Hillard, rather annoyed at the policeman's tone, "you don't think for an instant that I was directing this operetta?"

"Think? Where's your hat?"

Hillard ran his hand over his head. The policeman had him here. "I did not bring it out."

"Too warm and summery; huh? It don't look good. I've been watchin' these parts fer a leddy. They call her Leddy Lightfinger; an' she has some O' the gents done to a pulp when it comes to liftin' jools an' trinkets. Somebody fergits to lock the front door, an' she finds it out. Why did you come out without yer lid?"

"Just forgot it, that's all."

"Which way'd she go?"

"You'll need a map and a search-light. I started to run after her myself. I heard a voice from my window; I saw a woman; I made for the street; *niente*!"

"Huh?"

"*Niente*, nothing!"

"Oh! I see; Dago. Seems to me now that this woman was singin' I-taly-an, too." They were nearing the light, and the policeman gazed intently at the hatless young man. "Why, it's Mr. Hillard! I'm surprised. Well, well! Some day I'll run in a bunch o' these chorus leddies, jes' fer a lesson. They git lively at the restaurants over on Broadway, an' thin they raise the dead with their singin', which, often as not, is anythin' but singin'. An' here it is, after one."

"But this was not a chorus lady," replied Hillard, thoughtfully reaching into his vest for a cigar.

"Sure, an' how do you know?" with renewed suspicions.

"The lady had a singing voice."

"Huh! They all think alike about that. But mebbe she wasn't bad at the business. Annyhow... ."

"It was rather out of time and place, eh?" helpfully.

"That's about the size of it. This Leddy Lightfinger is a case. She has us all thinkin' on our nights off. Clever an' edjicated, an' jabbers in half a dozen tongues. It's a thousan' to the man who jugs her. But she don't sing; at least, they ain't any report to that effect. Perhaps your leddy was jes' larkin' a bit. But it's got to be stopped."

Hillard passed over the cigar, and the policeman bit off the end, nodding with approval at such foresight. The young man then proffered the coal of his pipe and the policeman took his light therefrom, realizing that after such a peace-offering there was nothing for him to do but move on. Yet on dismal lonesome nights, like this one, it is a godsend and a comfort to hear one's own voice against the darkness. So he lingered.

"Didn't get a peep at her face?"

"Not a single feature. The light was behind her." Hillard tapped one toe and then the other.

"An' how was she dressed?"

"In fog, for all I could see."

"On the level now, didn't you know who she was?" The policeman gave Hillard a sly dig in the ribs with his club.

"On my word!"

"Some swell, mebbe."

"Undoubtedly a lady. That's why it looks odd, why it brought me into the street. She sang in classic Italian. And what's more, for the privilege of hearing that voice again, I should not mind sitting on this cold curb till the milkman comes around in the morning."

"That wouldn't be fer long," laughed the policeman, taking out his watch and holding it close to the end of his cigar. "Twenty minutes after one. Well, I must be gittin' back to me beat. An' you'd better be goin' in; it's cold. Good night."

"Good night," Hillard responded cheerfully.

"Say, what's I-taly-an fer good night?" still reluctant to go on.

"*Buona notte.*"

"Bony notty; huh, sounds like Chinese fer rheumatism. Been to Italy?"

"I was born there," patiently.

"No! Why, you're no Dago!"

"Not so much as an eyelash. The stork happened to drop the basket there, that's all."

"Ha! I see. Well, Ameriky is good enough fer me an' mine," complacently.

"I dare say!"

"An' if this stogy continues t' behave, we'll say no more about the vanishin' leddy." And with this the policeman strolled off into the fog, his suspicions in nowise removed. He knew many rich young bachelors like Hillard. If it wasn't a chorus lady, it was a prima donna, which was not far in these degenerate days from being the same thing.

Hillard regained his room and leaned with his back to the radiator. He had an idea. It was rather green and salad, but as soon as his hands were warm he determined to put this idea into immediate use. The Voice had stirred him deeply, stirred him with the longing to hear it again, to see the singer's face, to learn what extraordinary impulse had loosed the song. Perhaps it was his unspoken loneliness striving to call out against this self-imposed isolation; for he was secretly lonely, as all bachelors must be who have passed the Rubicon of thirty. He made no analysis of this new desire, or rather this old desire, newly awakened. He embraced it gratefully. Such is the mystery and power of the human voice: this one, passing casually under his window, had awakened him.

Never the winter came with its weary round of rain and fog and snow that his heart and mind did not fly over the tideless southern sea to the land of his birth if not of his blood. Sorrento, that jewel of the ruddy clifts! There was fog outside his window, and yet how easy it was to picture the turquoise bay of Naples shimmering in the morning light! There was Naples itself, like a string of its own pink coral, lying crescent-wise on the distant strand; there were the snowcaps fading on the far horizon; the bronzed fishermen and their wives, a sheer two hundred feet below him, pulling in their glistening nets; the amethyst isles of Capri and Ischia eternally hanging midway between the blue of the sky and the blue of the sea; and there, towering menacingly above all this melting beauty, the dark, grim pipe of Vulcan. How easily, indeed, he could see all these things!

With a quick gesture of both hands, Latin, always Latin, he crossed the room to a small writing-desk, turned on the lights and sat down. He smiled as he took up the pen to begin his composition. Not one chance in a thousand. And after several attempts he realized that the letter he had in mind was not the simplest to compose. There were a dozen futile efforts before he produced anything like satisfaction. Then he filled out a small check. A little later he stole down-stairs, round the corner to the local branch of the post-office, and returned. It was only a blind throw, such as dicers sometimes make in the dark. But chance loves her true gamester, and to him she makes a faithful servant.

"I should be sorely tempted," he mused, picking up a novel and selecting a comfortable angle in the Morris, "I should be sorely tempted to call any other man a silly ass. Leddy Lightfinger—it would be a fine joke if my singer turned out to be that irregular person."

He fell to reading, but it was not long before he yawned. He shied the book into a corner, drew off his boots and cast them into the hall. A moment after his valet appeared, gathered up the boots, tucked them under his arm, and waited.

"I want nothing, Giovanni. I have only been around to

the post-office."

"I heard the door open and close four times, signore."

"It was I each time. If this fog does not change into rain, I shall want my riding-breeches to-morrow morning."

"It is always raining here," Giovanni remarked sadly.

"Not always; there are pleasant days in the spring and summer. It is because this is not Italy. The Hollander wonders how any reasonable being can dwell in a country where they do not drink gin. It's home, Giovanni; rain pelts you from a different angle here. There is nothing more; you may go. It is two o'clock, and you are dead for sleep."

But Giovanni only bowed; he did not stir.

"Well?" inquired his master.

"It is seven years now, signore."

"So it is; seven this coming April."

"I am now a citizen of this country; I obey its laws; I vote."

"Yes, Giovanni, you are an American citizen, and you should be proud of it."

Giovanni smiled. "I may return to my good Italia without danger."

"That depends. If you do not run across any official who recognizes you."

Giovanni spread his hands. "Official memory seldom lasts so long as seven years. The signore has crossed four times in this period."

"I would gladly have taken you each time, as you know."

"Oh, yes! But in two or three years the police do not forget. In seven it is different."

"Ah!" Hillard was beginning to understand the trend of

this conversation. "So, then, you wish to return?"

"Yes, signore. I have saved a little money," modestly.

"A little?" Hillard laughed. "For seven years you have received fifty American dollars every month, and out of it you do not spend as many copper centesimi. I am certain that you have twenty thousand lire tucked away in your stocking; a fortune!"

"I buy the blacking for the signore's boots," gravely.

Hillard saw the twinkle in the black eyes. "I have never," he said truthfully, "asked you to black my boots."

"Penance, signore, penance for my sins; and I am not without gratitude. There was a time when I had rather cut off a hand than black a boot; but all that is changed. We of the Sabine Hills are proud, as the signore knows. We are Romans out there; we despise the cities; and we do not hold out our palms for the traveler's pennies. I am a peasant, but always remember the blood of the Cæsars. Who can say? Besides, I have held a sword for the church. I owe no allegiance to the puny House of Savoy!" There was no twinkle in the black eyes now; there was a ferocious gleam. It died away quickly, however; the squared shoulders drooped, and there was a deprecating shrug. "Pardon, signore; this is far away from the matter of boots. I grow boastful; I am an old man and should know better. But does the signore return to Italy in the spring?"

"I don't know, Giovanni, I don't know. But what's on your mind?"

"Nothing new, signore," with eyes cast down to hide the returning lights.

"You are a bloodthirsty ruffian!" said Hillard shortly. "Will time never soften the murder in your heart?"

"I am as the good God made me. I have seen through blood, and time can not change that. Besides, the Holy Father will do something for one who fought for the cause."

"He will certainly not countenance bloodshed, Giovanni."

"He can absolve it. And as you say, I am rich, as riches go in the Sabine Hills."

"I was in hopes you had forgotten."

"Forgotten? The signore will never understand; it is his father's blood. She was so pretty and youthful, eye of my eye, heart of my heart! And innocent! She sang like the nightingale. She was always happy. Up with the dawn, to sleep with the stars. We were alone, she and I. The sheep supported me and she sold her roses and dried lavender. It was all so beautiful … till he came. Ah, had he loved her! But a plaything, a pastime! The signore never had a daughter. What is she now? A nameless thing in the streets!" Giovanni raised his arms tragically; the hoots clattered to the floor. "Seven years! It is a long time for one of my blood to wait."

"Enough!" cried Hillard; but there was a hardness in his throat at the sight of the old man's tears. Where was the proud and stately man, the black-bearded shepherd in faded blue linen, in picturesque garters, with his reed-like pipe, that he, Hillard, had known in his boyhood days? Surely not here. Giovanni had known the great wrong, but Hillard could not in conscience's name foster the spirit which demanded an eye for an eye. So he said: "I can give you only my sympathy for your loss, but I abhor the spirit of revenge which can not find satisfaction in anything save murder."

Giovanni once more picked up the boots. "I shall leave

the signore in the spring."

"As you please," said Hillard gently.

Giovanni bowed gravely and made off with his boots. Hillard remained staring thoughtfully at the many-colored squares in the rug under his feet. It would be lonesome with Giovanni gone. The old man had evidently made up his mind.... But the Woman with the Voice, would she see the notice in the paper? And if she did, would she reply to it? What a foundation for a romance!... Bah! He prepared for bed.

To those who reckon earthly treasures as the only thing worth having, John Hillard was a fortunate young man. That he was without kith or kin was considered by many as an additional piece of good fortune. Born in Sorrento, in one of the charming villas which sweep down to the very brow of the cliffs, educated in Rome up to his fifteenth year; taken at that age from the dreamy, drifting land and thrust into the noisy, bustling life which was his inheritance; fatherless and motherless at twenty; a college youth who was for ever mixing his Italian with his English and being laughed at; hating tumult and loving quiet; warm-hearted and impulsive, yet meeting only habitual reserve from his compatriots whichever way he turned; it is not to be wondered at that he preferred the land of his birth to that of his blood.

All this might indicate an artistic temperament, the ability to do petty things grandly; but Hillard had escaped this. He loved his Raphaels, his Titians, his Veroneses, his Rubenses, without any desire to make indifferent copies of them; he admired his Dante, his Petrarch, his Goldoni, without the wish to imitate them. He was full of sentiment without being sentimental, a poet who thought but never indited verses. His father's blood was in his veins, that is to say, the salt of restraint; thus, his fortune grew and multiplied. The strongest and reddest corpuscle had been the gift of his mother. She had left him the legacy of loving all beautiful things in moderation, the legacy of gentleness, of charity, of strong loves and frank hatreds, of humor, of living out in the open, of dreaming great things and accomplishing none of them.

The old house in which he lived was not in the fashionable quarter of the town; but that did not matter. Nor did it vary externally from any of its unpretentious neighbors. Inside, however, there were treasures priceless and unique. There was no woman in the household; he might smoke in any room he pleased. A cook, a butler, and a valet were the sum-total of his retinue. In appearance he resembled many another clean-cut, clean-living American gentleman.

Giovanni sought his own room at the end of the hall, squatted on a low stool and solemnly began the business of blacking his master's boots. He was still as lean and tall as a Lombardy poplar, this handsome old Roman. His hair was white; there was now no black beard on his face, which was as brown and creased as Spanish levant; and some of the fullness was gone from his chest and arms; but for all that he carried his fifty-odd years lightly. He worked swiftly to-night, but his mind was far away from his task.

There was a pitiful story, commonplace enough. A daughter, a loose-living officer, a knife flung from a dark alley, and sudden flight to the south. Hillard had found him wandering through the streets of Naples, hiding from the *carabinieri* as best he could. Hillard contrived to smuggle him on the private yacht of a friend. He found a peasant who was reconsidering the advisability of digging sewers and laying railroad ties in the Eldorado of the West. A few pieces of silver, and the passport changed hands. With this Giovanni blandly lied his way into the United States. After due time he applied for citizenship, and through Hillard's influence it was accorded him. He solemnly voted when elections came round, and hoarded his wages, like the thrifty man he was. Some day he would return to Rome, or Naples, or Venice, or Florence, as the case might be; and then!

When the boots shone flawlessly, he carried them to Hillard's door and softly tiptoed back. He put his face against the cold window. He, too, had heard the Voice. How his heart hurt him with its wild hope! But only for a moment. It was not the voice he hungered for. The words were Italian, but he knew that the woman who sang them was not!

Chapter 2 OBJECT, MATRIMONY

Winter fogs in New York are never quite so intolerable as their counterparts in London; and while their frequency is a matter of complaint, their duration is seldom of any length. So, by the morrow a strong wind from the west had winnowed the skies and cleared the sun. There was an exhilarating tingle of frost in the air and a visible rime on the windows. Hillard, having breakfasted lightly, was standing with his back to the grate in the cozy breakfast-room. He was in boots and breeches and otherwise warmly clad, and freshly shaven. He rocked on his heels and toes, and ran his palm over his blue-white chin in search of a possible slip of the razor.

Giovanni came in to announce that he had telephoned, and that the signore's brown mare would be at the park entrance precisely at half-after eight. Giovanni still marveled over this wonderful voice which came out of nowhere, but he was no longer afraid of it. The curiosity which is innate and child-like in all Latins soon overcame his dark superstitions. He was an ardent Catholic and believed that a few miracles should be left in the hands of God. The telephone had now become a kind of plaything, and Hillard often found him in front of it, patiently waiting for the bell to ring.

The facility with which Giovanni had mastered English amazed his teacher and master; but now he needed no more lessons, the two when alone together spoke Giovanni's tongue: Hillard, because he loved it, and Giovanni because the cook spoke it badly and the English butler not at all.

"You have made up your mind to go, then, *amico*?" said Hillard.

"Yes, signore."

"Well, I shall miss you. To whom shall I talk the tongue I love so well, when Giovanni is gone?" with a lightness which he did not feel. Hillard had grown very fond of the old Roman in these seven years.

"Whenever the signore goes to Italia, he shall find me. It needs but a word to bring me to him. The signore will pardon me, but he is like—like a son."

"Thanks, Giovanni. By the way, did you hear a woman singing in the street last night?"

"Yes. At first—" Giovanni hesitated.

"Ah, but that could not be, Giovanni; that could not be."

"No, it could not be. But she sang well!" the old servant ventured.

"So thought I. I even ran out into the street to find out who she was; but she vanished like the lady in the conjurer's trick. But it seemed to me that, while she sang in Italian, she herself was not wholly of that race."

"*Buonissima!*" Giovanni struck a noiseless brava with his hands. "Have I not always said that the signore's ears are as sharp as my own? No, the voice was very beautiful, but it was not truly Roman. It was more like they talk in Venice. And yet the sound of the voice decided me. The hills have always been calling to me; and I must answer."

"And the unforgetting *carabinieri*?"

"Oh, I must take my chance," with the air of a fatalist.

"What shall you do?"

"I have my two hands, signore. Besides, the signore has said it; I am rich." Giovanni permitted a smile to stir his thin lips. "Yes, I must go back. Your people have been good to me and have legally made me one of them, but my heart is never here. It is always so cold and every one moves so quickly. You can not lie down in the sun. Your police, bah! They beat you on the feet. You remember when I fell asleep on the steps of the cathedral? They thought I was drunk, and would have arrested me!"

"Everybody must keep moving here; it is the penalty of being rich."

"And I am lonesome for my kind. I have nothing in common with these herds of Sicilians and Neapolitans who pour into the streets from the wharves." Giovanni spoke scornfully.

"Yet in war time the Neapolitans sheltered your pope."

"Vanity! They wished to make an impression on the rest of the world. It is dull here, besides. There is no joy in the shops. I am lost in these great palaces. The festa is lacking. Nobody bargains; nobody sees the proprietor; you find your way to the streets alone. The butcher says that his meat is so-and-so, and you pay; the grocer marks his tins such-and-such, and you do not question; and the baker says that, and you pay, pay, pay! What? I need a collar; it is *quindici*—fifteen you say! I offer *quattordici*. I would give interest to the sale. But no! The collar goes back into the box. I pay *quindici*, or I go without. It is the same everywhere; very dull, dead, lifeless."

Hillard was moved to laughter. He very well understood the old man's lament. In Italy, if there is one thing more than another that pleases the native it is to make believe to himself that he has got the better of a bargain. A shrewd purchase enlivens the whole day; it is talked about, laughed over, and becomes the history of the day that Tomass', or Pietro, or Paoli, or whatever his name may be, has bested the merchant out of some twenty centesimi.

"And the cook and the butler," concluded Giovanna; "we do not get on well."

"It is because they are in mortal fear of you, you brigand! Well, my coat and cap."

Hillard presently left the house and hailed a Fifth Avenue omnibus. He looked with negative interest at the advertisements, at the people in the streets, at his fellow-travelers. One of these was hidden behind his morning paper. *Personals.* Hillard squirmed a little. The world never holds very much romance in the sober morning. What a stupid piece of folly! The idea of his sending that personal inquiry to the paper! To-morrow he would see it sandwiched in between samples of shop-girl romance, questionable intrigues, and divers search-warrants. Ye gods! "Will the blonde who smiled at gentleman in blue serge, elevated train, Tuesday, meet same in park? Object, matrimony." Hillard fidgeted. "Young man known as Adonis would adore stout elderly lady, independently situated. Object, matrimony." Pish! "Girlie. Can't keep appointment to-night. Willie." Tush! "A French Widow of eighteen, unencumbered," and so forth and so on. Rot, bally rot; and here he was on the way to join them! "Will the lady who sang from *Madame Angot* communicate with gentleman who leaned out of the window? J.H. Burgomaster Club." Positively asinine! The man opposite folded the paper and stuffed it into his pocket, and its disappearance relieved Hillard somewhat.

There was scarce one chance in a thousand of the mysterious singer's seeing the inquiry, not one in ten thousand of her answering it. And the folly of giving his club address! That would look very dignified in yonder agony column! And then he brightened. He could withdraw it; and he would do so the very first thing when he went down-town to the office. "Object, matrimony!" If the woman saw it she would only laugh. It was all a decent woman could do. And certainly the woman of the past night's adventure was of high degree, educated; and doubtless the spirit which had prompted the song was as inexplicable to her this morning as it had been to him last night. He had lost none of the desire to meet her, but reason made it plain to him that a meeting could not possibly be arranged through any personal column in the newspaper. He would cancel the thing.

He dropped from the omnibus at the park entrance, where he found his restive mare. He gave her a lump of sugar and climbed into the saddle. He directed the groom to return for the horse at ten o'clock, then headed for the bridle-path. It was heavy, but the air was so keen and bracing that neither the man nor the horse worried about the going. There were a dozen or so early riders besides himself, and in and out the winding path they passed and repassed, walking, trotting, cantering. Only one party attracted him: a riding master and a trio of brokers who were verging on embonpoint, and were desperate and looked it. They stood in a fair way of losing several pounds that morning. A good rider always smiles at the sight of a poor one, when a little retrospection should make him rather pitying. Hillard went on. The park was not lovely; the trees were barren, the grass yellow and sodden, and here and there were grimy cakes of unmelted snow.

"She is so innocent, so youthful!"

He found himself humming the refrain over and over. She had sung it with abandon, tenderness, lightness. For one glimpse of her face! He took the rise and dip which followed. Perhaps a hundred yards ahead a solitary woman cantered easily along. Hillard had not seen her before. He spurred forward, only faintly curious. She proved to be a total stranger. There was nothing familiar to his eye in her figure, which was charming. She rode well. As he drew nearer he saw that she wore a heavy grey veil. And this veil hid everything but the single flash of a pair of eyes the color of which defied him. Then he looked at her mount. Ha! there was only one rangy black with a white throat; from the Sandford stables, he was positive. But the Sandfords were at this moment in Cairo, so it signified nothing. There is always some one ready to exercise your horses, if they happen to be showy ones. He looked again at the rider; the flash of the eyes was not repeated; so his interest vanished, and he urged the mare into a sharp run. Twice in the course of the ride he passed her, but her head never turned. He knew it did not because he turned to see.

So he went back to his tentative romance. She had passed his window and disappeared into the fog, and there was a reasonable doubt of her ever returning from it. The Singer in the Fog; thus he would write it down in his book of memories and sensibly turn the page. Once down-town he would countermand his order, and that would be the end of it. At length he came back to the entrance and surrendered the mare. He was about to cross the square, when he was hailed.

"Hello, Jack! I say, Hillard!"

Hillard wheeled and saw Merrihew. He, too, was in riding-breeches.

"Why, Dan, glad to see you. Were you in the park?"

"Riverside. Beastly cold, too. Come into the Plaza and join me in a cup of good coffee."

"Had breakfast long ago, boy."

"Oh, just one cup! I'm lonesome."

"That's no inducement; but I'll join you," replied Hillard cheerfully.

The two entered the café, sat down, and Merrihew ordered Mocha.

"How are you behaving yourself these days?" asked Merrihew. He drank more coffee and smoked more cigars than were good for him. He was always going to start in next week to reduce the quantity.

"My habits are always exemplary," answered Hillard. "But yours?"

Merrihew's face lengthened. He pulled the yellow hair out of his eyes and gulped his coffee.

"Kitty Killigrew leaves in two weeks for Europe."

"And who the deuce is Kitty Killigrew?" demanded Hillard.

"What?" reproachfully. "You haven't heard of Kitty Killigrew in *The Modern Maid*? Where've you been? Pippin! Prettiest soubrette that's hit the town in a dog's age."

"I say, Dan, don't you ever tire of that sort? I can't recall when there wasn't a Kitty Killigrew. What's the attraction?" Hillard waved aside the big black cigar. "No heavy tobacco for me in the morning. What's the attraction?"

Merrihew touched off a match, applied it to the black cigar, took the cigar from his teeth and inspected the glowing end critically. He never failed to go through this absurd pantomime; he would miss a train rather than omit it.

"The truth is, Jack, I'm a jackass half the time. I can't get away from the glamour of the footlights. I'm no Johnny; you

24

know that. No hanging round stage-entrances and buying wine and diamonds. I might be reckless enough to buy a bunch of roses, when I'm not broke. But I like 'em, the bright ones. They keep a fellow amused. Most of 'em speak good English and come from better families than you would suppose. Just good fellowship, you know; maybe a rabbit and a bottle of beer after the performance, or a little quarter limit at the apartment, singing and good stories. What you've in mind is the chorus-lady. Not for mine!"

Hillard laughed, recalling his conversation with the policeman.

"Go on," he said; "get it all out of your system, now that you're started."

"And then it tickles a fellow's vanity to be seen with them at the restaurants. That's the way it begins, you know. I'll be perfectly frank with you. If it wasn't for what the other fellows say, most of the chorus-ladies would go hungry. And the girls that you and I know think I'm a devil of a fellow, wicked but interesting, and all that."

Hillard's laughter broke forth again, and he leaned back. Merrihew would always be twenty-six, he would always be youthful.

"And this Kitty Killigrew? I believe I've seen posters of her in the windows, now that you speak of it."

"Well, Jack, I've got it bad this trip. I offered to marry her last night."

"What!"

"Truth. And what do you think? Dropped me very neatly two thousand feet, but softly. And I was serious, too."

"It seems to me that your Kitty is not half bad. What

would you have done had she accepted you?"

"Married her within twenty-four hours!"

"Come, Dan, be sensible. You are not such an ass as all that."

"Yes, I am," moodily. "I told you that I was a jackass half the time; this is the half."

"But she won't have you?"

"Not for love or money."

"Are you sure about the money?" asked Hillard shrewdly.

"Seven hundred or seven thousand, it wouldn't matter to Kitty if she made up her mind to marry a fellow. What's the matter with me, anyhow? I'm not so badly set-up; I can whip any man in the club at my weight; I can tell a story well; and I'm not afraid of anything."

"Not even of the future!" added Hillard.

"Do you really think it's my money?" pathetically.

"Well, seven thousand doesn't go far, and that's all you have. If it were seventy, now, I'm not sure Kitty wouldn't reconsider."

Merrihew ran his tongue along the cigar wrapper which had loosened. He had seven thousand a year, and every January first saw him shouldering a thousand odd dollars' worth of last year's debts. Somehow, no matter how he retrenched, he never could catch up. It's hard to pay for a horse after one has ridden it to death, and Merrihew was always paying for dead horses. He sighed.

"What's she like?" asked Hillard, with more sympathy than curiosity.

Merrihew drew out his watch and opened the case. It was

a pretty face; more than that, it was a refined prettiness. The eyes were merry, the brow was intelligent, the nose and chin were good. Altogether, it was the face of a merry, kindly little soul, one such as would be most likely to trap the wandering fancy of a young man like Merrihew.

"And she won't have you," Hillard repeated, this time with more curiosity than sympathy.

"Oh, she's no fool, I suppose. Honest Injun, Jack, it's so bad that I find myself writing poetry on the backs of envelopes. And now she's going to Europe!"

"London?"

"No. Some manager has the idea in his head that there is money to be made in Italy and Germany during the spring and summer. American comic-opera in those countries; can you imagine it? He has an angel, and I suppose money is no object."

"This angel, then, has cut out a fine time for his bank account, and he'll never get back to heaven, once he gets tangled up in foreign red-tape. Every large city in Italy and Germany has practically its own opera troupe. In full season it is grand opera, out of season it is comic-opera, not the American kind; *Martha*, *The Bohemian Girl*, *The Mascotte*, *The Grand Duchess*, and the like. And oh! my boy, the homeliest chorus you ever dreamed of seeing; but they can sing. It's only the ballerina who must have looks and figure. Poor angel! Tell your Kitty to strike for a return ticket to America before she leaves."

"You think it's as bad as that?"

"Look on me as a prophet of evil, if you like, but truthful."

"I'll see that Kitty gets her ticket." Merrihew snapped the case of his watch and drew his legs from under the table. "I lost a hundred last night, too."

"After that I suppose nothing worse can happen," said Hillard cheerily. "You will play, for all my advice."

"It's better to give than receive ... that," replied Merrihew philosophically. "I've a good mind to follow the company. I've always had a hankering to beat it up at Monte Carlo. A last throw, eh? Win or lose, and quit. I might."

"And then again you mightn't. But the next time I go to Italy, I want you to go with me. You're good company, and for the pleasure of listening to your jokes I'll gladly foot the bills, and you may gamble your letter of credit to your heart's content. I must be off. Who is riding the Sandfords' black?"

"Haven't noticed. What do you think of Kitty?"

"Charming."

"And the photo isn't a marker."

"Possibly not."

"Lord, if I could only hibernate for three months, like a bear! My capital might then readjust itself, if left alone that length of time. Jack, why the deuce haven't I a relation I never heard of, who would politely die to-morrow and leave me that beggarly thousand? I'm not asking for much. The harder I chase it, the faster it runs ahead." Merrihew thwacked his boots soundly with his crop.

"Some day I'm going to enter that thousand in the Suburban handicap. And won't there be a killing!"

"It wouldn't do you any good to borrow it?"

"In that case I should owe two thousand instead of one. No, thank you. Shall I see you at the club to-night?"

"Perhaps. Good-by."

They nodded pleasantly and took their separate ways.

Merrihew stood very high in Hillard's regard. He was a lovable fellow, and there was something kindred in his soul and Hillard's, possibly the spirit of romance. They had met years before, at a commencement, Merrihew in his mortar-board and gown and Hillard as an old graduate, renewing his youth at the fountains. What drew them together, perhaps more than anything else, was their mutual love of out-door pleasures. Their first meeting was followed by many hunting and fishing expeditions, and many long rides on horseback. Take two men and put them on good horses, send them forth into the wilds to face all conditions of weather and inconveniences, and if they are not fast friends at the end of the journey, rest assured that they never will be.

For all his aversion to cards, there was a bit of the gamester in Hillard; as, once in his office, he decided on the fall of a coin not to withdraw his personal from the paper. He was quite positive that he would never hear that Voice again, but having thrown his dice he would let them lie.

Now, at eleven o'clock that same morning two distinguished Italians sat down to breakfast in one of the fashionable hotels. The one nor the other had ever heard of Hillard, they did not even know that such a person existed; and yet, serenely unconscious, one was casting his life-line, as the palmist would say, across Hillard's. The knots and tangles were to come later.

"The coffee in this country is abominable!" growled one.

"Insufferable!" assented his companion.

The waiter smiled covertly behind his hand. He had a smattering of all tongues, being foreign born. These Italians and these Germans! Why, there is only one place in the world where both the aroma and the flavor of coffee are preserved; and it is not, decidedly not, in Italy or Germany. And if his tip exceeded ten cents, he would be vastly surprised. The Italian is always the same, prince or peasant. He never wastes on necessities a penny which can be applied to the gaming-tables. And these two were talking about Monte Carlo and Ostend and the German *Kursaalen*.

The younger of the two was a very handsome man, tall, slender and nervous, the Venetian type. His black eyes were keen and energetic and roving, suggesting a temper less calculating than hasty. The mouth, partly hidden under a graceful military mustache, was thin-lipped, the mouth of a man who, however great his vices, was always master of them. From his right cheek-bone to the corner of his mouth ran a scar, very well healed. Instead of detracting from the beauty of his face it added a peculiar fascination. And the American imagination, always receptive of the romantic, might readily and forgivably have pictured villas, maids in durance vile, and sword-thrusts under the moonlight. But the waiter, who had served his time in one or another of the foreign armies, knew that no foil or rapier could have made such a scar; more probably the saber. For the Italian officer on horseback is the maddest of all men, and in the spirit of play courts hazards that another man might sensibly avoid in actual warfare.

His companion was less handsome but equally picturesque. His white head and iron-grey beard placed him outside the active army. He wore in his buttonhole a tiny bow of ribbon, the usual badge of the foreign service.

"I'm afraid, Enrico, that you have brought me to America on a useless adventure," said the diplomat, lighting a thin, strong cigarette.

"She is here in New York, and I shall find her. I must have money, must! I owe you the incredible amount of one hundred thousand lire. There are millions under my hand, and I can not touch a penny."

"Do not let your debt to me worry you."

"You are so very good, Giuseppe!"

"Have we not grown up together? Sometimes I think I am partly to blame for your extravagance. But a friend is a friend, or he is not."

"But he who borrows from his friend, loses him. Observe how I am placed! It is maddening. I have had a dozen opportunities to marry riches. This millstone is eternally round my neck. I have gone through my part of the fortune which was left us independently. She has all of hers, and that is why she is so strong. I am absolutely helpless."

"Poor friend! These American women! They all believe that a man must have no peccadillos, once he has signed the marriage contract. Body of Bacchus! the sacrament does not make a man less human than he was before. But this one is clever. She might be Italian born."

"Her mother was Italian. It is the schooling in this country that has made her so clever. The only thing Italian about her is her hatred. She is my countrywoman there. Without her consent I can touch nothing; and if I divorce her, pouff! all goes to the State. Sometimes I long to get my two hands round her white throat. One mistake, one little mistake! I am willing to swear that she loved me in the beginning. And I was a fool not to profit by this sentiment. Give me patience, patience. If I say to her, so much and you may have your freedom, there is always that cursed will. The crown of Italy will never withdraw its hand; no. With his wife's family on his hands, especially her brother, the king will never waive his rights."

"Zut! softly, softly!"

"Oh, I speak with no disrespect. But let me find her."

"I doubt it. And remember, we have but ten days."

"We shall not find time heavy. I know a few rich butchers and grocers who call themselves the aristocracy."

They laughed.

"And some of them play bridge and écarté."

The diplomat jingled his keys. He was not averse to adding a few gold pieces to his purse.

"I have followed her step by step to the boat at Naples. She is here. She is not so inconspicuous that she will be hard to find. She has wealthy friends, and from these I shall learn her whereabouts."

"You say she is beautiful; I would that I had seen her."

"Yes, she is beautiful; and a beautiful woman can not hide, even in a city so big and noisy as this. Think of it! Châteaux and villas and splendid rents, all waiting to be gormandized by the State! I have lied to her, I have humiliated myself, I have offered all the reparation a gentleman possibly could. Nothing, nothing! She knows; it is money, and she knows it is money. The American native shrewdness! My father was a fool and so was hers. And on July first comes the end! Let us get out into the air before I become excited and forget where I am."

"As you wish, *amico*." The diplomat beckoned to the waiter.

The waiter stepped forward with the coats and hats. His tip was exactly ten cents, and out of this the head waiter must have his percentage.

Three nights later, as Hillard and Merrihew were dining together at the club, the steward came into the grill-room and swept his placid eye over the groups of diners. Singling out Hillard, he came solemnly down to the corner table and laid a blue letter at the side of Hillard's plate.

"I did not see you when you came in, sir," said the steward, his voice as solemn as his step. "The letter arrived yesterday."

"Thank you, Thomas." With no small difficulty Hillard composed his face and repressed the eagerness in his eyes. She had seen, she had written, the letter lay under his hand! Who said that romance had taken flight? True, the reading of the letter might disillusion him; but always would there be that vision and the voice coming out of the fog. Nonchalantly he turned the letter face downward and went on with the meal.

"I did not know that your mail came to the club," said Merrihew.

"It doesn't. Only rarely a letter drifts this way."

"Well, go on and read it; don't let me keep you from it. Some charmer, I'll wager. Here I pour all my adventures into your ear, and I on my side never so much as get a hint of yours. Go on, read it."

"Adventures, fiddlesticks! The letter can wait. It is probably a bill."

"A bill in a fashionable envelope like that?"

Hillard only smiled, tipped the cradle and refilled Merrihew's glass with some excellent Romanee Conti. "When does Kitty sail?" he asked, after a while of silence.

"A week from this Saturday, February second. What the

deuce did you bring up that for? I've been trying to forget it."

"Where do they land?"

"Naples. They open in Rome the first week in March. All the arrangements and bookings seem to be complete. This is mighty good Burgundy, Jack. I don't see where you pick it up." After coffee Merrihew pushed back his chair. "I'll reserve a table in the billiard-room while you read your letter."

"I'll be with you shortly," gratefully.

So, with the inevitable black cigar between his teeth, Merrihew sauntered off toward the billiard-room, while Hillard picked up his letter and studied it. His fingers trembled slightly as he tore open the envelope. The handwriting, the paper, the modest size, all these pointed to a woman of culture and refinement. But a subtle spirit of irony pervaded it all. She would never have answered his printed inquiry had she not laughed over it. For, pinned to the top of the letter was the clipping, the stupid, banal clipping— "Will the lady who sang from *Madame Angot* communicate with gentleman who leaned out of the window? J.H. Burgomaster Club." There was neither a formal beginning nor a formal ending; only four crisp lines. But these implied one thing, and distinctly: the writer had no desire for further communication "with gentleman who leaned out of the window." He read and re-read slowly.

I am sorry to learn that mysinging disturbed you.

Therewas a reason.

At that partic-

ular moment I was happy. That was all. It was enough. She had laughed; she was a lady humorously inclined, not to say mischievous. A comic-opera star would have sent her press agent round to see what advertising could be got out of the incident; a prima donna would have appealed to her primo tenore, for the same purpose. A gentlewoman, surely; moreover, she lived within the radius, the official radius of the Madison Square branch of the post-office, for such was the postmark. Common sense urged him to dismiss the whole affair and laugh over it as the Lady in the Fog had done. But common sense often goes about with a pedant's strut, and is something to avoid on occasions. Here was a harmless pastime to pursue, common sense notwithstanding. The vein of romance in him was strong, and all the commercial blood of his father could not subjugate it. To find out who she was, to meet her, to know her, if possible, this was his final determination. He rang for paper and a messenger, and wrote: "Madame Angot. There is a letter for you in the mail-department of this office." This time his initials were not necessary. Once the message was on its way, he sought Merrihew, whom he found knocking the balls about in a spiritless manner.

"A hundred to seventy-five, Dan."

"For what?"

"For the mere fun of the game, of course."

"Make it cigars, just to add interest."

"Cigars, then."

But they both played a very indifferent game. At ten-thirty Merrihew's eyes began to haunt the clock, and Hillard grew merciful for various reasons.

"What time does the performance end?" he asked.

"At ten-fifty, but it takes about twenty minutes to scrape off the make-up."

"Run along, then, my son; I can spare you. And you've a cigar coming."

Merrihew agreeably put his cue in the rack.

"Much obliged for the dinner, Jack. I'll return the favor any night you say." He made off for the coat-room.

Hillard laughed, and went up to the writing-room to fulfil a part of his destiny. He took the letter out and read it again. A woman of wit and presence; a mighty good dinner companion, or he was no judge of women. He replaced the letter in its blue covering, and then for the first time his eye met the superscription. Like a man entranced he sat there staring. The steward had brought the letter to him, and in his first excitement this had made no impression upon his mind; he had seen nothing peculiar nor strange. And here it was, not his initials, but his name in full.

She knew who he was!

Chapter 3 MADAME ANGOT

In a fashionable quarter of the city there stood a brownstone house, with grotesque turrets, winding steps, and glaring polished red tiles. There was a touch of the Gothic, of the Renaissance, of the old English manor; just a touch, however, a kind of blind-man's-buff of a house. A very rich man lived here, but for ten months in the year he and his family fluttered about the social centers of the world. And with a house like this on his hands, one could scarce blame him. Twice a week, during this absence, a caretaker came in, flourished a feather duster, and went away again. Society reporters always referred to this house as "the palatial residence."

This morning a woman stood in the alcove-window and looked down into the glistening street. There was a smile on her lips, in her eyes, in the temporary little wrinkles on either side of her nose. The Venetian red of her hair trapped the reflected sunlight from the opposite windows, and two little points of silver danced in her blue eyes. Ah! but her eyes were blue; blue as spring-water in the morning, blue as the summer sky seen through a cleft in the mountains, blue as lapis-lazuli, with the same fibers of gold. And every feature and contour of the face harmonized with the marvelous hair and the wonderful eyes; a beautiful face, warm, dreamy, engaging, mobile. It was not the face of a worldly woman; neither was it the face of a girl. It was too emotional for the second, and there was not enough control for the first. It seemed as if she stood on the threshold of life, with one hand lingering regretfully in the clasp of youth and the other doubtfully greeting womanhood; altogether, something of a puzzle.

But the prophecy of laughter did not come to pass; the little wrinkles faded, the mouth grew sad, and the silver points no longer danced in her eyes. The pain in her heart was always shadowing; like a jailer it jealously watched and repressed the natural gaiety which was a part of her. Those who have been in serious wrecks are never quite the same afterward; and she had seen her fairest dream beaten and crumpled upon the reef of disillusion.

Yet again the smile renewed itself. She was a creature of varying moods. She twisted and untwisted the newspaper. Should she? Ought she? Was it not dreadfully improper and bizarre? Had she not always regretted these singular impulses? And yet, what harm to read this letter and return it to the sender? She was so lonely here; it was like being among a strange people, so long ago was it that her foot had touched this soil. Was it possible that she was twenty-five? Was there not some miscount, and was it not fifteen instead? As old and as wise as the Cumæan Sybil at one moment, as light and careless as a Hebe the next. Would not this war of wisdom and folly be decided ere long?

She opened the paper and smoothed out the folds. "Madame Angot. There is a letter for you in the mail-department of this office." It was so droll. It was unlike anything she had ever heard of. A personal inquiry column, where Cupids and Psyches billed and cooed, and anxious Junos searched for recreant Jupiters! The merest chance had thrown the original inquiry under her notice. Her answer was an impulse to which she had given no second thought till too late. She ought to have ignored it. But since she had taken the first step she might as well take the second. She was lonely; the people she knew were out of town; and the jest might amuse her.

This man was, in all probability, a gentleman, since he was a member of a gentlemen's club. But second thought convinced her that this proved nothing. Men are often called gentlemen out of compliment to their ancestors. Still, if this man only saw the affair from her angle of vision, the grotesque humor of it and not the common vulgar intrigue! She hesitated, as well she might. Supposing that eventually he found out who she was? That would never, never do. No one must know that she was in America, about to step into the wildest of wild adventures. No; she must not be found out. The king, who had been kind to her, and the court must never know. From their viewpoint they would have declared that she was about to tarnish a distinguished name, to outrage the oldest aristocracy in Europe, the court of Italy. But she had her own opinion; what she proposed to do was in itself harmless and innocent. But this gentleman who leaned out of the window? What should she do with him? What had possessed her to sing at that moment? A block above or below his window, and no one would have heard, not even the policeman. This time the laughter bubbled. It was all so funny. She had heard every word of their conversation. She had seen the match flare in the young man's face. Fortunately they had not thought to peer into the area-ways. Was it the face she had seen in that flash of light that interested her sufficiently to risk the note? Against the dark of the night it had appeared for an instant, clean, crisp, ruddy as a cameo. Sometimes a single glance is enough; the instinct of the heart is often surer than the instinct of the mind. She would not have been afraid had he found her. The face warranted confidence.

She had sung because she had been happy, happy with

that transient happiness which at times was her portion. Could she ever judge another man by his looks? She believed not. How she had run! The man, bareheaded, giving chase, and the burly policeman across the street! Chorus-ladies—what in the world were they?

She stepped down from the alcove, wound the grey veil round the riding-crop and tossed them into a corner. Somehow, in the daylight, the magic was gone from his face, for she had recognized him that first day in the park. He rode well. She knew that his interest in her had been only casual. She touched a bell. A maid appeared.

"Signora?"

"Bettina, you will go to the office of this newspaper and inquire for a letter addressed to Madame Angot. You can speak that much English. And be quick, for I may change my mind."

"I go at once, Signora." And she was back in less than half an hour.

"There was a letter, then?" The points were dancing again in the blue eyes.

"And here it is, signora." The maid's eyes sparkled, too. An intrigue! It would not be so dull hereafter.

"You may go. Perhaps," and Bettina's mistress smiled, "perhaps I may let you read it and answer it, after I am done with it. That would be rather neat."

"But it will be in English, signora; and that I can not read." Bettina's eyes filled with disappointment.

"You may use it as a lesson. In a few days you should be able to master it."

The slight nod was a dismissal, and the maid went about her duties, which were not many in this house. These were terrible days; the two of them alone in this strange *palazzo*, and the stuffy, ill-smelling *trattoria* they dined at! *Che peccato!* And that she should sit side by side with her mistress! *Santa Maria*, what was the good world coming to? And the ban on the familiar tongue! English? She despised it. German? She detested it. But to be allowed to speak in French, that alone made conversation tolerable. And this new mad whim! Oh, yes; the signora was truly mad this time.

Meanwhile the lady with the Venetian hair toyed with the letter. Club paper. Evidently he was not afraid to trust her. But would he amuse her? Would he have anything to say that would interest her? She ran the paper-knife under the flap. The contents gave her a genuine surprise. She ran to the window. Italian! It was written in Italian, with all the flourishes of an Italian born. She turned to the signature. Hillard; so he had signed his name in full? She ruminated. How came such a name to belong to a man who wrote Italian so beautifully? Here was something to ponder over. She smiled and looked at the signature again... . John, Giovanni. She would call him Giovanni. She had been rather clever. To have had the wit to look in the library for the blue book and the club list; not every woman would have thought of that. Then a new inspiration came to her, and she struck the bell again. She sent Bettina for the card-basket in the lower hall. She scattered the contents upon the floor, touched up the wood fire, and sat down Turkish-wise. She sorted the cards carefully, and lo! she was presently rewarded. She held up the card in triumph. He had called at this house on Thanksgiving Day. He was known, then, to the master and mistress, this Giovanni with the Irish surname. Very good. She now gave her full attention to the letter, which, incredible as it may seem, she had not yet perused.

To the Lady in the Fog—To begin with, let me say that I, too, have laughed. But there was some degree of chagrin in my laughter. On my word of honor, it was a distinct shock to my sense of dignity when I saw that idiotic personal of mine in the paper. It is my first offense of the kind, and I am really ashamed. But the situation was not ordinary. Ordinary women do not sing in the streets after midnight. As you could not possibly be ordinary, my offense has greater magnitude. To indite a personal to a gentlewoman! A thousand pardons! I doubted that it would come under your notice; and even if it did, I was sure that you would ignore it. And yet I am human enough to have hoped that you wouldn't. When I found your note, it was a kind of vindication; it proved that a singular episode had taken place. To find a woman with an appreciable sense of humor is rare; to find one who couples this with initiation is rarer still. I do not refer to wit, the eternal striving to say something clever, regardless of cost. How you found out my name confuses me.

"Indeed!" murmured the lady.

Doubtless you have the club list in your house. Do you know, when the letter was brought me, I saw nothing unusual about the address. It was only when I began this letter that I comprehended how clever you were. There are half a dozen J.H's at the club. I tell you truthfully, over my own name, that your voice startled me. It would have startled me under ordinary circumstances. In New York one does not sing in the streets. It is considered bad form by the police.

"Thanks! I must remember that."

I was startled, then, because my thoughts were far away. I

was dreaming of Italy, where I was born, though there is no more Italian blood in my veins than there is in yours.

The ruddy head became erect and the blue eyes searched the glowing seams in the logs. Here was a riddle.

"What made him think that, I wonder?"

I therefore write this in a language familiar to us both, certain you could not sing Lecocq's songs in Italian if you did not speak and understand it thoroughly. Signora or signorina, whichever it may be, have we no mutual friends? Are you not known to some one who knows me? Some one who will speak for me, my character, my habits? Modesty forbids that I myself should dwell upon my virtues. I could refer you to my bankers, but money does not recommend the good character of a man. It merely recommends his thrift, or more generally that of his father.

"That will pass as wit," said the lady. "But it is rather a dull letter, so far. But, then, he is wandering in the dark."

You say you sang because at that moment you were happy. This implies that you are not always so. Surely, with a voice like yours one can not possibly be unhappy. If only I might meet you! Will you not do me that honor? I realize that this is all irregular, out of fashion, obsolete. But something tells me that neither of us is adjusted properly to prosaic environments. Isn't there just a little pure, healthy romance waiting to be given life? Your voice haunts me; out of every silence it comes to me— "She is so innocent, so youthful!"

John Hillard.

The letter fluttered into her lap. She leaned on her elbows. It was not a bad letter; and she rather liked the boyish tone of it. Nothing vulgar peered out from between the lines. Did he really love music? He must, for it was not every young man who could pick out the melody of an old, forgotten opera. She shivered, but the room was warm. Had fate or chance some ulterior purpose behind this episode? Rather than tempt fate she decided not to answer this letter; aside from her passive superstition, it would be neither wise nor useful. She desired to meet no strangers; to be left to herself was all she wished. Her voice, it was all she had that afforded her comfort and pleasure.

Romance! The word came back to her. With an unmusical laugh she stood up, shaking the letter to the floor. Romance! She was no longer a girl; she was a woman of five and twenty; and what should a woman know of romance? Ah, there had been a time when all the world was romance, romance; when the night breeze had whispered it under her casement-window, when the lattice-climbing roses had breathed it, when the moon and the stars had spelled it. Romance! She hated the word not less than she hated the Italian language, the Italian people, the country itself. She spurned the letter with her foot and fed the newspaper to the fire. She would let Bettina answer the letter.

She went down-stairs to the piano and played with strong feeling. Presently she began to sing a haunting melancholy song by Abt. From Abt she turned to Flotow; from Offenbach to Rossini; from Gounod to Verdi. The voice was now sad or gay, now tender or wild. She was mistress of every tone, every shade, every expression.

The door opened gradually. The little maid's face was moved to rapture over these exquisite sounds.

Crash! It was over.

"Bettina? Bettina, are you listening?"

"I am always listening." Bettina squeezed into the room. "I had not the heart to interrupt. It is beautiful, beautiful! To sing like that!" Then, with a burst of confidence: "There will be kings and dukes at your feet!"

"Enough!"

"Pardon, signora, I forgot. But listen; I bring a message. A boy came to say that the rehearsal will be at four this afternoon. It is now after twelve."

"So late? I did not know. We must be off to lunch."

"And the letter up-stairs on the floor?"

"Some day, Bettina, you will enter the Forbidden Chamber, and I shall have to play Bluebeard. This time, however, I do not mind. Leave it there or burn it," indifferently.

Bettina knew her mistress. She thought best to leave the letter where it lay, forgotten for the time being.

Chapter 4 BLINDFOLDED

For two days the club steward only nodded when Hillard came in; he had no letters to present.

"I am thirty-three years old," Hillard mused, as he sought the reading-room. "Down-town I am looked upon as a man of affairs, a business man, with the care of half a dozen fortunes on my hands. Now, what's the matter with me? I begin to tremble when I look that sober old steward in the face. If he had handed me a letter to-night, I should have had to lean against the wall for support. This will never do at all. I have not seen her face, I do not know her name; for all I know, she may be this Leddy Lightfinger.... No, that would be impossible. Leddy Lightfinger would have made an appointment. What possesses me to dwell in this realm of fancy, which is less tangible than a cloud of smoke? Have I reached my dotage by the way of the seven-league boots? Am I simply bored with the monotony of routine, and am I groping blindly for a new sensation?" He smoked thoughtfully. "Or, am I romantic? To create romance out of nothing; I used to do that when I was a boy. But I'm a boy no longer. Or, *am* I a boy, thirty-three years old?... She does not answer my letter. Sensible woman. In her place I shouldn't answer it. But in my place I want her to. Two weeks ago I was haunting the curio-shops for a Roman cameo two thousand years old; to-night I might take it as a gift. I have ceased to be interested in something that has always interested me. Something is wrong; what is it? She sent for my letter. That indicates that she read it. Well, well!" reaching for the *London Illustrated News*; "let's see what their Majesties have been doing the past fortnight."

The King of England was preparing to descend to the

Riviera; the King of Spain was killing pigeons; the Kaiser was calling for more battleships; the Czar of all the Russias was still able to sit for his photograph; the King of Italy was giving a fête; and Leopold of Belgium was winning at Monte Carlo. Among the lesser nobles the American duchesses were creating a favorable impression in spite of their husbands.

"What a fine sensation it must be," Hillard murmured, "to be able at any time to plunge one's noble white hand into a sack of almost inexhaustible American dollars!"

He dropped the paper. The same old stories, warmed over. There was really nothing new in the world. If Giovanni returned to Italy in the spring, he was of a mind to go with him. He looked up and was glad to see Merrihew in the doorway.

"Been looking for you, Jack. Want your company tonight. Kitty Killigrew is giving a little bite to eat after the performance, and has asked me to bring you along. Will you come?"

"With pleasure, Dan. Are you dining with any one tonight?" Hillard was lonesome.

"Yes. A little bridge till eleven."

"You're hopeless. I can see you in limbo, matching coffin-plates with Charon. I'll hunt you up at eleven."

"Heard the talk?"

"About what?"

"Why, some one in the club has been using the agony column. The J.H's are being guyed unmercifully, and you'll come in for it presently. It's a case of wine on the man who did it."

Hillard felt of his collar and drew down his cuffs. "Probably some joke," he ventured tentatively.

"If it isn't, the man who would stoop to such tommyrot and tack the name of his club to it must be an ass."

"No doubt about that. Odd that this is the first time I have heard about it." But silently Hillard was swearing at his folly. There was one crumb of comfort: the incident would be forgotten in a few days.

"I may depend upon you to-night, then?" said Merrihew.

"I shall be pleased to meet Miss Killigrew," which was a white one. Hillard would have paid court to a laundress rather than offend Merrihew.

And promptly at eleven he went up to the card-room and dragged Merrihew away. Merrihew gave up his chair reluctantly. He was winning. He would have been just as reluctant, however, had he been losing. The amateur gambler never wants to stop.

On the way to the Killigrew apartment, Merrihew's moods varied. At one moment he was on the heights, at the next in the depths. He simply could not live without Kitty. Perhaps if this trip abroad turned out badly she might change her mind. Seven thousand *could* be made to muster. Twice Hillard came very near making his friend a confidant of his own affair; but he realized that, while Merrihew was to be trusted in all things, it was not yet time.

He found a pleasing and diverting company. There was Mère Killigrew, a quaint little old lady who deplored her daughter's occupation but admitted that without her success, Heaven only knew how they would have got along. There was the genial Thomas O'Mally, a low-comedian of genuine ability, whom Hillard knew casually; Smith, a light-comedian; and Worth, a moderately successful barytone to whom Hillard took one of those instant and unaccountable dislikes. These three and

Kitty were going abroad. And there were several members of *The Modern Maid* company, which went on tour the following Monday.

Kitty fancied Hillard from the start; and he on his side found her well educated, witty and unaffected. She was even prettier than her photograph. Merrihew's face beamed upon them both, in a kind of benediction. He had known all along that once Jack saw Kitty, he would become a good ally in fighting down her objections.

"Think of singing in Italy!" cried Kitty. "Isn't it just wonderful?"

"And has Merrihew told you to get a return ticket before you sail?" with half a jest.

"Don't you think it will be successful?" a shade of disappointment. "There will be thousands of lonesome Americans over there. Out of patriotism, if for nothing else, they ought to come and see us."

"They certainly ought to. But I'm an old killjoy."

"No, no; go on and tell me all your doubts. You have been over there so many times."

"Well, supposing your tourists are tired, after having walked all day through the churches and galleries? They may want to go to bed early. But you never can tell till you try. You may become the rage on the continent. Yet, you go into the enemy's country. It isn't the same as going to London, among tolerant cousins. In Italy and in Germany there is always so much red tape, blundering, confusing red tape, custom duties, excessive charges. But your manager must know what he is doing."

"He has everything in black and white, I believe. But

your advice is sensible."

"Do you know anything about Italy or Germany?"

"Only what I learned in my geographies," laughing. "Rome, Florence, Genoa, Venice, Nice, Milan, Strasburg, Cologne, and on to Berlin! It is like a fairy story come true."

"Who is your prima donna?" he asked.

"Ah!" Kitty's face became eager with excitement. "Now you have put your finger on the mystery that is bothering us all. Not one of us has seen her or knows her name. She has not rehearsed with us and will not till we reach Naples, where we rest a week. When we speak of her, the manager smiles and says nothing; and as none of us has seen the backer, Mr. Worth thinks that she herself is the prima donna and backer in one. We think that she is some rich young woman who wishes to exploit her voice. There's a lot of them in the world. I wish I knew her. I am dying of curiosity. The manager is not a man to fool away his time. She doubtless can act and sing. Little has been said about the venture in the papers, and I'm glad. We may prove a perfect fizzle, and the less said the better. As we can't walk back, I must learn to swim…. Lunch is ready, every one!"

The mummers and the outsiders flocked into the small dining-room. There was plenty to eat—beer, soda, whisky, and two magnums of champagne, Merrihew's contribution to the feast. Hillard listened with increasing amusement to the shop-talk. Such and such a person (absent) never could act; such and such a composer (absent) was always giving the high note to the wrong singer; such and such a manager (absent) never staged the opera right. It was after one when they returned to the sitting-room, where the piano stood. The wine was now opened and toasts were drunk. O'Mally told inimitable stories. There was something exceedingly droll in that expressive Irish face of his and the way he lingered over his wine.

"There is nothing so good as a glass of champagne," he observed, "unless it is another."

Worth did not drink, but Hillard did not like his handsome face any the more for this virtue. He sang remarkably well, however, and with a willingness Hillard had not believed he possessed. He wondered vaguely why he disliked the man. He had never met him before, and knew nothing at all about him. It was one of those inexplicable things which can not be answered. Otherwise Hillard enjoyed himself vastly. He found these people full of hope, light-hearted, generous, intelligent, and generally improvident.

"Mr. Merrihew has been telling me all about you," said Kitty.

"You mean, of course, my good qualities," replied Hillard.

"To hear him talk, one would think that you possessed nothing else. But I am sure that you have glaring faults, such as a man might pass over and a woman go round."

"I believed that Merrihew had a serious fault till to-night," he said; and he made no attempt to disguise the admiration in his eyes.

She looked at him quickly and colored. It was a good sign.

"Has the foolish boy been telling you that I refused to marry him? I like him very much," she added gravely; "but I shall never marry any man till I have ceased to love the stage. Just now I can not wisely love anything else."

"I understand," he said.

"I am not a whit less extravagant than he is. How could the two of us live on an income which he himself admits that he can not live within? But that isn't it; a million would not make any difference. I am like a young colt; I have no desire to be harnessed yet. A month after I am gone he will forget all about me; or, at least, he will only recollect me with a sigh of relief. There will be others; only I hope they will treat him as frankly as I have done."

"Merrihew is the most loyal man I know," Hillard declared, bound to defend his comrade against this shrewd insight to his character.

"Of course he is loyal! And he is always in earnest—for the moment." She laughed. "But if he marries any one while I am gone, I shall hate him."

And then they both laughed.

"I'll wager another magnum," cried Merrihew from across the room, "that I'm the subject under discussion."

"Another magnum!" murmured O'Mally rapturously.

"No more magnums," said Kitty resolutely.

"On abstract principles, then!" insisted Merrihew.

"You win," Kitty replied merrily. "We have been saying only nice things about you."

It was outrageously late, nearly four, when the revelers took leave of their hostess. Merrihew was happy with that evanescent happiness which goes hand in glove with late suppers and magnums. In the morning he would have a headache.

"Isn't she a little wonder, Jack? Do you blame me?"

"Not at all, Dan. It might be a good thing for you to marry a sensible little woman like that. But she won't have you."

"No, she won't." Merrihew reached for his watch. "Four

A.M. Wonder if we can't find another bottle somewhere."

"You are going home, my boy."

"All right, if you say so,"—good-humoredly. "Say, what do you think of that man Worth?"

"Very good voice; but he's too handsome. Being a plain duffer myself, I don't take kindly to handsome men."

"Oh, go on! You're as fine a looking chap as there's in New York. But this man Worth has the looks of a lady-killer. He's been eying Kitty, but it doesn't go. Hang it, I can't see why she won't marry me now. She's got to, some time or other."

"You must have patience."

"Or more money. Can't O'Mally tell a good story, though?"

"Good company, too; but I should hate to turn him loose in my wine-cellars. I imagine that he's not a connoisseur, and will praise anything that's good to drink, unless it's water."

Merrihew roared.

"Well, here's your station, Dan. You go home like a good boy. Shall I see you to-morrow?"

"Eight-thirty in the park. Gallop off headache. Nothing like a horse for a headache. Good night."

Merrihew climbed the elevated stairs and vanished. Hillard arrived home tired and sleepy; but as he saw a letter on the stand in the hall, his drowsiness passed quickly. There was no other blue envelope like it. She now had his house address; she was interested enough to look it up. She did not follow his lead and write in Italian; she wrote in English—crisp English, too. Again there was neither beginning nor ending. But this was a letter; there was something here of the woman, something to read and read again.

I had told the maid to burn your letter. But she left it on the floor where I had thrown it, and I came across it this morning. It looked rather pathetic. So I am writing you against my better judgment. Yes, I know your name; I find that I am well acquainted with people you know. I am a woman who often surrenders to the impulse of the moment; I may or may not answer any future letter from you. You write very good Italian; but it will surprise you to learn that I detest all things that are Italian. Once I loved them well. Why should you wish to know me? Our ways are as divergent as the two poles. Happy because I sing? There are some things over which we can sing or laugh, but of which we can not speak without crying. Happy or unhappy, what can this matter to you? To you I shall always remain the Lady in the Fog. Are you rich, young, talented? I care not in the least. Perhaps it amuses me to add to your confusion. Find me? I think not. Seek me? Do so; I permit you to. And would you know me if you found me? Misguided energy!

Hillard put the letter away, extinguished the lights, and passed up to his room. She defied him to find her? This was a direct challenge. He would accept it. This time he would use no personal to tell her that a letter awaited her. She should make the inquiries herself. And from the mail-clerk he would obtain a description of the elusive Madame Angot. Next morning he rode in the park with Merrihew. Again he saw the veiled lady on the Sandford black. Out of normal curiosity he telephoned the stables and made inquiries. The reply was short. No one at the stables knew the lady, but she rode the horse on proper authority.

That night he wrote:

I shall keep on writing till you cease to reply. Let me be frank with you. I am bored; so are you. The pleasure you derive in keeping up this mystery engages you. You bid me to find you. I accept the challenge. You must understand at once that it is the mystery that interests me. It is the unknown that attracts me. I am mentally painting you in all sorts of radiant colors. You defy me to find you. There is nothing so reliable as the unexpected, nothing so desperately uncertain as a thing assured. I warn you that I shall lay all manner of traps, waylay your messengers, bribe them. I shall find out where you live. The rest will be simple.

She replied:

I have no desire to alleviate your confessed boredom. Your persistence would be praiseworthy if well directed. Waters wear away stone, the wind crumbles the marble, but a woman is not moved till she wishes to be. I never thought that I should dabble in an intrigue of this sort, and I am surprised at the amusement it affords me. I really owe you some gratitude. The few I have met who know you tell me that you are a "nice young man."

He rebelled at the adjective. Every man has some portion of self-love. So his next effort was a passionate denial that he was nice. When should he meet her? The postman brought him a letter which contained one word—*Nimmer!* He sent her four pages, a frank and witty description of himself and friends, his past and some of theirs.

On the day she received this letter a cablegram came to her from the far Mediterranean. Whatever it contained had the effect to cause all restraint to disappear from the tone of her letters. They became charming; and more and more Hillard found himself loving a Voice. All his watching, all his traps, came to no successful end. She was too clever for him. He sought the mail-department of the great newspaper; the clerk couldn't remember, there were so many calling for mail. Letters passed to and fro daily now, but always she declared that it was impossible for them to meet. To write a letter was one thing, to meet a strange man in an unconventional manner was another. No, it was out of the question to dine with him in a restaurant. It was equally out of the question to cook a dinner where she lived, as she and her maid dined at a small restaurant near-by. Would he not be content with the romance and let the reality go? Finally he proposed to bring the dinner all cooked from the club. Two days went by without a sign; then the blue letter came.

I surrender. The most fatal thing in life is curiosity. It has the power to lead us into all manner of trouble. And I have my share of curiosity. Remember, you never would have found me. I may dwell in a garret; I may be hideous; perhaps nothing remains to me but my voice. Whatever you have painted me in your imagination, I tell you that I shall prove directly the opposite. And now the terms. And if you do not follow them confidently and blindly, your dinner will grow cold in the carriage. Dinner will be at eight, February first. At seven a carriage will call for you. The messenger will blindfold you. He will then proceed to the club and take the dinner, and bring you here. Be warned! If you so much as lift the corner of the bandage, the romance will end then and there. It is necessary to enforce these conditions, but it is not necessary to explain why. I realize that I am doing something very foolish and unwise. But, as you say, I am a woman who has seen much of the world. Thus I have my worldly side. I shall use it as a buffer.

"Blindfolded!" Hillard scrubbed his chin. All these precautions! Who was she? What was she? An ordinary young woman, full of mischief, or was she what he hoped, a real mystery? He was well on the way to find out. Since there was no escape, blindfolded he would go.

At half after six, on the night of the first of February, then, he began to dress. It was some time since he had taken such particular care.

"The signore seems in high spirits to-night," observed Giovanni, as he laid out the linen.

"Man, I'm happy and greatly excited. Do you recollect the lady who sang under my window? I am going to meet her to-night. The mystery will be a mystery no longer."

"Who is she?" asked Giovanni sharply. It was rarely he asked a question with such directness.

But his master was too excited to note it. "On my word, I don't know who she is, Giovanni. She has written such charming letters! She may be only a singer; she may be a Russian princess in exile; she may be an adventuress of the most formidable type; she may be an American girl. One thing, she is not English. English women as I have found them lack the essential spirit of adventure."

"Ah!" Giovanni stroked his lips doubtfully. "It is not like the signore to plunge blindly into adventures like this."

"The very word, blindly. I go blindfolded, *amico*. What do you think of that?"

"Blindfolded?" Giovanni was horrified. "It is a trap!" he

cried. "They will assassinate you! No, you shall not go! In Rome, at the carnivals, it is an old game. They will rob you."

"You are dreaming. This is America; things are not done that way here. And nothing now can turn me aside." Hillard was all the while finishing his toilet.

"I suppose not. But blindfolded!"

"Take the number of the cab as I get in. If anything should happen, give the number to the police."

Giovanni, with a sharp movement of the hands, expressed his resignation to the worst. He knew the futility of arguing with his master. But he followed him down to the hall and tied on the bandage himself. He was honest about it, too, for Hillard could see nothing. Then the messenger-boy took him by the hand and led him to the carriage. As the two were climbing in, Giovanni spoke rapidly in his native tongue.

"There is no number on the carriage!"

"Too late to bother now."

The carriage rolled off toward the club, where the dinner, hot and smoking, was taken on.

"Joinin' th' Elks?" asked the boy, when they were well under way once more.

"No, it's a séance. They are going to call up my fate round a table."

"Huh? Aw, go-wan! Dey don't call up no ghosts wit' French cider and hot boids." The boy relapsed into silence.

Hillard tried to follow the turns of the carriage, but these were too many; and so he resigned himself to become totally lost. By and by the carriage stopped.

"Dis is where we alights, me loid!" the boy jeered. "An' no lookin', mind."

Hillard found the carriage steps and landed safely. He stood for a moment, listening. They were in a quiet part of the city; no elevated or surface cars were near. He was assured that the location was exclusive. Garrets are not to be found in quiet places.

"Look out fer th' steps," said the boy, again taking Hillard by the hand.

"And you be careful of that basket."

"I ain't lettin' it drop any."

Winding steps, thought the blindfolded man. He could recollect none. It seemed to him that they stood there five minutes before the door opened. When it did, the boy passed in the basket and resolutely pushed Hillard into the hall. The door closed gently, and the adventure was begun. Whither would it lead him?

"Take off the bandage the signore may now," said a voice in broken English.

"Thanks!" He tore the handkerchief from his eyes and blinked. The hall was so dimly lighted that he could see nothing distinctly.

"The signore's coat and hat."

He passed over these articles, shook the wrinkles from his trousers, smoothed his chin, and stood at attention. The maid eyed him with abundant approval, then knocked timidly on the door leading to the drawing-room. He was sure of one thing: this was some millionaire's home. What if he should see in the drawing-room a party of his intimate friends, ready to plague and jest? He shuddered. He never had entertained such an appalling probability.

"*Avanti!*" called a soft voice from within.

Hillard gathered in his courage, opened the door and stepped inside. A single lamp in a far corner drew his glance, which roved a moment later. On a divan near this lamp sat a woman in black. Only a patch of white throat could be seen, for her shoulders were not bare and her arms only to the elbows. Her back was turned squarely. He could see nothing of her face. But what a head! He caught his breath. It glowed like a copper-beech in the sunshine. What was it? There was something, something he could not see.

"Madame?" he faltered. He had had a gallant Italian phrase to turn for her benefit. He spoke English instead, and not very firmly.

The woman turned. Hillard took a step backward and blundered against a pedestal.

She was masked!

Chapter 5 THE MASK

Masked! Only her mouth and chin were visible, and several little pieces of court-plaster effectually disguised these. There *was* a mystery. He to come blindfolded and she to wear a mask! Extraordinary! There was something more than a jest: she really did not wish to be known, and the reason lay far back of all this, beyond his grasp. He stood there dumfounded. She rose. The movement was elegant.

"And this," she said ironically, "is the gentleman who leaned out of the window?"

He brought all his faculties together, for he knew that he would need them in this encounter. "Supposing I had fallen out of it? Well, it could not have mattered. I should not have been more at your feet than I am now." This was very good, considering how dry his tongue was.

"If you had fallen out? I had not thought of that. A modern Ulysses, house-broken, and an itinerant siren! You had been wise to have stuffed your ears that night."

"My mythology is rusty. And I much prefer Penelope. She interests me vastly more than the ancient prize-fighter."

"But sit down, Mr. Hillard, sit down." The lady with the mask motioned him to a chair directly under the light. She wished to study his face while she talked.

Hillard reached the chair successfully enough, but he never could recollect how. He sat down as a bashful man sits down in a crowded ball-room, with his knees drawn in tightly and his feet at sympathetic angles. He knew that she would have the best of him in this engagement. All the bright things to say would come to him after he had gone home. It was far easier to write letters. That mask! One might as well converse with the Sphinx. His face was hers to study; her emotions would be wholly her own.

Presently she laughed with malice.

"You are not comfortable in that chair."

"That is true; and yet it is soft and roomy. I am uneasy. Perhaps you recall to my subconsciousness a period in my former existence on earth; or, if you will, one of my ancestors."

"I fail to understand."

"Well, a Hillard two hundred years ago had his head cut off by an ax. His executioner wore a mask."

"A mistake. Your ancestor should have been hanged."

"And I along with him, you would imply?"

"Are you not Irish? I have known Irishmen by the name of Hillard."

"They were in disguise. But I have a generous strain of Irish blood in me. Otherwise I shouldn't have had the courage to follow up an adventure like this."

"Thanks. The compliment is rather ambiguous."

"My compliments can not possibly be more ambiguous than your appearance. Surely, there will be an hour for unmasking."

"It has already begun, Mr. Hillard."

"So I am the one who is to be unmasked? Well, I have only the mask nature gave to me. I wish she had been more liberal. But I shall see what can be done with it."

"Is there any mask quite so terrible, quite so deceptive, as this very mask nature gives us? Can it not lie adroitly, break hearts, overthrow empires? You can judge a character by this mask sometimes, but never the working of the mind behind it."

She resumed her seat on the divan.

"I wish I could read yours."

"And much good it would do you." She smiled, rather ruefully Hillard thought.

He took note of her teeth, and felt a sudden tinge of regret. One may disguise the face and hair, but the teeth are always the same. Two lower teeth on the right side appeared to be gone; the others were firm and glistening white. It was a pity, for a woman's teeth are as much her glory as her hair.

"I am curious to learn what you brought for dinner."

He enumerated the delicacies.

"You have evidently studied your Lucullus," she said.

Silence. The ruddy light on her hair fascinated him.

"What is it?" she demanded.

"Your hair," with a simplicity which silenced her. "You have the most beautiful hair I have ever seen."

"Thank you. And yet, for all you know, it may be a fine wig."

"If it is, I shall never be sure of anything again. Am I in prosaic New York? Have you not, by some carpet-magic, transported me to old Europe? If a dozen conspirators came in in cowls to render me the oath, I should not be at all surprised."

"There is no magic; only a mask."

"And there is no way of seeing behind that?"

"None, absolutely none. I am told that you are a gentleman; so I am confident that you will not stoop to use force."

"Only the force of eloquence, if ever I may lay claim to that again."

"You are beginning well. For I tell you, Mr. Hillard, I

shall expect but the most brilliant wit from you to-night. As for me, I shall only interpolate occasionally. Now, begin."

"I am not used to dancing without the pole."

"You must learn. Dance!"

"Upon what—nothing? And how shall I know that my dancing pleases you?"

"I agree to tell you. I wear this mask to-night because I am taking a surreptitious leaf out of my book of cares."

"Cares? Have you any?"

"If I were without cares it would not be necessary to seek diversions of this equivocal character." She crossed her arms. The magic of old Venice seemed at that moment to enfold her.

"You are, then, seeking a diversion?"

"Nothing more or less. Do not flatter yourself that there is anything personal or romantic on my side. I am bored."

"I am wholly in your hands," he said; "and they are very beautiful hands."

"Is there anything more beautiful than a cat's paw, when the claws are hidden? Never judge a woman by her hands." Nevertheless she buried her hands in the depths of a down-pillow. She had forgotten her rings. She slipped them off and managed to hide them.

"I promise to remember. Your letters—" he began diffidently. Where the deuce was his tongue? Was he to be tongue-tied all the evening before this Columbine, who, with the aid of her mask, was covertly laughing at his awkwardness?

"My letters? A woman often writes what she will not say, and says what she will not write. Did you not ask me to disillusion you?"

"Yes, but softly, softly. I begin to believe one thing: you

brought me here to teach me a lesson. Gentlemen should never use the personal column."

"Nor should ladies read it. I am not saving any mercy for myself!" with laughter.

"Shall I begin with my past?"

"Something less horrifying, if you please!"

"I object to the word nice," he said, seeking a new channel, for he was not steering very well in those he had so far selected.

"The word was employed negligently. Your friends used the word."

"I should have preferred milksop!" He was growing impatient. "Hadn't you better try some new kind of torture?"

"This is only a skirmish; your real torture hasn't even begun yet. But this will give you an appetite. I do not drink champagne, but the chambertin will do nicely. Oh, I propose that you shall pay for this dinner, Mr. Hillard; pay for the privilege of sharing it with me."

"Bring on the check. I should like to settle the bill at once, and have it off my mind."

"You may take off your gloves," she countered. "I know that you must feel uncomfortable with them on. To clasp one's own hands is a kind of personal sympathy. Try it."

He drew them off, not ungracefully, and tucked them away. He spread his thin brown muscular fingers a few times, then folded his arms.

"You look quite Napoleonic in that pose."

"If this were only Elba and not St. Helena! I should be coming back to you some day."

"I shall credit that against the partridges."

This time her laughter was relaxed and joyful. And somehow he felt more at ease. He was growing accustomed to the mask. He stretched his legs and fingered his nether lip.

"Have you not somewhere an invisible cloak?"

"I had one that night, which nature lent me," she answered readily. "I was so invisible to you that I heard the policeman call out your name. I thank you for insisting that I was not a chorus-lady."

Here was a revelation which accounted for many things. "I haven't been very fortunate so far in this adventure."

"That is rank ingratitude. I am of the opinion that fortune has highly favored you."

"But the mask, the mask! If you heard the policeman call my name, you must have heard him speak of one Leddy Lightfinger."

"I did indeed. And is it not possible that I am that very person?"

Hillard dropped his hand toward his watch. "Why do you hate Italy?"

She sat straight, and what little he could see of her mouth had hardened.

"There will be no retrospection this evening, if you please," her voice rather metallic.

The mystery lifted its head again. One does not hate a country without a strong and vital reason. Was Giovanni partly right, after all? Was this a kind of trap, a play to gain his interest? Was her singing under his window purely accidental? She hated Italy. The State or the Church? More likely the State. And what had the State done to her or she to the State? A conspirator, in need of funds and men? If this was the case, she was not going about her cause scientifically. Italy had no hold upon anything of his save his love of beauty. Perhaps her reason for hating Italy was individual and singular: as she would have hated any other country, had her unhappiness originated there.

"Will you not sing?" he asked. This was an inspiration. Music might assist in melting her new reserve.

"You recollect, then, that I possess a voice?"

"It is all I have to recollect. Tell me, whither is all this to lead?"

"To the door, and into the fog again."

"On my word, I'm half inclined to believe you to be an anarchist or a Red, or something on that order."

"On account of my hair?" She laughed again. "Put yourself at ease. I am neither Leddy Lightfinger nor a socialist. There are no dynamite bombs in this house. I despise any organization which aims to destroy society. Society is bad enough as it is; but think of trying to readjust it!"

"I give up the puzzle."

"That is better."

It is difficult to seek and hold a pair of eyes partly hidden behind a mask. Several times he made the attempt, but his eyes were first to lower.

Her severity, her irony and her apparent lack of warmth were mere matters of calculation. Her plan was to inspire him with trepidation, to keep him always at arm's length, for his own safety as well as hers. She knew something of men. Even the best, if suddenly thrown into an affair so strange as this, might commit an irreparable blunder; and this she did not want Hillard to do. She was secretly pleased with his strong face and shapely head. There was neither beard nor mustache to hide the virtues or defects. The chin was square but not heavy, the mouth humorous, kindly and firm, the nose bridged; and the brown eyes, sleepy yet with latent fires, were really handsome. She knew all about him; she was not afraid to be alone with him; nor was it really necessary to wear a mask. But the romance in her heart, that she believed to be dead, was not dead, only waiting to be rekindled. True, they were never to meet again; it was all to begin to-night and end to-night. No man was likely to forget a face met under such whimsical and extraordinary circumstances; so he must not have hers to remember. She arose.

"I will sing!"

"That is more than I dared to hope." He made as though to rise.

"Sit down. I do not play by note; my memory is very good. While I am singing I should much prefer you to remain where you are."

He obeyed without protest, and she went to the piano. Above the instrument was a rare old Venetian mirror; in it he could see her face fairly well. And where had he seen that mirror before?

"What shall it be?" she asked, and he forgot the mirror.

"The song you sang under my window."

"But that is for the male voice!"

"You sang it very well, nevertheless. I have a good memory, too." He leaned forward, his arms crossed on his knees. Was there ever, in all the world, such an Arabian night?

She sang, but without that buoyant note of the first night. One after another he called out the popular airs of the old light operas. She had them all on her tongue's end.

"Light opera appeals to you?" She had followed in the

mirror his slightest move. Was she disappointed?

Where had he seen that copy of Botticelli before? If only there was a little more light.

"Pardon me," he said. "You asked—?"

She repeated her question, wondering what had drawn his attention.

"I like my grand opera after dinner. After dinner I shall want Verdi, Berlioz, Gounod."

"But after dinner I may not care to sing." She spoke in German.

He was not expecting this tongue; besides, his German had never been a finished product. For all that, he made a passable reply.

"You speak as many languages as a Swiss hotel-concierge."

"I wish I did. My mother had one idea in regard to my youth: I should speak four languages and eventually become a great diplomat. As it stands, I speak indifferent French and German, and am not in the diplomatic service. My mother had one of the loveliest voices. It was a joy to hear her speak, now Italian, now German, now French. She understood that in these days one does not travel far with Greek and Latin, though they come in handy when you strike old inscriptions. We were great comrades. It was rare fun to go with her on an antique-hunting expedition. They never fooled her nor got the better of her in a bargain."

She liked the way he spoke of his mother.

"But you," he said; "you are not Italian."

She smiled.

"You are neither French, German nor English."

She still smiled, but to the smile she added a gentle shrug.

"You are American—like myself!" he hazarded.

Her fingers stirred over the keys again, and Grieg's *Papillon* fluttered softly from flower to flower.

Chapter 6 INTO THE FOG AGAIN

He sat there, waiting and listening. From the light and airy butterfly, the music changed to Farwell's *Norwegian Song*. Hillard saw the lonely sea, the lonely twilight, the lonely gull wheeling seaward, the lonely little cottage on the cliffs, and the white moon in the far east. And presently she spoke, still playing softly.

"My father was an American, my mother Italian. But I have lived in Europe nearly all my life. There! You have more of my history than I intended telling you." The music went dreamily.

"I knew it. Who but an American woman would have the courage to do what you are doing to-night? Who but one of mine own countrywomen would trust me so wholly and accept me so frankly for what I am, an American gentleman?"

"Softly!" she warned. "You will dig a pit for your vanity."

"No. I am an American gentleman, and I am proud of it; though this statement in your ears may have a school-boy ring."

"A nobility in this country? Impossible!"

"Not the kind you find in the *Almanach de Gotha*. I speak of the nobility of the heart and the mind." He was very much in earnest now.

"Indeed!" The music stopped, and she turned. She regarded his earnestness with favor.

"I have traveled much; I have found noblemen everywhere, in all climes, and also I have found beasts. Oh, I confess that my country is not wholly free from the beast. But the beast here is a beast; shunned, discredited, outcast. On the other side, if he be mentioned in the *Almanach*, they give him sashes and decorations. And they credit us with being money-mad! It is not true. It is proved every day in the foreign cables that our love for money is not one-tenth so strong as that which our continental cousins evince."

"But if you are not money-mad, why these great fortunes?" dubiously.

"At a certain age a fortune in this country doubles itself without any effort on the part of the owner. Few of us marry for money; and when we do, we at least have the manhood to keep the letter of our bargain. We do not beat the wife, nor impoverish her, nor thrust opera-singers into the house she shares with us."

"And when you marry?"

"Well, it is generally the woman we love. Dowries are not considered. There is no social law which forbids a dowerless girl to marry a dowerless man," laughing. "But over there it is always and eternally a business contract simply. You know that."

"Yes, a business contract," listlessly.

"And yet these foreigners call us a business nation! Well, we are, outside our homes. But in the home we are husbands and fathers; most of us live cleanly and honestly; we make our homes our havens and our heavens. But of course there is always the beast. But they talk of nobility on the other side. That is it; they talk, talk. Italy, France, Germany! Why, I had rather be the son of an English farmer than a prince on the continent. And I had rather be what I am than the greatest nobleman in England."

"Go on, go on! I like it. What do you call it—jingo?"

"Call it what you will. Look at the men we produce. Three or four hundred years ago Europe gave us great poets, great artists, great soldiers, great churchmen, and great rascals. I admire a great rascal, when he is a Napoleon, a Talleyrand, a

Machiavelli; but a petty one! We have no art, no music, no antiquity; but we have a race of gentlemen. The old country is not breeding them nowadays."

"No, she simply prints new editions of the *Almanach*. Continue; I am becoming illumined."

"If I am boring you?"

"No. I have the greatest admiration for the American gentleman. My father was one. But I have met Americans who are not so loyal as you are, who see no good in their native land."

"I said we have beasts; I forgot to mention the cads. I am perfectly frank. Italy is the most beautiful country in the world; France is incomparable; Germany possesses a rugged beauty which I envy for my country's sake. Every square foot of it is cultivated; nowhere the squalidity one sees among the farm-houses of this country. Think of the histories, the romance, the art, the music! America has little history; and, saving the wildernesses, it is not beautiful; but it is generous and bountiful and healthy mentally. Europe is a story-world, and I should like nothing better than to read it to the end of my days."

"Signora, dinner is served!" The little maid stood between the sliding doors which gave entrance to the dining-room.

Signora! thought Hillard. He certainly would look at her hands again.

"After you, Mr. Hillard," she said.

He bowed and passed on before her. But not till he had passed did he understand the manoeuver. To follow her would have been nothing less than the temptation to pluck at the strings of her mask. Would he have touched it? He could not say, the temptation not having been his.

That dinner! Was he in New York? Was it not Bagdad, the

bottle and the genii? Had he ever, even in his most romantic dreams, expected to turn a page so charming, so enchanting, or so dangerous to his peace of mind? A game of magical hide-and-seek? To see, yet to be blindfolded! Here, across the small table, within arm's length, was a woman such as, had he been a painter, he must have painted; a poet, he must have celebrated in silken verse. Three-and-thirty? No, he was only a lad this night. All his illusions had come back again. At a word from this mysterious woman, he would have started out on any fool's errand, to any fool's land.

And she? A whim, a fantastic, unaccountable whim; the whim of a woman seeking forgetfulness, not counting the cost nor caring; simply a whim. She had brought him here to crush him for his impertinence; and that purpose was no longer in her mind. Was she sorry? Did he cause her some uneasiness, some regret and sadness? It was too late. There could be no Prince Charming in her world. He had tarried too long by the way. Not that there was the least sentiment in her heart regarding him; but his presence, his freshness, his frank honesty, these caused her to resort to comparisons. It was too late indeed.

On the little table was a Tuscany brass lamp of three wicks, fed by olive oil. It was sufficient to light the table, but the rest of the room was sunk in darkness. He half understood that there was a definite purpose in this semi-illumination: she had no wish that he should by chance recognize anything familiar in this house. Dimly he could see the stein-rack and the plate-shelf running around the walls. Sometimes, as the light flickered, a stein or a plate stood out boldly, as if to challenge his memory.

He watched her hands. The fingers were free from rings. Was she single or married? The maid had called her signora; but that might have been a disguise, like the mask and the patches of court-plaster.

"May I ask you one question?"

"No," promptly. There was something in his eyes that made her grow wary of a sudden.

"Then I shan't ask it. I shall not ask you if you are married."

"And I shall not say one way or the other."

She smiled and he laughed quietly. He had put the question and she had answered it.

Neither of them ate much of this elaborate dinner. A game like this might easily dull the sharpest appetite. He studied her head, the curves of her throat, the little gestures, the way her shoulders seemed to narrow when she shrugged; and all these pictures he stored away for future need. He would meet her again; a touch of prescience told him this. When, where, did not matter.

A running conversation; a fencing match with words and phrases. Time after time she touched him; but with all his skill he could not break through her guard. Once or twice he thrust in a manner which was not in accord with the rules.

"And that interesting dissertation on the American gentleman?" she said icily, putting aside each thrust with a parry of this kind.

"That's the trouble with posing as a moralist; one must live up to the precepts. Would you believe me if I told you that, at the age of three-and-thirty, I am still heart-whole?"

She parried: "I trust you will not spoil that excellent record by making love to me." She reached for the matches, touched off one, watched it burn for a moment, extinguished it, and then deliberately drew a line across the center of the table-cloth.

"Now what might that represent?" he asked curiously.

"A line, Mr. Hillard. The moment you cross that line, that moment you leave this house. On guard!"

"Come, that is not brave. You can retreat till your shoulders touch the mat, but I must stand this side of the line, unable to reach you. And you have the advantage of the mask besides. You are not a fair fencer."

"The odds should be in my favor. I am a woman. My wrist is not so strong as yours."

"Physically, of course, I may pass the line; to reach the salt, for instance. Will that be against the rules?"

"To a certain extent, no."

"You make it very hard. You have put temptation in my path."

"Bid Satan get behind thee."

"But supposing he should take it into his head to—shoulder me forward?"

"In that case, under the new rules, I should referee the matter."

"I wish I knew the color of your eyes. Behind those holes I see nothing but points of fire, no color. Are they blue, brown, grey?"

"They are blue. But supposing I wear this mask because my face is dreadfully scarred, and that I have some vanity?"

"Vanity, yes; but scars, never; at least never so deep as you yourself can make. You do not wear that mask to cover defects, but out of mercy to me."

And so the duel went on. Sometimes the heat of the mask

almost suffocated her, and she could hardly resist the desire to tear it from her face. Yet, in spite of this discomfort, she was enjoying herself. This adventure was as novel to her as it was to him. Once she rose and approached the window, slyly raising the mask and breathing deeply of the cold air which rushed in through the crevices. When she turned she found that he, too, had risen. He was looking at the steins, one of which he held in his hand. Moreover, he returned and set the stein down beside his plate.

"Tell me, why do you do that?" There was an anxious note in her voice.

"I have an idea. But let us proceed with the dinner. This salad—"

"I am more interested in the idea." She pushed aside the salad and took a sip of the ruby Burgundy. Had he discovered something?

"May I smoke?" he asked.

"By all means."

He lighted a cigarette and put the case near the line.

"Do you not enjoy a cigarette?"

"Sometimes," she answered. "But that idea—"

"Will you not have one?" He moved the case still nearer to the line.

She reached out a firm round white arm.

"One moment," he said; "let us understand each other thoroughly."

"What do you mean?" her arm poised in mid-air. "To touch a cigarette you must cross the line to this side."

She withdrew her arm slowly.

"I shall not smoke. If I crossed the line I should establish a dangerous precedent. A good stroke. Now, the idea. I must have that idea."

He blew the smoke toward the lamp; it sailed over the flaming wicks and darted into the dark beyond.

"The mirror over the piano confused me. I had seen it somewhere before. Then, there was that old copy of Botticelli. The frame was familiar, but I could not place it. This stein, however!" He laughed; the laughter was boyish, even triumphant.

"Well, that stein?" She was now leaning across the table, her fingers tense on the cloth.

"I bought that stein two seasons ago. This is the Sandfords' place, and you are the veiled lady who has been riding Mrs. Sandford's favorite hunter in the park."

"And so?"

"I shall find out who you are presently."

"How?"

"That shall be my secret. Mutual friends, indeed! You will not have to send me home blindfolded."

"That is precisely what I shall do, in a certain sense. My name? Perhaps. But you will never know my face."

"Suppose I should determine to cross the line, despite your precepts?"

They stood up simultaneously. In a matter of this sort he was by far the quicker. In an instant he had caught her by the wrist, at the same time drawing her irresistibly round the table toward him. His grasp was not rough, only firm. She ceased to pull against him.

"I must see your face. I shall never be at peace if I do not."

"Certainly you will never know any peace if you do. Be careful!"

His free hand stole toward the strings of her mask. She moved not. His face was very close to hers now. If only she would struggle! Yes, he was certain now that her eyes were blue. But they looked at him with a menace which chilled his ardor. He dropped the hand from the mask and released her wrist.

"No, I haven't the courage. If I take that mask from your face, it will be the end. And I do not want this ever to end. If you will not let me see your face of your own free will, so be it. I shall see it some day, mark me. Fate does not cross two paths in this manner without a purpose." He stepped back slowly. "You do not understand the lure of that mask."

"Perhaps I do. I am beginning to admire your self-control, Mr. Hillard; I am beginning to admire it very much. But I am tired now, and I must ask you to go."

"Once more, will you let me see your face?"

"No. If, as you say, fate intends for us to meet again, you will see it. But I have my doubts. So it is my will to pass out of your life as completely as though I had never entered it; from one fog into another. No, I am not a happy woman; I am not happy in my friendships. Listen to me," and her voice grew low and sweet. "Let me appeal to your imagination. This light adventure shall be a souvenir for your old age. One night Romance stepped into your life and out of it. Think! There will always be the same charm, the same mystery, the same enchantment. Knowing nothing of me, there will follow no disillusions, no disenchantments; I shall always be Cinderella, or the Sleeping Beauty, or what your fancy wills. Do you understand me?"

He nodded.

"Nothing," she proceeded, "nothing lasts so long in the recollection as a pleasant mystery. In other days, in other times…. Well, on my side I shall recall this night pleasantly. Without knowing it, you have given me a new foothold in life. I did not believe that there lived a single man who could keep to the letter of his bargain. Presently you will forget the chagrin. Good night! And do not lean out of any more windows," she added lightly.

"You are right," he said reluctantly. "Something to dream over in my old age. And certainly I shall dream of it; a flash of sunlight in the shadow."

Then slowly he reached down toward her wine-glass. She understood his purpose and essayed to stop him.

"Do not deny me this little thing," he said.

She let her hand fall. He took the glass, held it against the light to see where her lips had touched it. Carefully he poured out the wine from the opposite side and kissed the rim.

"I shall keep this glass. I must have some visible object to make sure that this hasn't been a dream. Mrs. Sandford may send me the bill."

"You may kiss my hand, Mr. Hillard."

He bent quickly and kissed, not the hand, but the wrist where the marks of his fingers still remained faintly. He squared himself, and gazed long and steadfastly into her eyes. In that moment he seemed to her positively handsome; and there was a flutter in her heart that she was unable to define. On his part he realized the sooner he was gone the better; there was a limit to his self-control…. He gained the street somehow. There he stopped and turned. Did the curtain move? He wasn't sure; but he raised his hat, settled it firmly on his head, and walked rapidly away. He was rather proud of himself. He had conquered a hundred temptations. And he confidently knew that it would be many a day before she ceased to think of him. Was she single or married? Well, it mattered not, one way or the other; he knew that long years ago this night had been written and his fate summed up. Unhappy? There was more than one mask. Once in his own room, however, the longing to see her face grew terribly strong. He stood the glass on the mantel and stared at it. Why must she go out of his life? What obstacle was there to stand between them and a kindly friendship?

There was little sleep for him that night; and in the morning the first thing he did was to pick up the wine-glass. It was all true. And then his good resolutions melted and vanished. He must have one more word with her, happen what might. So at ten o'clock he called a cab and drove rapidly to the Sandford place. Snow had fallen during the night, and many of the steps were still spotless white. Impossible! He leaned from the cab and rubbed his eyes. Absolutely impossible! For, what did he see? Wooden shutters over all the lower windows and the iron gates closed before the doors! And not a footprint anywhere. This was extraordinary. He jumped from the cab, ran up the steps, and rang the bell, rang it ten times with minute intervals. And no one answered. Then he heard a call from across the street. A man stood in one of the area-ways.

"Nobody home!" he shouted. "Gone to Egypt."

"But there was some one here last night," Hillard shouted back.

"Last night? Guess you've got the wrong street and wrong house, young man."

"But this is the Sandford place?"

"Nothing else."

"I was here last night."

"Dreaming. That house has been empty since November. I happen to be the caretaker."

Hillard went back to his cab, dazed. No one there last night? Come, come; there was a mistake somewhere. It was out of the question that he had been in another house. He would soon find out whether or not he had dined there the night before.

"A cable-office!" he cried to the cabby. "Hurry!"

Once there he telephoned down-town and secured Sandford's cable address. Then he filled out a blank which cost him ten dollars. Late that night at the club he received his reply. It was terse.

You are crazy. House absolutely empty. SANDFORD.

Chapter 7 THE TOSS OF A COIN

Hillard made an inexcusably careless shot. It was under his hand to have turned an even forty on his string. He grounded his cue and stood back from the table. That was the way everything seemed to go; at tennis, at squash, at fencing, at billiards, it was all the same. The moment victory was within his grasp his interest waned. Only last night he had lost his title as the best fencer in the club; disqualified in the preliminaries, too, by a tyro who would never cease to brag about the accident.

"I say, Jack, what's the matter with you, anyhow?" asked Merrihew, out of patience. "A boy could have made that three-cushion, his hands tied behind him."

"It was bad," Hillard agreed. "Perhaps I am not taking the interest in the game that I formerly took."

"I should say not. You lost me fifty last night. Corlis has no more right to cross foils with you than I have; and yet he goes in for the finals, while you are out of it. Where's your eye? Where's your grip?"

Hillard chalked his cue silently.

"And when I make a proposition," pursued Merrihew, "to ride to the Catskills and back—something you would have jumped at a year ago—you shake your head. Think of it! Through unbroken roads, nights at farm-houses, old feather beds, ice in the wash-basin, liver and bacon for breakfast, and off again! Snow or rain! By George, you had a bully time last year; you swore it was the best trip we ever took on the horses. Remember how we came back to town, hungry and hardy as Arctic explorers? Come on; everything is dull down-town. Where's your spirit of adventure?"

"I'm sure I don't know where it is. Shall we finish the game?"

"Not if you're going to throw it like this," declared Merrihew. He was proud of his friend's prowess in games of skill and strength, and he was wroth to see him lose all interest unaccountably.

"Ten and a string against your half a string," said Hillard, studying the score. "I'll bet a bottle that I beat you."

"Done!" said Merrihew. Being on his mettle, he made a clean score of twenty, five to go. "I can see you paying for that check, Jack."

But the odds tingled Hillard's blood. He settled down to a brilliant play and turned sixty-one in beautiful form. There were several shots which caused Merrihew to gasp.

"Well, it's worth the price of the bottle. If only you had had that eye last night! We'll have the bottle in the alcove at the head of the stairs. I want to talk to you."

So the two passed up-stairs to the secluded alcove, and the bottle shortly followed. Merrihew filled the glasses with the air of one who would like to pass the remainder of his days doing the same thing. Not that he was overfond; but each bottle temporarily weeded out that crop of imperishable debts, that Molochian thousand, that Atalanta whose speed he could not overtake, having no golden apples. To him the world grew roseate and kindly, viewed through the press of the sparkling grape, and invariably he saw fortune beckoning to the card-tables.

"Now, then, Jack, I've got you where I want you. Who is she?"

"On my word, I don't know," answered Hillard, stirring

restlessly.

"Then there is a woman!" cried Merrihew, astonished at his perspicacity. "I knew it. Nothing else would so demoralize your nerve. Shall we drink a health to her?"

Hillard raised his glass and touched that of his comrade. For the good of his soul and the peace of his mind, he then and there determined to tell Merrihew the whole adventure, without a single reservation.

"To the Lady in the Fog!" he said.

"Fog?" blankly.

"Well, the Lady in the Mask."

"Fog, mask? Two of them?"

"No, only one. Once I met her in the fog, and then I met her in the mask."

"I'll drink to her; but I'm hanged if I don't believe you're codding me," said Merrihew disappointedly. "This is New York."

"I know it; and yet sometimes I doubt it. Here's to the lady."

They drank. Hillard set down his glass; Merrihew refilled his.

"The whole story, Jack, details and all; no half-portions."

Hillard told the yarn simply, omitting nothing essential. He even added that for three weeks he had been the author of the personal inquiry as to the whereabouts of one Madame Angot. More than that, he was the guilty man who had set the club by the ears.

"I don't know, Dan, but this has taken so strong a hold on me that I shan't forget it soon. Imagine it yourself. Oh, but she could sing! I am a man not to be held in the leash of an adventure like this; but she held me. How? By the hope that one day I might see her face, with no veil of mystery to hold her off at arm's length."

Merrihew was greatly excited. He was for ordering a second bottle, but Hillard stayed him.

"By George! And you are sure that it was at the Sandfords'?"

"I am positive. But there is a puzzle that I have failed to solve: Sandford's cable and the caretaker's declaration. I know that I was in that house. I ran across a stein which I had given Sandford. I have inquired of the police; they had been requested to watch the house in the absence of the owner. The patrolman says that he has seen no light in the house since the family sailed for Africa. I sleep soundly; never have nightmares. And yet, but for her letters and the fact that Giovanni heard her sing under my window, I might almost believe I've been dreaming. It is no dream; but it begins to look as if I were the victim of some fine hoax."

"And Sandford mixed up in it," supplemented Merrihew.

"Sandford and I are good friends, but we are not so intimate that he'd take the pains to work out a hoax of this magnitude. It did not originate with him, and his wife is altogether out of the picture. If I had only seen her face, I might have forgotten all about her in a few days. But the mask, the charm, the mystery! I can't get her out of my thoughts; I am irrational in all I do; an absolute failure in the office."

"It is more than a hoax, in my opinion. Wait till Sandford returns and finds his silver gone!"

Hillard started.

"And his gold-plate," continued Merrihew, pleased with

the idea. "My boy, that's what it is; the best dodge I ever heard of. But how did they get into the house, she and her maid? It will make a good story for the Sunday papers. You won't be in it, unless she ropes you in as an accomplice. That would be rich!"

"I'm a romantic ass!" Hillard sighed. Leddy Lightfinger! If this turned out to be the case, he would never trust a human being again; he would take to breeding dogs.

"Let's take that ride on the horses," Merrihew urged. "That'll clear your brain of this sentimental fog."

"No!" Hillard struck his hands together. "I've a better idea than that, and it has just come to me. I shall go to Italy in March, and you, my boy, shall go with me."

"Impossible! Why, I'm all but broke." Merrihew shook his head decidedly.

"I'll take you as a companion. I'm a sick man, Dan. I'm likely to jump overboard if some one isn't watching me every minute."

"I'd like to go, Jack; Heaven and earth, but I should! But I can't possibly go to Italy with a letter of credit no more than twenty-five hundred, and that's all there is in the exchequer at present."

"Between such friends as we are—"

"That racket won't work. I could not take a moment's peace if I did not feel independent. Supposing I wanted to come home and you didn't, or you did and I didn't? No, Jack; nothing to it that way." And Merrihew was right.

"But I'm not going to give it to you!" Hillard protested. He was determined to break down Merrihew's objections if it took all night. "I am going to lend it to you."

"And could I ever pay you back if I accepted the loan?"

humorously. "You'll have to invent some other scheme."

"There's Monte Carlo; you might pull down a tidy sum," said the tempter.

"That's the way, you beggar; hit me on the soft side." But Merrihew was still obdurate. To go to Europe was out of the question.

"Now listen to reason, Dan. If you wait for the opportunity to go to Europe, you'll wait in vain. You must make the opportunity. One must have youth to enjoy Italy thoroughly. The desire to go becomes less and less as one grows older. Besides, it completes every man's education; it broadens his charity and smooths down the rough edges of his conceit. I'll put the proposition in a way you can't possibly get round. You've simply got to go. You will always have that thousand, so don't worry about that. You have twenty-five hundred on hand, you say. With that you can see Italy like a prince for three months. I know the tongue and the country; I know what you would want to see, what to avoid, where to stop."

"What's the proposition?" Merrihew drained the bottle.

"This: I'll agree to take not a penny more than twenty-five hundred myself. We'll go on equal terms. Why," confidently, "besides living like a prince, you'll have four hundred to throw away at roulette. Boy, you have never seen Italy; therefore you do not know what beauty is. When we eventually land at Bellaggio, on Lake Como, and I take your lily-white hand in mine and lead you up to the terrace of Villa Serbelloni, and order tea, then you will realize that you have only begun to live. Gardens, towering Alps, the green Lecco on one side and the green Como on the other; and Swiss champagne at a dollar-forty the quart! Eh?"

Merrihew produced his black cigar. This matter needed some deep reflection, and could not be determined offhand. The ash turned white on the end of the cigar before he replied.

"If you weren't Irish, you'd just naturally be Dago," he said with a laugh. "But it isn't fair to shoot me up this way, with flowery speeches."

"And then, besides all these things," Hillard added, "there's Kitty Killigrew, singing her heart out to a people who can't understand a word she's singing. Kitty Killigrew!"

"Can it be done for twenty-five hundred?"

"He's melting!" murmured Hillard jubilantly. "He's melting!"

"For a small amount I'd punch your head!" Merrihew chewed his cigar with subdued fierceness. He knew very well that he was destined to go to Europe. Kitty Killigrew, who had promised to mail the route they were to play, and hadn't!

"It is written, Dan, that you shall go with me. Think of running into the theater and seeing Kitty! I begin to like the music of that name."

"We'll settle this argument right here and now." Merrihew drew out a coin. "Call it!" he cried recklessly.

"Heads!"

The coin flickered in the light, fell, and proved that all money is perverse, by rolling under the davenport upon which they were sitting. An amusing hunt followed. They ran their hands over the floor, turned the rug, pulled out the davenport and looked behind, burnt innumerable matches, and finally rang for the attendant. The situation was explained, and he procured a candle. He was ultimately successful.

"Here it is, sir."

"Don't touch it!" warned Hillard.

"What is it, head or tail?" asked Merrihew weakly.

"Heads, sir," said the attendant, picking up the coin and offering it to the owner.

"Keep it," said Merrihew generously, even sadly. He never got up a game of chance that he did not get the worst of it. And now, Italy! All that way from home! "Boy, bring up a bottle of '96."

"Dan!"

"You be still," said Merrihew savagely. "You've roped me in nicely, and I'm game to go; but I'll have that bottle if I have to drink it all alone."

But he did not drink it all alone. Hillard was too wise to permit that. Merrihew might wish to add a few hundred to his letter of credit, via the card-room.

"And the Lady in the Mask?" asked Merrihew, as they at length stood up, preparatory to going down-stairs.

"I must relegate her to the fog she came out of. But it would be a frightful thing if—if—" He hesitated to form the words.

But Merrihew had no such scruple. "If the silver and plate were missing when the Sandfords return?"

"Oh, bosh! It's all some joke, and I'm the butt of it. She was in that house by the same authority she rode the horse."

"A woman of that sort would have no difficulty in hoodwinking the stablemen," declared Merrihew, certain that he had solved the riddle.

"And so you add forgery? Not a shred of my romance left!" Hillard spoke jestingly, but like a man who covers up a sudden twinge of pain.

"We'll know all about it in the fall. And ten to one, my theory will be the correct one."

"That's better. I have some hope now. You never won a bet in all your life."

"I know it; but this may be the one time. By the way, received a postal from Kitty this morning. From Gibraltar. Fine trip. Visited the gun-galleries and the antique furniture shops. Says no sign of prima donna as yet, but believes her to be on board. O'Mally's on the water-wagon. But Kitty aggravates me."

"What has she done now—refused you by Marconigraph?"

"No; but she promised me her address."

"Address her care Cook's, Florence, Rome, Venice. It's the popular mail-box of Europe; and if she has given them the address, they will forward."

"That helps considerably. I'm glad there's one Cook which can be relied on."

"In the morning I'll arrange for passage. We'll try the Celtic."

"I'll leave the business end of the trip to you."

"The first Saturday in March, then, if we can get booking. That will be in less than two weeks."

"I'm game. Shall I pack up my riding-breeches?"

"Prepare for everything except automobiles."

"Bah! I wouldn't take one as a gift."

"You couldn't afford to, if what I hear about them is true. Though you might be able to sell the gift and wipe out that thousand."

"Hang the thousand! I had almost forgotten it again."

In the lobby of the club, as they were about to enter the

coat-room, Hillard ran into one of several gentlemen issuing.

"Pardon me," he said, stepping aside.

"*Non un importa!*" said the stranger with a graceful wave of the hands.

Hillard looked quickly into the gentleman's face. "I am clumsy," he said in Italian.

Then the other stared at him, and smiled. For a moment there was a brief tableau, in which each took the other's measure and noted the color of the eyes. The man was an exceedingly handsome Italian, for all that a scar ran from his check to his chin. It was all over in a moment; and Hillard and Merrihew proceeded to the street.

"Handsome duffer," was Merrihew's comment. "But you never can tell a man by his looks. Gaze on me, for instance. I'm a good example of handsome is as handsome does." He was growing merry.

"Go home!" Hillard slapped him jovially on the shoulder.

"Home? Ah, yes! But shall I have a home to go to when I get back? You have roped me in nicely. My poor little twenty-five hundred! But Swiss champagne at a dollar-forty the quart! Well, every cloud has its lining. Say, Jack, how much brighter the world looks after a magnum! And a funny story's twice as funny. Good night. As for the Lady in the Fog, take the cash and let the credit go. That's my motto."

As Hillard never received any answer to his personal, he discontinued it. Truly, she had returned to the fog out of which she had come. But it was no less difficult for him to take up the daily affairs again; everything was so terribly prosaic now; the zest was gone from work and play. Italy was the last resort; and the business of giving Merrihew a personally conducted tour would occupy his mind. Always he was asking: Who was she? What mystery veiled her? Whither had she gone? We never can conjure up a complete likeness. Sometimes it is the eyes, again the mouth and chin, or the turn of the throat; there is never any ensemble of features and adornments. And as for Hillard, he really had nothing definite to recall, unless it was the striking color of her hair or the mellow smoothness of her voice. And could he really remember these? He often wished that she had sung under any window but his.

Giovanni was delighted when he heard the news. He would go, too, and act as valet to the signore and his friend till they put out for Rome. Then, of course, he would be obliged to leave them. Occasionally Hillard would reason with him regarding his deadly projects. But when a Latin declares that he has seen through blood, persuasions, arguments, entreaties, threats do not prevail. He comforted himself with the opinion, however, that Giovanni's hunt would come to no successful end.

"You will surely fall into the hands of the police."

"What God wills comes true. But by this time they will have forgotten me."

"But you have not forgotten."

"*Padre mio*, that is different. One obeys the civil law from habit. Between me and the *carabinieri* there is nothing personal. Thus it is easy for them to forget. Still, I shall not announce my approach, that I am Giovanni l'Aguello, returned for arrest. I shall take good care to keep out of their way."

"The eagle; that is a good name for you."

"And once I was as tame as a dove."

"But your man might be dead."

"He is not dead. If he were, something would tell me."

"It is a bad business, and I wish you no luck."

Giovanni smiled easily. Wishes seldom interfere with any one.

"I will double your wages," said Hillard, "if you will go where I go and return with me when I come back to America."

A deprecating movement. "Money? It is nothing. I am rich, after my kind."

"Are you still in the Church?"

"I confess regularly once a week. Oh, I am a good Catholic."

"Take yourself off. I am displeased with you."

The few days before sailing found Merrihew in a flutter of intense excitement. He carried his letter of credit about in order to convince himself during the day that he was really and truly going to Italy. He forswore the bottle and the illumined royalty of the card-deck, and spent his evenings "studying up" the lay of the land. To be sure, there was one grand dinner the night before they sailed. Suppose, Merrihew advanced, for the sake of argument, suppose the ship went down or he never came back, or he was ill all the way over? There would be one good dinner to remember, anyhow.

It was a drizzling, foggy morning when they drove down to the boat. There are seldom bright sailing days in the forepart of March. But the atmospheric effects made no impression on the volatile Merrihew. It was all very interesting to him. And he had an eye for all things, from the baskets of fruit and flowers, messengers with late orders from the stores, repeated farewells, to the squalling babies in the steerage. Even in the impudent shrieking tugboats he found a measure of delight; and the blur on the water was inviting.

At four o'clock they were on the high seas, heading for the Azores. Hillard was dreaming and Merrihew was studiously employed over a booklet on *How to Speak Italian in One Day.* There was a moderate sea on.

By and by Giovanni, who had spent most of the time arranging the luggage in the adjoining staterooms, came up on deck. He had two packets of letters and telegrams. One he gave to Merrihew and the other to his master.

"I forgot to give the signore his mail at breakfast. The boat-mail has just been distributed." He then went forward.

Merrihew was greatly pleased with his packet. There were humorous letters and cheery telegrams, containing all sorts of advice in case of seasickness, how to slip cigars through the customs, where to get the best post-cards, and also the worst.

Hillard found among his a bulky envelope post-marked Naples. After he opened it he lay back in his chair and contemplated the ruffled horizon. Naples! He sat up. It had been addressed to the house and the address typewritten.

"Dan?"

"What is it?"

"Look at this!"

"Good Lord!" Dan gasped, his feet coming down to the deck.

For Hillard was holding up for his inspection a crumpled black silk mask.

Chapter 8 WHAT MERRIHEW FOUND

The great ship had passed the Isle of Ischia, and now the Bay of Naples unfolded all its variant beauties. Hillard had seen them many times before, yet they are a joy eternal, a changing joy of which neither the eye nor the mind ever grows weary. Both he and Merrihew were foremost in the press against the forward rail. To the latter's impressionable mind it was like a dream. In fancy he could see the Roman galleys, the fighting triremes, the canopied pleasure-craft, just as they were two thousand years ago. Yonder, the temples and baths of Nero of the Golden House; thither, the palaces of the grim Tiberius; beyond, Pompeii, with Glaucus, lone, and Nydia, the blind girl. The dream-picture faded and the reality was no less fascinating: the white sails of the fishermen winging across the sapphire waters, leaving ribboned pathways behind that crossed and recrossed like a chart of the stars; proud white pleasure-yachts, great vessels from all ports in the world; and an occasional battle-ship, drab and stealthy. And the hundred pink and white villages, the jade and amethyst of the near and far islands, the smiling terraces above the city, the ruined temples, the grim giant ash-heap of Vesuvius!

"That is it," said Merrihew, whose flights of rhetoric were most simplified.

"*Vedi Napoli e poi mori!*" replied Hillard.

"Hold on," exclaimed Merrihew. "Pass it out slowly. What's that mean?"

"See Naples and die."

"I prefer to see it and live. But I am kind of disappointed in Vesuvius. It's not the terrible old Moloch of my geographies that gobbled up cities and peoples. And nobody seems to be afraid of it," with a gesture toward the villages nestling with the utmost confidence at the circling base. "Not a bit of smoke anywhere."

"No, my boy, don't speak slightingly of old Vesuvius. It is one of the great mysteries of the world. To-morrow that mountain may swallow up the whole bay, or it may never wake up again. Respect it; I do. When I recall Herculaneum and Pompeii—"

"Two thousand years ago; that's different. I'm never satisfied, I know, but I should like to see it blow its head off while I'm here."

"Not I! As I grow older I like comfort and security more and more. See that village on the cliffs toward the south? That's Sorrento, where I was born. The eruption of '72 happened while I was there, but I was too young to take any particular notice. Sh! Look at Giovanni."

Merrihew looked at the old Roman. Tears were running down his cheeks, and his gaze strove to pierce the distance to the far-off Sabine Hills. Italy! Yonder his heart and soul had taken root; his native land, his native land, and condemned to live in exile from it! Hillard leaned over and touched him on the arm, and he started.

"Take care, Giovanni."

"Pardon! I am weak this day, but to-morrow I shall be strong. Seven years! Have you not longed for it yourself? Has not your heart gone out many times across the seas to those cliffs?" pointing to Sorrento.

"Many times, Giovanni. But remember and control yourself. Presently the *carabinieri* will come on board. You will see that all our luggage goes promptly to the Bristol, once we are through the customs."

"Trust me, signore."

They landed at the custom-house at two in the afternoon, and passed without any difficulty. Naples is the easiest port in the world, if you are not a native and you chance to be an uncommercial traveler who is willing to purchase salt and tobacco of the State. The Italian tobacco is generally bad, and formerly one had to smoke it or go without; but now the best of imported cigars may be found in all the large cities, cheaper in some respects than those in America, and not a whit inferior, since there is no middleman's profit, buying, as one does, direct from the State. The hotels, however, sell the same brands at an outrageous advance; the proprietor must have his commission, the concierge, the head-waiter, the waiters, the porters, and the chef, for this slight favor to the guest. Commission! It means something in sunny Italy. All this Hillard explained to Merrihew as they were awaiting the examination. Merrihew, holding grimly on to his hand-luggage, stood waiting for Hillard at the iron gates fronting the railroad. Suddenly a brilliantly uniformed man rushed up to him, bowed, and insisted on taking the luggage. Merrihew protested feebly.

"But you are Meestaire Merrihoo, the friend of Meestaire Hil*lar*?"

"Yes."

"It is all right, then." The brilliant uniform prevailed, and Merrihew surrendered the luggage, marveling. Hillard seemed to know every one over here.

"Beautiful weather," said the uniform, as they passed through the gates.

"Fine," said Merrihew. From the corner of his eye he inspected the man at his side. Certainly he could be no less than a captain in the navy, with those epaulets and sleeve-bands.

"This is your first trip to Italy?"

"Yes. You people are very courteous here."

"Oh, we make that a part of our business."

A hundred cabmen yelled and shouted; but at a sign from Merrihew's new acquaintance they subsided or turned their attention elsewhere. This sign of respect made a still deeper impression on Merrihew.

"I'll bet a dollar he's an admiral!" he thought.

At length they came to an omnibus. The admiral beckoned to Merrihew to step in. The luggage was thrown on top.

"I am very grateful to you," said Merrihew, offering his hand.

The admiral shook it somewhat doubtfully, tipped his cap, and went hurriedly back to the *dogana*, or custom-house.

Shortly after Hillard appeared.

"We shan't go up in the omnibus," he said. "We'll take a carriage."

Merrihew looked around in vain for his distinguished acquaintance.

"What did you give the porter?" Hillard asked as they drove off.

"Porter? I didn't see any porter."

"Why, the chap who took your luggage from the customs."

"Good Lord! was that the porter? Why, I thought he was a personal friend of yours and an admiral in the Italian navy. I shook hands with him!"

Hillard shouted with laughter.

What a noisy, smelly, picturesque city it was! The cries of the hawkers, the importunities of the guides, the venders and cabmen, the whining beggars; the clatter of horses and carriages and carts; strolling singers, goats with tinkling bells, the barking of outcast dogs, and the brawling and bawling of children, hundreds upon hundreds of children! Merrihew grew dizzy trying to absorb the whole canvas at once. How the sturdy little campagna ponies ran up and down the narrow winding streets! Crack-crack! went the driver's lash. It possessed a language all its own. It called, it warned at the turning of the corners, it greeted friends, it hurled curses at rivals. Crack-crack! till Merrihew's ears ached. It was all very crowded and noisy till they reached the upper terrace of the Corso Vittorio; then the sounds became murmurous and pleasing.

Their rooms were pleasantly situated, looking out upon the sparkling bay. Giovanni began at once to unpack the trunks, happy enough to have something to occupy him till after dark, when he determined to venture forth. The dreaded *carabinieri* had paid him not the slightest attention; so far he was as safe as though he were in New York.

It was yet so early in the day that the two young men sallied forth in quest of light adventure. Besides, Merrihew was very eager to find some Roman and Florence newspapers. The American Comic Opera Company was somewhere north. They found stationed outside the hotel a rosy-cheeked cabby who answered to the name of Tomasso, or Tomass', as the Neapolitans generally drop the finals. He carried a bright red lap-robe and blanket, spoke a little English, and was very proud of the accomplishment. He was rather disappointed, however, when Hillard bargained with him in his own tongue. He saw at once that there would be no imposing on the young *Americano*. The two harangued for a while, on general principles. Twice words rose so high that Merrihew thought they were about to come to blows. Tomass' shook his fingers under Hillard's nose and Hillard returned the compliment. Finally Tomass' compromised on one-lira-fifty per hour, with fifty centesimi *pourboire*. Crack-crack! Down the hill they went, as if a thousand devils were after them.

"By George!" gasped Merrihew, clutching his seat; "the fool will break our necks!"

"They are always like this," laughed Hillard. "Slowly, slowly!" he called.

Tomass' grinned and cracked his whip. He did not understand the word slowly in his own tongue or in any other; at least, not till he reached the shops. It was business to go slowly there. A dozen times, on the Via Roma, Merrihew yelled that they would lose a wheel. But Tomass' knew the game. A man on foot could not have eluded collisions more skilfully. Merrihew never saw such driving. Nor had he ever seen such shops. Coral, coral, wherever the eye roamed. Where did they get it all and to whom did they sell it? Necklaces, tiaras, rings, brooches, carved and uncarved; were there women enough in the world to buy these things?

"If I had a wife… " he began.

"Well?"

"I'd feel devilish sorry for her husband at this moment."

"But isn't the color great?" said Hillard. It was good to be in Naples again.

Indeed, on a sunny afternoon, the traveler will find no other street offering such a kaleidoscope of luxuriant colors as the Via Roma of Naples. Behold the greens, the flowers, the cheeses, the shining fish, the bakestuffs, the silver- and goldsmiths, the milliners, the curio-dens! And the people! Dark-eyed beauties on foot or driving, handsome bearded men, monks, friars, priests, an archbishop in his splendid carriage, a duke driving tandem, nuns, and children. And uniforms as thick as poppies in a wheat-field. Officers rode past in their light blue capes, their gold and scarlet braids and polished scabbards; the foot-soldiers with their flowing green cock-feathers, policemen with their short swords, the tall and dignified *carabinieri* (always in pairs) with their cocked hats and crimson pompons towering above the sea of hats. It seemed to Merrihew that a rainbow had been captured and trained accordingly.

"I never saw so many kids," he observed; "so many dirty ones," he added. "Herod would have had his work cut out for him here. Now, where can we get some newspapers? I must know where she is."

"Presently," said Hillard. "The Piazza dei Martin," he directed Tomass'. Then he turned to Merrihew solemnly. "My boy, if you are to travel with me, beware of the Tauchnitz edition."

"What's that?"

"It's good reading in paper-covers. It is easier to sit in the hotel all day and read Tauchnitz than it is to tramp through churches and galleries and museums."

"No Tauchnitz; I promise." And Merrihew was an inveterate novel reader.

At the book-shop in the Piazza they found the Rome and

Florence papers. Hillard went through them thoroughly, but nowhere did he see anything relative to the doings of the American Comic Opera Company.

"Not a line, Dan."

"But there must be something in the Florence paper. They should be playing there yet."

"Nothing; these papers are two weeks old."

Merrihew stared blankly at the sheet. "I should like to know what it means."

"We will write to the consulate in Rome. If there has been any trouble he will certainly notify us. I'll write to-night. Now, here's Cook's next door. We'll ask if there is any mail for Kitty Killigrew."

But there wasn't, nor had there been; and the name was not on the forwarding books.

"Looks as if your Kitty were the needle in the haystack."

"Hang the luck!" Merrihew jammed his hands into his pockets and sulked with the world.

"It is evident that Kitty will not have you."

"Cut it!" savagely. Pictures and churches and museums were all well enough, but Merrihew wanted Kitty Killigrew above all the treasures of earth. It was no longer a passing fancy; he was downright in love.

When they turned down to the Via Caracciolo, with the full sweep of the magnificent bay at their feet, Merrihew's disappointment softened somewhat. It was the fashionable hour. The band was playing near-by in the Villa Nazionale. Americans were everywhere. Occasionally a stray princess or countess flashed by, inert and listless against the cushions, and invariably over-dressed. And when men accompanied them, the men (if they were husbands) lolled back, even more listless. And beggars of all sorts and descriptions besieged the "very great grand rich Americans." To the Neapolitan all Americans are rich; they are the only *forestieri* who are always ready to throw money about, regardless of results. The Englishman, now, when the *poveretto* puts out his unlovely hand, looks calmly over his head and drives on. The German (and in the spring there are more Germans in Italy than Italians!) is deep in his Koran, generally, his Karl Baedeker, or too thrifty to notice. It is to the American, then, that the beggar looks for his daily macaroni.

They were nearly a week in Naples. They saw the galleries, the museums and churches; they saw underground Naples; they made the weary and useless ascent of Vesuvius; and Merrihew added a new smell to his collection every hour. Pompeii by moonlight, however, was worth a thousand ordinary dreams; and Merrihew, who had abundant imagination, but no art with which to express it—happily or unhappily—saw Lytton's story unfold in all its romantic splendor. In the dark corners he saw Glaucus, and Sallust, and Arbaces; he could hear the light step of the luxurious Julia, and the tramp of the gladiators; he could hear Ione's voice in song and the low whisper of Nydia with her roses. "To the lions! Glaucus to the lions!" It would have been perfect had Vesuvius blown off the top of its head at that moment.

They lingered at Amalfi three days, and dreamed away the hours under the white pergola. Merrihew was loath to leave; but Hillard was for going on to Sorrento, for which his heart was always longing.

A spring rain fell as they took the incline, and it followed them over the mountains and down into Sorrento. The ruddy oranges hung in clusters over the old walls which lined both sides of the road, walls so old that history stops before them doubtfully. And the perfume of the sweet rain mingling with that of the fruit was like nothing Merrihew had ever sensed before. They finally drew up in the courtyard of the Hotel de la Sirena, and the long ride was at an end. The little garden was white and pink with roses and camellias, and the tubbed mandarins were heavy with fruit.

"And this is March!" said Merrihew, his thought traveling back to his own bleak country, where winter is so long and summer is so short.

Their rooms were on the northeast corner, on the first floor; and from the windows they could look down upon the *marina piccola*and the tideless sea, a sheer hundred and fifty feet below. Everybody welcomed the Signore Hillard; the hotel was his, and everything and everybody in it. Fire? It was already burning in the grate; orange wood, too, the smoke of which leaves no strong acidulous odor on the air. The Signore Hillard had only to speak, he had only to express a wish; they would scour the village to gratify it. Hillard accepted all these attentions as a matter of course, as a duke or a prince might have accepted them.

"By George!" whispered Merrihew; "they treat you like a prince here."

Later, when they were alone, Hillard began to explain.

"They remember my father; he used to live like a prince in Sorrento. Every time I come here I do the best I can to keep the luster to his name. To-morrow I shall point out to you the villa in which I was born. A Russian princess owns it now. You will know the place by the pet monkey which is always clambering about the balconies near the porter's lodge. More than that, if the princess is not on the Riviera, I'll take you there to tea some afternoon."

"A real live princess!" said Merrihew. "Is she beautiful?"

"Once upon a time," returned Hillard, laughing. "And, now, what do you say to a game of penuchle till dinner, a penny a point?"

Merrihew found two decks of cards, arranged them, and the game began. It was all very cheerful, the fire in the grate, the rain on the casement-windows, the blur on the bay, and the fragrance of two well-filled pipes.

There is very little to do in Sorrento at night; no theaters, no bands, no well-lighted cafés, nothing save wandering companies who dance the tarantella in the lobbies of the hotels, the men clumsy in their native costumes and the girls with as much grace and figure as so many heifers. It is only in Sicily that the Latin has learned to dance. But the tarantella is a novelty to the sight-seeing tourist, who believes he must see everything in order to be an authority when he gets back home.

Giovanni did not return till late that night, and on the morrow Hillard questioned him.

"I have been to see a cousin," said Giovanni, "who lives on the way to El Deserta."

"Ah! So you have a cousin here?"

"Yes, signore."

How old he looked, poor devil! Hillard had not taken particular notice of him during the past week's excursions. Giovanni had aged ten years since they landed.

"And was this cousin glad to see you? And is he to be trusted?"

"Both, signore. He had some news. She is — dancer in one of the Paris music-cafés."

Hillard kindled his pipe thoughtfully. And patiently Giovanni waited, knowing that shortly his master would offer some suggestion.

"Would you like me to give you the necessary money to go to Paris and bring her back to the Sabine Hills?" he asked softly.

"I shall go to Paris, signore — after."

"You will never find him."

"Who can say?"

"What is his name?" Hillard had never till this moment asked this question.

"I know it; that is sufficient. He is high, signore, very high; yet I shall reach him. If I told you his name — "

"There would be the possibility of my warning him."

"That is why I hesitate."

"You are a Catholic, Giovanni."

Giovanni signified that he was.

"Does not the God of all Catholics, of all Christians, in fact, does He not say that vengeance is His and that He will repay?"

"But there are so many of us, signore, so many of us small and of slight importance, that, likely enough, God with all His larger cares has not the time to remember us. What may happen to him in the hereafter does not concern me; for he will certainly be in the purgatory of the rich and I in the purgatory of the poor. It must be now, now!"

"Go your own way," said Hillard, dismissing him; "I shall never urge you again."

Giovanni gone, Hillard leaned against the casement. The sun was bright this morning and the air was clear. He could see Naples distinctly. Below, the fishermen and their wives, their bare feet plowing in the wet sands, were drawing in the nets, swaying their bodies gracefully. Presently the men in the boat landed the catch, and the net sparkled with living silver. So long as Giovanni was with him, he would be morally responsible for his actions. He would really be glad when the grim old Roman took himself off on his impossible quest.

How the sight of this beach recalled his boyhood! How many times had he and his brilliant mother wandered over these sands, picking up the many-colored stones, or baiting a young star-fish, or searching the caverns of the piratical Saracens that honeycombed the clifts, or yet, again, taking a hand at the nets! Sometimes he grew very lonely; for without a woman, either of one's blood or of one's choice, life holds little. Ah, that woman in the mask, that chimera of a night, that fancy of an hour!

And then Merrihew burst in upon him, wildly excited, and flourished the hotel register.

"Look at this!" he cried breathlessly. He flung the book on the table and pointed with shaking finger.

Hillard came forward, and this is what he saw:

Thomas O'Mally
James Smith
Arthur Worth
La Signorina Capricciosa
Kitty Killigrew
Am. Comic Opera Co., N.Y.   "Kitty has been here!"

"Perfectly true. But I wonder."

"Wonder about what?" asked Merrihew.

"Who La Signorina Capricciosa is. Whimsical indeed. She must be the mysterious prima donna."

He studied the easy-flowing hand, and ran his fingers through his hair thoughtfully. Then he frowned.

"What is it?" asked Merrihew curiously.

"Nothing; only I am wondering where I have seen that handwriting before."

Chapter 9 MRS. SANDFORD WINKS

A week in Sorrento, during which Merrihew saw all the beautiful villas, took tea with the Russian princess, made a martyr of himself trying to acquire a taste for the sour astringent wines of the country, and bought inlaid-wood paper-cutters and silk socks and neckties and hat-bands, enough, in truth, to last him for several generations; another week in Capri, where, at the Zum Kater Hidigeigei, he exchanged compliments with the green parrot, drank good beer, played *batseka* (a game of billiards) with the exiles (for Capri has as many as Cairo!) and beat them out of sundry lire, toiled up to the ledge where the playful Tiberius (see guide-books) tipped over his whilom favorites, bought a marine daub; and then back to Naples and the friendly smells. His constant enthusiasm and refreshing observations were a tonic to Hillard.

At the hotel in Naples they found a batch of mail. There was a letter which held particular interest to Merrihew. It was from the consul at Rome, a reply to Millard's inquiries regarding the American Comic Opera Company.

"We'll now find out where your charming Kitty is," Hillard said, breaking the seal.

But they didn't. On the contrary, the writer hadn't the slightest idea where the play-actors were or had gone. They had opened a two weeks' engagement at the Teatro Quirino. There had been a good house on the opening night; the remainder of the week did not show the sale of a hundred tickets. It was a fallacy that traveling Americans had any desire to witness American productions in Italy. So, then, the managers of the theater had abruptly canceled the engagement. The American manager had shown neither foresight nor common sense. He had, in the first place, come with his own scenery and costumes, upon which he had to pay large duties, and would have to pay further duties each time he entered a large city. His backer withdrew his support; and the percentage demanded by the managers in Florence, Genoa, Milan and Venice was so exorbitant (although they had agreed to a moderate term in the beginning) that it would have been nothing short of foolhardiness to try to fill the bookings. The singing of the prima donna, however, had created a highly favorable impression among the critics; but she was unknown, and to be unknown was next to positive failure, financially. This information, the writer explained, had been obtained by personal investigation. The costumes and scenery had been confiscated; and the manager and his backer had sailed for America, leaving the members of the company to get back the best way they could. As none of the players had come to the consulate for assistance, their whereabouts were unknown. The writer also advised Mr. Hillard not to put his money in any like adventure. Italy was strongly against any foreign invasion, aside from the American trolley-car.

"That's hard luck," growled Merrihew, who saw his hopes go down the horizon.

"But it makes me out a pretty good prophet," was Hillard's rejoinder. "The Angel's money gave out. Too many obstacles. To conquer a people and a government by light opera —it can't be done here. And so the American Comic Opera Company at the present moment is vegetating in some little *pensione*, waiting for money from home."

Merrihew gnawed the end of his cane. All his pleasant dreams had burst like soap-bubbles. Had they not always done so? There would be no jaunts with Kitty, no pleasant little excursions, no little suppers after the performance. And what's a Michelangelo or a Titian when a man's in love?

"Brace up, Dan. Who knows? Kitty may be on the high seas, that is, if she has taken my advice and got a return-ticket. I'll give you a dinner at the Bertolini to-night, and you may have the magnum of any vintage you like. We'll have Tomass' drive us down the Via Caracciolo. It will take some of the disappointment out of your system."

"Any old place," was the joyless response. "Seems to me that Italy has all the cards when it comes to graft."

"America, my boy, is only in the primary department. Kitty's manager forgot the most important thing of the whole outfit."

"What's that?"

"The Itching Palm. Evidently it had not been properly soothed. Come on; we may run across some of our ship-acquaintances. To-morrow we'll start for Rome, and then we shall add our own investigations to those of the consul."

They had ridden up and down the Via Caracciolo twice when they espied a huge automobile, ultramarine blue. It passed with a cloud of dust and a rumble which was thunderous. Hillard half rose from his seat.

"Somebody you know?" asked Merrihew.

"The man at the wheel looked a bit like Sandford."

"Sandford? By George, that would be jolly!"

"Perhaps they will come this way again. Tomass', follow that motor."

Sure enough, when the car reached the Largo Vittoria, it wheeled and came rumbling back. This time Hillard had no doubts. He stood up and waved his arms. The automobile barked and groaned and came to a stand.

"Hello, Sandford!"

"Jack Hillard, as I live, and Dan Merrihew! Nell?" turning to one of the three pretty women in the tonneau. "What did I tell you? I felt it in my bones that we would run across some one we knew."

"Or over them," his wife laughed.

In a foreign land one's flag is no longer eyed negligently and carelessly, as though it possessed no significance; it now becomes a symbol of the soil wherein our hearts first took root. A popular tune we have once scorned, now, when heard, catches us by the throat; the merest acquaintance becomes a long-lost brother; and persons to whom we nod indifferently at home now take the part of tried and true friends. But when we meet an old friend, one who has accepted our dinners and with whom we have often dined, what is left but to fall on his neck and weep? There was, then, over this meeting, much ado with handshaking and compliments, handshaking and questions; and, as in all cases like this, every one talked at once. How was old New York? How was the winter in Cairo? And so forth and so on, till a policeman politely told them that this was not a private thoroughfare, and that they were blocking the way. So they parted, the two young men having promised to dine with the Sandford party that evening.

"What luck, Dan!" Hillard was exuberant.

"Saves you the price of a dinner."

"I wasn't thinking of that. But I shall find out all about her to-night."

"Who?"

"The Lady in the Fog, the masquerading lady!"

"Bah! I should prefer something more solid than a vanishing lady."

"Look here, Dan, I never throw cold water on you."

"There have been times when it would have done my head good."

Sandford knew how to order a dinner; and so by the time that Merrihew had emptied his second glass of Burgundy and his first of champagne, he was in the haze of golden confidence. He would find Kitty, and when he found her he would find her heart as well.

"Say, Jack," said Sandford, "what did you mean by that fool cable, anyhow?"

Hillard had been patiently waiting for an opening of this sort. "And what did you mean by hoaxing me?"

"Hoaxing you?"

"That's the word. I was in your house that night; I was there as surely as I am here to-night."

"Nell, am I crazy, or is it Jack?"

"Sometimes," said Mrs. Sandford, "when you put the chauffeur in the tonneau, I'm inclined to think that it is you."

Hillard looked straight into the placid grey eyes of his hostess. Very slowly one of the white lids drooped. His heart bounded.

"But really," continued Sandford seriously, "unless you bribed the caretaker, you could not possibly have entered the house. You have been dreaming."

"Very well, then; it begins to look as if I had." It was apparent to Hillard that Sandford was not in his wife's confidence in all things. He also saw the wisdom of dropping the subject while at the table. To take up the thread of that romance again! He needed no wine to tingle his blood.

They took coffee and liqueur in the glass-inclosed balcony. All Naples sparkled at their feet, and the young moon rose over the Sorrentine Hills. Sandford and Merrihew and the other two ladies began an animated exchange of experiences. Hillard found a quiet nook, not far from the lift. He saw that Mrs. Sandford's chair was placed so that she could get a good view of the superb night. He sat down himself, sipped his liqueur meditatively, drank his coffee, and, as she nodded, lighted a cigarette.

"Well?" she said, smiling into his brown eyes. She was rather fond of Hillard; a gentleman always, and one of excellent taste. There was never any wearisome innuendo in his wit nor suggestion in his stories.

"You deliberately winked at me," he began.

"I deliberately did."

"Sandford is in the dark; I suspected as much."

"Regarding the wink?"

"Regarding the mysterious woman who occupied your house by your express authority, and who rode the hunter in the park."

"Was there ever a more beautiful picture?" sweeping her hands toward the city.

"The beauty of it will last several hours yet. Who and what was she?"

"I wish I could find you a wife; you would make a good husband."

"Thank you. I am even willing, with your assistance, to prove it. Who was she, and how came she in your house?"

"She wished that favor, and that her presence in New York should not be known. Now, describe to me exactly what happened. I am worrying about the plate and the silver."

He laughed. "And you will meet me half-way?"

"I promise to tell you all I ... dare."

"There is a mystery?"

"Yes. So begin with your side of it."

He was a capital story-teller. He recounted the adventure in all its color; the voice under his window, the personals in the paper, the interchange of letters, the extraordinary dinner, the mask in the envelope. She followed him with breathless interest.

"Charming, charming!" She clapped her hands. "And how well you tell it! You have told it just as it happened."

"Just as it happened!" confounded for a moment.

"Exactly. I have had a letter, two, in fact. You did not see her face?"

"Only the chin and mouth. But if I ever meet her again I shall know her by her teeth."

"Heavens! And how?"

"Two lower ones are gone; otherwise they would be beautiful."

"Poor man! You have builded your house upon the sands. Her teeth are perfect. She has fooled you."

"But I saw with these two eyes!"

"There is a preparation which theatrical people use; a kind of gum. She mentioned the trick. Isn't she clever?"

"Yet I shall know her hair," doggedly.

She put her hands swiftly to her head. "Now, you have known me for years. What is the color of my hair?"

"Why, it is blond."

"Nothing of the kind. It is auburn. If you can not tell mine, how will you tell hers?"

"I shall probably run after every red-headed woman in Europe till I find her," humorously.

"If you can keep out of jail long enough."

"I shall at any rate remember her voice."

"That is better. Our ears never deceive half so often as our eyes."

"Her face is not scarred, is it?"

"Scarred!" indignantly. "She is as beautiful as a Raphael, as lovely as a Bouguereau. If I were a man I should gladly journey round the world for the sight of her."

"I am willing, even anxious."

"I should fall in love with her."

"I believe I have."

"And I should marry her, too."

"Even that."

"Come, Mr. Hillard; I am just fooling. You are too sensible a man to fall in love with a shadow, a mask. Your fancy has been trapped, that is all. One does not fall in love that way."

"You ought to know," with a sidelong glance at Sandford.

As her glance followed his, hers grew warm and kindly. Sandford, by chance meeting the look, smiled back across the room. This little by-play filled Hillard with a sense of envy and loneliness. At three-and-thirty a bachelor realizes that there is something else in life besides business and travel.

"It is quite useless to ask who she is?" he inquired of his hostess.

"Quite useless."

"She is married?"

"Certainly I have not said so."

He flicked the ash from his cigarette. What was the use of trying to trap a woman into saying what she did not propose to say?

"Have you those letters?"

"One of them I'll show you."

"Why not the other?"

"It would be wasting time. It merely relates to your adventure. She sailed the day after you dined with her."

"That accounts for the shutters. The police and the caretaker were bribed."

"I suspect they were."

"If I were a vain man, and you know I am not, I might ask you if she spoke well of me in this letter. Understand, I am not inquiring."

"But you put the question as adroitly as a woman. We are sure of vanity always. Yes, she spoke of you. She found you to be an agreeable gentleman. But," with gentle malice, "she did not say that she wished she had met you years ago, under more favorable circumstances, or that she liked your eyes, which are really fine ones."

He had to join in her laughter.

"Come, give me the death-stroke and have done with it. Tell me what you dare, and I'll be content with it."

She opened her handkerchief purse and delved among the various articles therein.

"I expected that you would be asking questions, so I came prepared. I did not tell my husband for that very reason. He would have insisted upon knowing everything. Here, read this. It is only a glimpse."

He searched eagerly for the signature.

"Don't bother," she said. "The name is only a nickname we gave her at school."

"School? Do you mean to tell me that you went to school with her? Where?"

"In Pennsylvania first; then in Milan. Read."

O Cara Mia—If only you knew how sorry I am to miss you! Why must you sail at once? Why not come to my beautiful Venice? True, I could not entertain you as in the days of my good father. But I have so much to say to you that can not be written. You ask about the adventure. Pouf! goes my little dream of greatness. It was a blank failure. Much as I knew about Italy I could not know everything. The officials put unheard-of obstacles in our path. The contracts were utterly disregarded. In the first place, we had not purchased our costumes and scenery in Italy.

"Costumes and scenery?" Hillard sought the signature again. Mrs. Sandford was staring at the moonlit bay.

That poor manager! And that poor man who advanced the money! They forgot that the booking is as nothing, the incidentals everything. The base of all the trouble was a clerk in the consulate at Naples. He wrote us that there would be no duties on costumes and scenery. Alas! the manager and his backer are on the way to America, sadder and wiser men. We surrendered our return tickets to the chorus and sent them home. The rest of us are stranded—is not that the word?—here in Venice, waiting for money from home. If I were alone, it would be highly amusing; but these poor people with me! There is only one way I can help them, but that, never. You recollect that my personal income is quarterly, and it will be two months before I shall have funds. I could get it advanced, but I dare not. There are persons moving Heaven and earth to find me. My companions haven't the least idea who I am; to them I am one of the profession. So here we all are, wandering about the Piazza San Marco, calling at Cook's every day in hopes of money, and occasionally risking a penny in corn for the doves. I am staying with my nurse, my mother's maid, in the Canipo Santa Maria Formosa, near our beloved Santa Barbara. Very quietly I have guaranteed the credit of my unfortunate companions, and they believe that Venetians are very generous people. Generous! Think of it! Come to Venice, dear; it is all nonsense that you must return to America. Perhaps you will wonder how I dared appear on the stage in Italy. A black wig and a theatrical make-up; these were sufficient. A duke sent me an invitation to take supper with him, as if I were a ballerina! I sent one of the American chorus girls, a little minx for mischief. She ate his supper, and then ran away. I understand that he was furious. Only a few months more, Nell, and then I may come and go as I please. Come to Venice. Capricciosa.

Hillard did not stir. Another labyrinth to this mystery! Capricciosa; Kitty Killigrew's unknown prima donna; and all he had to do was to take the morning train for Venice, and twenty-four hours later he would be prowling through the Campo Santa Maria Formosa. Though his mind was busy with a hundred thoughts, his head was still bent and his eyes riveted upon the page.

Mrs. Sandford observed him curiously, even sadly. Why couldn't his fancy have been charmed by an every-day, sensible girl, and not by this whimsical, extraordinary woman who fooled diplomats, flaunted dukes, and kept a king at arm's length as a pastime? And yet—!

"Capricciosa," he mused aloud. "That is not her name."

"And I shall not tell it you."

"But her given name? Just a straw; something to hold on; I'm a drowning man." Hillard's pleadings would have melted a heart of stone.

"It is Hilda."

"That is German."

"She prefers it to Sonia."

"Sonia Hilda; it begins well. May I keep this letter?"

"Certainly not. With that *cara mia*? Give it to me."

He did so. "Shall I seek her?"

"This is my advice: don't think of her after to-night. If you ever see or recognize her, avoid her. It may sound theatrical, but she is the innocent cause of two deaths. These men sought her openly, too."

"What has she done?"

"She made a great, though common, mistake."

"Political?"

Her lips closed firmly, but a smile lurked in the corners.

He sighed.

"Don't be foolish. I am sorry I let you see the letter. I forgot that she told me her hiding-place."

"Her hiding-place?"

"Mr. Hillard, she is as far removed from your orbit as Mars' is from Jupiter's. Forget her."

"My orbit is not limited. I shall seek her; when I find her I shall ... marry her."

But her lips closed again.

"Sphinx!" he murmured with reproach.

"I like you too much, Mr. Hillard, to stand by and see you break your heart against a stone wall."

"Don't you see, the deeper the mystery is the more powerful the attraction becomes?"

The door to the lift opened and closed noisily, and Hillard turned negligently. A man sauntered through the room. The moment he came into the light Hillard's interest became lively enough: It was the handsome Italian with the scar.

"Who is that man?" he whispered. "Only a few weeks ago I bumped into him on coming out of the club."

A swift glance, then her eyes grew unfriendly, her shoulders rigid and repellent.

"Do not attract his attention," she answered in a low tone. "Yes, I know him, and I do not wish him to see me."

"Who is he?" he repeated.

"A Venetian officer, and a profligate. I entertained him once, but I learned from him that I had been ill-advised."

Hillard saw that this subject would admit of no further questions. The man with the scar had committed some inexcusable offense, and Mrs. Sandford had crossed him off the list. He knew that the Italian officer is, more or less, a lady's man; and the supreme confidence he has in the power of brass buttons and gold lace makes him at times insufferable.

It was after ten when Hillard and his friend took their leave. They would not see their host and hostess again till they reached New York. Upon coming out on the Corso, Hillard whistled merrily.

"Pleasant evening," was Merrihew's comment.

Hillard continued to whistle.

"Good dinner, too."

The whistle went on serenely, in spite of Merrihew's obvious attempts to choke it off.

"You seemed to have a good deal to say to Mrs. Sandford. She knows the lady who was in the house?"

Still the whistle.

"Say, wake up!" cried Merrihew impatiently.

"We shall leave in the morning for Venice," said Hillard, taking up the tune again.

"Venice? How about Rome and Florence?"

"Which would you prefer: Rome and the antiquities, or Venice and—Kitty Killigrew?"

"Kitty in Venice? Are you sure?"

"She is there with La Signorina Capricciosa. Oh, this is a fine world, after all, and I was wrong to speak ill of it this morning."

"If Kitty's in Venice, I'm an ungrateful beggar, too. But I do not see why Kitty's being in Venice excites you."

"No? Well, fate writes that Kitty's mysterious prima donna and my Lady of the Mask are one and the same person."

"No!"

The two, without further words, marched along the middle of the Corso to the hotel, which was only a few steps away. They entered. The concierge started toward them as if he desired to impart some valuable information, but suddenly reconsidered, and retreated to his bandbox of an office and busied himself with the ever-increasing *debours*. The strangeness of his movements passed unnoticed by the two men, who continued on through the lobby, turning into the first corridor.

Hillard inserted his key in the door of his room, unlocked it, and swung it inward. This done, he paused irresolutely on the threshold, and with good cause.

"What the devil can this mean?" he whispered to Merrihew, who peered over his shoulder.

Two dignified *carabinieri* rose quickly and approached Hillard. There was something in the flashing eyes and set jaws that made him realize that the safest thing for him to do at that moment was to stand perfectly still!

Chapter 10 CARABINIERI

"Signori," began Hillard calmly, "before you act, will you not do me the honor to explain to me the meaning of this visit?"

"It is not he!" said one of the *carabinieri*. "It is the master, and not the servant. This is Signore Hil*lar*, is it not?" he continued, addressing himself to Hillard.

"Yes."

"The signore has a servant by the name of Giovanni?"

"Yes. And what has he done to warrant this visit?" Hillard asked less calmly.

"It is a matter of seven years," answered the spokesman. "Your servant attempted to kill an officer in Rome. Luigi here, who was then interested in the case in Rome, thought he recognized Giovanni in the street to-day. Inquiries led us here."

"Ah!" Hillard thought quickly. "I am afraid that you have had your trouble for nothing. Giovanni is now a citizen of the United States, under full protection of its laws, domestic and foreign. It would not be wise for you to touch him."

The *carabinieri* stared at each other. They shrugged.

"Signore, we recognize no foreign citizenship for our countrymen who, having committed a crime, return to the scene of it. We are here to arrest him. He will be tried and sentenced. But it is possible that he may be allowed to return to America, once he has been proved guilty of intent to kill."

Hillard flushed, but he curbed the rise in his temper. It was enough that the United States was made the dumping-ground of the criminal courts of Europe, without having it forced upon him in this semi-contemptuous fashion. The *carabinieri* saw the effort.

"The signore speaks Italian so well that he will understand that we have nothing to do with deportation. Our business is simply to arrest offenders against the State. It is to the State you must look for redress; and here the State is indifferent where the offender goes, so long as it is far away." The speaker bowed ceremoniously.

"Yes, I understand. But I repeat, my servant is a legal citizen of the United States, and there will be complications if you touch him."

"Not for us. That rests between you and the State. Our orders are to arrest him."

"At any rate, it looks as though Giovanni had been forewarned of your visit. And may I ask, what is the name of the officer Giovanni attempted to kill?"

"It is not necessary that you should know."

Hillard accepted the rebuke with becoming grace.

"And now, signore," with the utmost courtesy, "permit us to apologize for this intrusion. We shall wait in the hall, and if we find Giovanni we shall gladly notify you of the event."

The two officers bowed and passed out into the corridor. Hillard raised his hat, and closed the door.

"Now, what the deuce has all this powwow been about?" demanded Merrihew; for he had understood nothing, despite his *How to Speak Italian in One Day*.

"It's that rascal Giovanni."

"Did he find his man and cut him up?"

"No. It seems that these carabinieri have remark-able memories; the old affair. Poor devil! I can't imagine how they traced him here. But I repeatedly warned him about going abroad in the daylight. Hello, what's this?" going to the table. It was a note addressed to him; and it was from the fugitive.

My kind master—The *carabinieri* are after me. But rest easy. I was not born to rot in a dungeon. I am going north. As for my clothes, send them to Giacamo, the baker, who lives on the road to El Deserta. He will understand. May the Holy Mother guard you, should we never meet again!

Hillard passed the note to Merrihew.

"That's too bad. I've taken a great fancy to him. It seems that the peasant has no chance on this side of the water. His child a painted dancer in Paris, and a price on his own head! It's hard luck. And the fellow who caused all this trouble goes free."

"He always goes free, Dan, here or elsewhere."

"Why, we'd have lynched him in America."

"That's possible. We are such an impulsive race," ironically. "Yes, no doubt we'd have lynched him; and these foreigners would have added another ounce of fact to their belief that we are still barbarians."

"I hadn't thought of that," Merrihew admitted. Till now he had never cared particularly whether a foreigner's opinion was favorable or not.

"No, but when you start for home you will always think of it. Our reporters demand of the foreigner, barely he has stepped ashore, what he thinks of the United States; and then nearly every one he meets helps to form the opinion that we are insufferably underbred. Ours is not studied incivility; it is worse than that; it is downright carelessness."

"I am beginning to see things differently. When the concierge tips his hat, I tip mine. Since Giovanni is gone, suppose we pack up? There's little to do, as the trunks are as we left them.

But I say, how is it that all these *carabinieri* we see are so tall? The Neapolitan is invariably short and thick-set."

"They come from the north as far as Domo d'Ossola; mountaineers. Italy has a good policy regarding her military police. The Neapolitan is sent north and the Venetian and Tuscan south, out of reach of family ties and feuds. Thus, there is never any tug between duty and friendship. The truth is, the Italian is less inclined toward duty than toward friendship. This isolation makes the *carabinieri* the right hand of the army, and no other soldier in Europe is half so proud of his uniform, not even the German. The people smile as they pass, you will notice always in pairs; but when they are in trouble, these weather-vane people, they fly straight to the *carabinieri*. Imagine the cocksureness and insolence we'd have suffered from two New York policemen, had we found them in our homes! Oh, I have a soft spot for the *carabinieri*. You will find no brigands in Italy now; that is because the *carabinieri* are everywhere, silent, watchful, on highways, in the mountains, in all villages and in all stations. I have never seen one of them ogle a woman. And never ask them where your hotel is, or the station, or such and such a street. They will always tell you, but they secretly resent it."

"I'll remember; but so far as I'm concerned, they'd have an easy time of it. Why, I couldn't ask a question in billboard Italian. Now, out with it; where and how did you learn that Kitty is in Venice?"

Hillard told him briefly.

"And so they are all in Venice, broke? By George, here's our chance; everlasting gratitude and all that. We'll bail 'em out and ship 'em home! How is that for a bright idea?" Merrihew had regained his usual enthusiasm.

"Let me see," said Hillard practically. "There are five of them: five hundred for tickets and doubtless five hundred more for unpaid hotel bills. It would never do, Dan, unless we wish to go home with them."

"But I haven't touched my letter of credit yet. I could get along on two thousand."

"Not with the brand of cigars you are smoking; a lira-fifty each."

"Well I'll try the native brand for a while, *Trabucos*."

"Not in my immediate vicinity," Hillard objected. "No, we can't bail them out, but we can ease up their bills till money comes from home. Not one of them by this time will have a watch. O'Mally will remain sober from dire necessity. Poor Kitty Killigrew! All the wonderful shops and not a stiver in her pockets!"

"Aren't they the most careless lot, these professional people? They never prepare for emergencies, and are always left high and dry. Instead of putting their cash in banks, they buy diamonds, with the idea that they have always something convertible into cash at a moment's notice."

"Usually at one-third of what the original price was." Hillard threw off his hat and coat and lighted his pipe.

Merrihew paced the floor for some time, his head full of impossible schemes. He stopped in the middle of the room with an abruptness which portended something.

"I have it. Instead of going directly to Venice, we'll change the route and go to Monte Carlo. I'll risk my four hundred, and if I win!"

"Then the announcement cards, a house-wedding, and pictures in the New York papers. Dan, you are impossible. You have gambled enough to know that when you are careless of results you win, but never when you need the cash. But it is Monte Carlo, if you say so. Two or three days there will cure you of your beautiful dream. After all," with a second thought, "it's a good cause, and it might be just your luck to win. The masquerading lady! I'll stake my word that there is comedy within comedy, and rare good comedy at that. Monte Carlo it is."

Merrihew danced a jig. Hillard stepped to the mirror and bowed profoundly. The jig ceased.

"Madame, permit me, a comparative stranger, to offer you passage money home. We won it at Monte Carlo; take it, it is yours. Polite enough," mused Hillard, turning and smiling; "but hanged if it sounds proper."

"To the deuce with propriety!" cried Merrihew buoyantly. "We'll start, then, at nine to-morrow?"

"At nine promptly."

"I'm off to bed, then." As Merrihew reached the door he paused. "I forgot to tell you. Do you recollect that Italian you ran into at the club that night? Saw him at the hotel to-night. He bowed to Sandford, and Sandford cut him dead. It set me thinking."

"The Sandfords entertained him somewhere, once upon a time, and he behaved like a cad. I don't know what about, and I don't care."

"Humph! I hope Giovanni gets off safely."

"I think he will."

When Merrihew had gone Hillard opened the shutters to clear the room of the tobacco smoke, and stood beside the sill, absorbing the keen night air and admiring the serene beauty of the picture which lay spread before him. The moon stood high and clear now, the tiled roofs shone mistily, and from some near-by garden came the perfume of boxwood and roses. All was silence; noisy Naples slept. He would see her face this time; he would tear aside the mystery. She had made a great mistake? That was of small consequence to him. He could laugh at Mrs. Sandford's warning. He was no green and untried youth; he was a man. Then he laughed aloud. It was so droll. Here was Merrihew in love with the soubrette, and he himself... . *Was* he in love, or was only his fancy trapped? A fine comedy! The soubrette and the prima donna! He closed the shutters, for the Neapolitan is naturally a thief, and an open window is as large as a door to him. He packed his cases, and this done, went to bed. For a time he could hear Merrihew in the adjoining room; but even this noise ceased. Hillard fell asleep and dreamed that he and Giovanni were being pursued by *carabinieri* in petticoats and half-masks, that Merrihew had won tons of napoleons at Monte Carlo, and that Kitty Killigrew was a princess in disguise. Such is the vagary of dreams.

Chapter 11 THE CITY IN THE SEA

From her window Kitty looked down on the Campo which lay patched with black shadows and moonshine. A magic luster, effective as hoar-frost, enveloped the ancient church, and the lines of the eaves and the turns of the corners were silver-bright. How still at night was this fairy city in the sea! Save for the occasional booming of bells—and in Italy they are for ever and ever booming—and the low warning cry of the gondoliers, there was nothing which spoke of life, certainly not here in the Campo Santa Maria Formosa. There were no horses clattering over the stone pavements, no trams, no omnibuses; the stillness which was of peace lay over all things. And some of this had entered Kitty's heart. She was not deeply read, but nevertheless she had her share of poetical feeling. And to her everything in the venerable city teemed with unexpressed lyric. What if the Bridge of Sighs was not true, or the fair Desdemona had not dwelt in a palace on the Grand Canal, or the Merchant had neither bought nor sold in the shadow of the Rialto bridge? Historians are not infallible, and it is sometimes easier and pleasanter to believe the poets.

But for one thing the hour would have been perfect. Kitty, ordinarily brave and cheerful, was very lonesome and homesick. Tears sparkled in her eyes and threatened to fall at any moment. It was all very well to dream of old Venice; but when home and friends kept intruding constantly! The little bank-account was so small that five hundred would wipe it out of existence. And now she would be out of employment till the coming autumn. The dismal failure of it all! She had danced, sung, spoken her lines the very best she knew how; and none had noticed or encouraged her. It was a bitter cup, after all the success at home. If only she could take it philosophically; like La Signorina! She shut her eyes. How readily she could see the brilliant, noisy, friendly Broadway, the electric signs before the theaters, the gay crowds in the restaurants! It was all very fine to see Europe on a comfortable letter of credit, but to see it under such circumstances as these, that was a different matter. To live in this evil-smelling old tenement, with seldom any delicacy to eat, a strange jabber-jabber ringing in one's ears from morning till night, and to wait day after day for that letter from home, was not a situation such as would hearten one's love of romance. The men had it much easier; they always do. There was ever some place for a man to go; and there were three of them, and they could talk to one another. But here, unless La Signorina was about—and she had an odd way of disappearing—she, Kitty, had to twiddle her thumbs or talk to herself, for she could understand nothing these people, kindly enough in their way, said to her.

She opened her eyes again, and this time the tears flowed unheeded. Of what use is pride, unless it be observed by others? She missed some one, a frank, merry, kind-hearted some one; and it was balm to her heart to admit it at last. Had he appeared to her at that moment, she must have fallen gratefully into his arms.

And there were so many things she could not understand. Why should La Signorina always go veiled? Why should she hide her splendid beauty? Where did she disappear so mysteriously in the daytime? And those sapphires, and diamonds, and emeralds? Why live here, with such a fortune hanging round her neck? Kitty forgot that, for the sake of sentiment, one will sometimes eat a crust when one might dine like a prince.

"Kitty?" The voice came from the doorway. Kitty was startled for a moment, but it was only La Signorina. Kitty furtively wiped her eyes.

"I am over here by the window. The moon was so bright I did not light the lamp."

La Signorina moved with light step to the window, bent and caught Kitty's face between her hands and turned it firmly toward the moon.

"You have been crying, *cara*!"

"I am very lonely," said Kitty.

"You poor little homeless bird!" La Signorina seized Kitty impulsively in her arms. "If I were not— " She hesitated.

"If you were not?"

"If I were not poor, but rich instead, I'd take you to one of the fashionable hotels. You are out of place here, in this rambling old ruin."

"Not half so much as you are," Kitty replied.

"I am never out of place. I can live comfortably in the fields with the peasants, in cities, in extravagant hotels. It is the mind, my dear, not the body. My mind is always at one height; where the body is does not matter much."

There was a subtle hauteur in the voice; it subdued Kitty's inquisitiveness. And no other woman had, till recently, accomplished this feat. Kitty was proud, but there was something in her companion that she recognized but could not express in words.

"Come!" said the older woman. "I myself am lonely and desperate to-night. I am going to throw away a precious bit of silver on a gondolier. We haven't been out three times together since we arrived. Perhaps it would have been better had we all remained in Rome; but there I could not have helped you. The band plays in the Piazza to-night. They are going to play light opera, and it will tone us both up a bit. More than that, we'll have coffee at Florian's, if we can find a table. To-morrow we may have to do without breakfast. But there's the old saying that he who sleeps dines. *Avanti!*"

"Sometimes," said Kitty, drying the final tear, "sometimes I am afraid of you."

"And wisely. I am often afraid of myself. I always do the first thing that enters my head, and generally it is the wrong thing. Never mind. The old woman here will trust us for some weeks yet." She leaned from the window and called. "Pomp-*e*-o!"

From the canal the gondolier answered.

"Now then!" said the woman to the girl.

Kitty threw a heavy shawl over her head and shoulders, while the other wound about her face the now familiar dark grey veil; and the two went down into the Campo to the landing. Kitty longed to ask La Signorina why she invariably wore that veil, but she did not utter the question, knowing full well that La Signorina would have evaded it frankly.

Pompeo threw away his cigarette and doffed his hat. He offered his elbow to steady the women as they boarded; and once they were seated, a good stroke sent the gondola up the canal. The women sat speechless for some time. At each intersection Pompeo called right or left musically. Sometimes the moon would find its way through the brick and marble cañon, or the bright ferrule of another gondola flashed and disappeared into the gloom. Under bridges they passed, they glided by little restaurants where the Venetians, in olden days, talked liberty for themselves and death to the Austrians, and at length they came out upon the Grand Canal where the Rialto curves its ancient blocks of marble and stalactites gleam ghostly overhead.

"There, this is better."

"It is always better when you are with me," said Kitty.

For years Kitty had fought her battles alone, independent and resourceful; and yet here she was, leaning upon the strong will of this remarkable woman, and gratefully, too. It is a pleasant thing to shift responsibility to the shoulders of one we know to be capable of bearing it.

"Now, my dear Kitty, we'll just enjoy ourselves to-night, and on our return I shall lay a plan before you, and to-morrow you may submit it to the men. It is as usual a foolish plan, but it will be something of an adventure."

"I accept it at once, without knowing what it is."

"Kitty Killigrew," mused La Signorina. "The name is as pretty as you are. Pretty Kitty Killigrew; it actually sings." Then she added solemnly: "Never change it. There is no man worth the exchange."

Kitty was not wholly sure of this, so she made no response.

"What a beautiful palace!" she cried presently, pointing to a house in darkness, not far from the house of Petrarch. It was only the interior of the house that was in darkness. The moon poured broadly upon it. The leaning gondola-posts stood like sleeping sentinels, and the tide murmured over the marble steps.

Pompeo, seeing Kitty's gesture and not understanding her words, swung the gondola diagonally across the canal.

"No, no, Pompeo!" La Signorina spoke in Italian. "I have

told you never to go near that house without express orders. Straight ahead."

The gondola at once resumed its former course. Never did Pompeo take a tourist down the Grand Canal that he did not exalt in his best Italian and French the beauties of yonder empty palace. Had he not spent his youth in the service of the family? It was only of late years that Pompeo had become a public gondolier, with his posts in the stand fronting the Hotel de l'Europe.

"*A-oel!* Look out!" he called suddenly. Another gondola scraped alongside and passed on.

"Who lives there?" asked Kitty.

"Nobody," answered La Signorina. "Though once it was the palace of a great warrior. How picturesque the gondolas look, with their dancing double lights! Those without numbers are private."

"The old palace interests me more than the gondolas," declared Kitty.

But La Signorina was not to be trapped.

Presently they passed the row of great hotels, with their balconies hanging over the water and their steps running down into it. Kitty eyed them all regretfully. She saw men and women in evening dress, and she was sure that they had dined well and were happy. Without doubt there were persons who knew her by name and had seen her act. From the Grand Canal they came out into the great Canal of San Marco, the beginning of the lagoon. Here Kitty forgot for the moment her troubles; her dream-Venice had returned. There were private yachts, Adriatic liners, all brilliant with illumination, and hundreds of gondolas, bobbing, bobbing, like captive leviathans, bunched round the gaily-lanterned barges of the serenaders. There was only one flaw to this perfect dream: the shrill whistle of the ferry-boats. They had no place here, and their presence was an affront.

"How I hate them!" said La Signorina. "The American influence! Some day they will be filling up the canals and running trams over them. What is beauty and silence if there be profit in ugliness and noise?"

"La Signorina—" began Kitty.

"There! I have warned you twice. The third time I shall be angry."

"Hilda, then. But I am afraid whenever I call you that. You do not belong to my world."

"And what makes you think that?" There was a smile behind the veil.

"I do not know, unless it is that you are at home everywhere, in the Campo, in the hotels, in the theater or the palace. Now, I am at home only in the theater, in places which are unreal and artificial. You are a great actress, a great singer; and yet, as O'Mally would say, you don't belong." Kitty had forgotten what she had started out to say.

La Signorina laughed. "Pouf! You have been reading too many novels. To the *molo*, Pompeo."

At the *molo*, the great quay of Venice, they disembarked. The whilom prima donna dropped fifty centesimi into Pompeo's palm, and he bowed to the very gunwale of the boat.

"*Grazie, nobilità.*"

"What does he say?" asked Kitty.

"He says, 'Thanks, nobility.' If I had given him a penny it would have been thanks only. For a lira he would have added *principessa*—princess. The gondolier will give you any title you desire, if you are willing enough to pay for it. We shall return on foot, Pompeo; this will be all for the night."

Pompeo lifted his hat again, and pushed off.

"He was very cheap," said Kitty. "Only ten cents for a ride like that!"

A ripple of laughter greeted this remark. "Pompeo can read human nature; he knows that I am honest. What I gave him was a tip."

"Aren't you laughing at me sometimes?"

"Disabuse your mind of that fancy, *cara*. It is a long time since I gave my affections to any one, and I do give them to you." With this she caught Kitty by the arm, and the two went up the Piazzetta leisurely toward the Piazza.

The Piazza San Marco, or Saint Mark, is the Mecca of those in search of beauty; here they may lay the sacred carpet, kneel and worship. There is none other to compare with this mighty square, with its enchanting splendor, its haunting romance, its brilliant if pathetic history. Light, everywhere light; scintillating, dancing, swinging light! Spars and lances of light upon the shivering waters, red and yellow and white! Light, the reflective radiance of jewels and happy eyes! Light, breaking against the pink and white marbles, the columns of porphyry, malachite, basalt, and golden mosaics! Let the would-be traveler dream of it never so well; he will come to find his dreams vanquished. Nothing changes in the Piazza San Marco, nothing save the tourists and the contents of the bewildering shops; all else remains the same, a little more tarnished by the sea-winds and the march of the decades, perhaps, but still the same. Read your poets and study your romances, but delve into no disillusioning guide-books. Let us put our faith in the gondolier;

for his lies are far more picturesque than a world of facts.

There were several thousand people in the square to-night, mostly travelers. The band was playing selections from Audran's whimsical*La Mascotte*. The tables of the many cafés were filled, and hundreds walked to and fro under the bright arcades, or stopped to gaze into the shop-windows. Here the merchant seldom closes his shop till the band goes home. Music arouses the romantic, and the romantic temperament is always easy to swindle, and the merchant of Venice will swindle you if he can.

The two women saw no vacant tables at Florian's, but presently they espied the other derelicts—O'Mally, Smith, and Worth—who managed to find two extra chairs. They learned that O'Mally had had two beers, a vast piece of recklessness. He was ripe for anything, and gaily welcomed his fellow unfortunates. He laughed, told funny stories, and made himself generally amusing. Smith made weak attempts to assist him. On the other hand, Worth seldom smiled and rarely spoke.

Through her veil their former prima donna studied them carefully, with a purpose in mind. The only one she doubted was Worth. Somehow he annoyed her; she could not explain, yet still the sense of annoyance was always there. It might have been that she had seen that look in other eyes, and that it usually led to the same end. She could not criticize his actions; he was always the perfection of courtesy to her, never overstepped, never intruded.

"Gentlemen," she said during a lull, "I have a plan to propose to you all."

"If it will get us back to old Broadway before we are locked up for debt, let us have it at once, by all means," said O'Mally.

"Well, then, I propose to wait no longer for letters from home. The last boat brought nothing; it will be fourteen days before the next arrives, since you all tell me that you wrote to have your mail sent by the Mediterranean. My plan is simple. They say that a gambler always wins the first time he plays. Taking this as the golden text, I propose that each of you will spare me what money you can, and Kitty and I will go to Monte Carlo and take one plunge at the tables."

"Monte Carlo!" O'Mally brought down his fist resoundingly. "That's a good idea. If you should break the bank, think of the advertisement when you go back to New York. La Signorina Capricciosa, who broke the bank at Monte Carlo, will open at the—"

"Be still," said Worth.

"Dash it, business is business, and without publicity there isn't any business." O'Mally was hurt.

"Mr. O'Mally is right," said La Signorina. "It would be a good advertisement. But your combined opinion is what I want."

The three men looked at one another thoughtfully, then drew out their wallets, thin and worn. They made up a purse of exactly one hundred and fifty dollars, not at all a propitious sum to trap elusive fortune. But such as it was, O'Mally passed it across the table. This utter confidence in her touched La Signorina's heart; for none of them knew aught of her honesty. She turned aside for a moment and fumbled with the hidden chain about her neck. She placed her hand on the table and opened it. O'Mally gasped, Smith opened his mouth, and Worth leaned forward. An emerald, a glorious green emerald, free from the usual cluster of diamonds, alone in all its splendor, lay in the palm of her hand.

"I shall give this to you, Mr. O'Mally," said the owner, "till I return. It is very dear to me, but that must not stand in the way."

"Ye gods!" cried O'Mally in dismay. "Put it away. I shouldn't sleep o' nights with that on my person. Keep it. You haven't the right idea. We'll trust you anywhere this side of jail. No, no! It wouldn't do at all. But you're a brick all the same." And that was as near familiarity as O'Mally ever came.

She turned to Smith, but he put out a hand in violent protest; then to Worth, but he smiled and shook his head.

"O'Mally is right," he said. "We need no guaranty."

She put the ring away. It was her mother's. She never would smile in secret at these men again. They might be vain and artificial and always theatrical, but there was nevertheless a warm and generous heart beneath.

"Thank you," she said quietly. "If I lose your money we will all go to Florence. I have another plan, but that will keep till this one under hand proves a failure. None of you shall regret your confidence in me."

"Pshaw!" said O'Mally.

"Nonsense!" said Smith.

And Worth smiled reassuringly.

O'Mally beckoned to a waiter. "*Oony* bottle *vino dee Asti, caldo, frappé*!" he said loudly, so that all might hear him give the order. A month in Venice, and he would be able to talk like a native. True, if any Italian spoke to him, he was obliged to shake his head; but that was a trifling matter.

"Tom!" warned Smith.

"You let me alone," replied O'Mally. "A quart of Asti

won't hurt anybody."

So the thin sweet wine of Asti was served, and La Signorina toasted them all gratefully.

Early the next morning she and Kitty departed for Monte Carlo in quest of fortune. Fortune was there, waiting, but in a guise wholly unexpected.

Chapter 12 *A BOX OF CIGARS*

On the way up to Rome Hillard and his pupil had a second-class compartment all to themselves. The train was a fast one; for the day of slow travel has passed in Italy and the cry of speed is heard over the land. The train stopped often and rolled about a good deal; but the cushions were soft, and there was real comfort in being able to stretch out full length. Hillard, having made this trip many times, took the forward seat and fell into a doze.

Merrihew was like a city boy taking his first trip into the country. He hung out of the window, and smoked and smoked. Whenever the train swept round a curve he could look into the rear carriages; and the heads sticking out of the thirds reminded him of chicken-crates. Never had he seen such green gardens, such orange and lemon groves, such forests of olives. Save that it was barren rock, not a space as broad as a man's hand was left uncultivated; and not a farm which was not in good repair. One saw no broken fences, no slovenly out-houses, no glaring advertisements afield: nobody was asked impertinently if Soandso's soap had been used that morning, nor did the *bambini* cry for soothing-syrups. Everything was of stone (for wood is precious in Italy), generally whitewashed, and presenting the smiling countenance of comfort and cleanliness. The Italian in the city is seldom clean; there, it is so easy to lie in the gutters under the sun. Reared and bred in laziness for centuries, dirt has no terrors, but water has. With his brother in the country it is different. Labor makes him self-respecting. Merrihew had seen so many dirty Sicilians and Neapolitans working on American railways that he had come to the conclusion that Italy was the most poverty-stricken country in the world. He was now forming new opinions at the rate of one every hour.

How pretty were the peasants in the fields with their bright bits of color, a scarlet shawl, a skirt of faded blue, a yellow kerchief round the head! And the great white oxen at the plows! Sometimes he saw a strange, phantom-like, walled town hanging to some cliffs far away. It disappeared and reappeared and disappeared again. Never a chimney with the curling black smoke of the factory did he see above any of these clustered cities. When he recalled to mind the pall of soft-coal smoke which hangs over the average American city, he knew that while Italy might be cursed with poverty she had her blessing in fine clear skies. And always, swinging down the great roads, he saw in fancy the ghosts of armies, crusaders, mercenaries, feudal companies, crossbowmen, and knights in mail.

It amused him to see the buxom women flagging the train at crossings. And the little stations, where everybody rushed out to buy a drink of bottled water! Suddenly the station-master struck a bell, the conductor tooted a horn, and the engine's shrill whistle shrieked; and off they flew again. No newsboy to bother one with stale gum, rank cigars, ancient caramels and soiled novels; nothing but solid comfort. And oh! the flashing streams which rushed under bridges or plunged alongside. Merrihew's hand ached to hold a rod and whip the green pools where the fallen olive leaves floated and swam like silver minnows. Half a dozen times he woke Hillard to draw his attention to these streams. But Hillard disillusioned him. Rarely were there any fish, nor were these waters drinkable, passing as they did over immense beds of lime.

There was a change of cars at Rome and a wait of two

hours. Hillard led the way to a popular café in the Piazza delle Terme, near the station. Here they lunched substantially. In that hour or so Merrihew saw more varied uniforms than he had seen in all his past life; perambulating parrakeets which glittered, smoked cigarettes or black cigars with straws in them, and drank coffee out of tumblers. He readily imagined that he was surrounded by enough dukes and princes and counts to run a dozen kingdoms, with a few left over for the benefit of the American market. He was making no mistakes now; he could distinguish a general from a hotel concierge without the least difficulty.

And still Americans, everywhere Americans; rich and poor Americans, loud and quiet Americans; Americans who had taste and education, and some who had neither; well-dressed and over-dressed, obtrusive and unobtrusive, parvenu and aristocrat. Once Merrihew saw a fine old gentleman wearing the Honor Legion ribbon in his buttonhole, and his heart grew warm and proud. Here was an order which was not to be purchased like the Order of Leopold and the French Legion of Honor. To win this simple order a man must prove his courage under fire, must be the author of an heroic exploit on the battle-field. And besides, there was this advantage: to servants in Europe a button or a slip of ribbon in the lapel signifies an order, a nobility of one sort or another, and as a consequence they treat the wearer with studied civility.

"I wish I had remembered," sighed Merrihew, after gazing at the old gentleman.

"Remembered what?"

"Why, I've got a whole raft of medals I won at college. I could wear them quite handily over here."

"Buy an order. Any pawnshop will have a few for sale. You could wear it in Switzerland or France, and nobody would be any the wiser."

"But I'm serious."

"So am I."

Merrihew brightened, reached into a vest pocket, and to Hillard's horror produced a monocle, which he gravely screwed in his eye.

"Where the—"

"Sh! If you make me laugh I'll drop it."

Merrihew stared about calmly and coldly, as he had seen some Englishmen do. A waiter, seeing the sun flash on the circle of crystal, hurried over, firmly believing he had been heliographed.

"*Niente*," said Merrihew, waving him aside. "You see?" he whispered to Hillard, who was rather amused at this tomfoolery. "Brings 'em without a word. Hanged if I don't wear it the rest of the trip. There's a certain—whatdyecallit?—eclaw about the demmed thing."

"Wear it, by all means. You'll be as amusing as a comic weekly. But if you ever drop it, I'll step on it accidentally."

"I can keep it in my eye all right," said Merrihew, "so long as I don't laugh. Now, while there's time, let us see some of the sights; the Golden House of Nero, for instance, and the Forum, the Colosseum, St. Peter's and the Vatican; just a passing glance at a few things, as it were." Merrihew as he spoke kept a sober countenance.

It deceived Hillard, who eyed him with unfeigned wonder, marveling that any rational mind should even think of such a thing, much less propose it.

"Why not run up to Venice and back?" he inquired sarcastically.

"Is it as far as that?" innocently. "Well, we'll make it just St. Peter's and the Vatican."

"Impossible! In the hour we have left we can see nothing, positively nothing. And even now we had better start for the station to get a compartment before the rush. St. Peter's and the Vatican! You talk like the Englishman who wanted to run over to San Francisco and back to Philadelphia in the morning."

A grin now spread over Merrihew's face. Hillard scratched his chin reflectively.

"I'll pay for the luncheon myself," he said.

"You had better. It was great sport to watch your face. I'll be in a happy frame of mind all day now."

After luncheon Merrihew secretly bought two boxes of cigars to carry along. They were good cigars and cost him fifteen dollars. He covered them with some newspapers, and at the station succeeded by some legerdemain in slipping them into one of his cases. Hillard would have lectured him on his extravagance, and this was a good way to avoid it. But some hours later he was going to be very sorry that he had not made a confidant of his guide. Merrihew had never heard of the town of Ventimiglia, which straddles the frontiers of France and Italy. As they were boarding the train they noticed two gentlemen getting into the forward compartment of the carriage.

"Humph! Our friend with the scar," said Hillard. "We do not seem able to shake him."

"I'd like to shake him. He goes against the grain, somehow." Merrihew swung into the compartment. "I wonder why the Sandfords dropped him?"

"For some good reason. They are a liberal pair, and if our friend forward offended them, it must have been something deliberate and outside the pale of forgiveness. But I should like to know where old Giovanni is. I miss him."

"Poor devil!" said Merrihew with careless sympathy. It is easy to be sympathetic with persons whose troubles are remote from our own.

The train started, and again they had the compartment.

"Monte Carlo! Gold, gold, little round pieces of gold!" Merrihew rubbed his hands like the miser in *The Chimes of Normandy*.

"Hard to get and heavy to hold!" quoted Hillard. "I suppose that you have a system already worked out."

"Of course. I shall win if I stick to it."

"Or if the money lasts. Bury your system, my boy. It will do you no good. Trust to luck only. Monte Carlo is the graveyard of systems."

"But maybe my system is the one. You can't tell till I have tried it."

Merrihew lighted a cigar, and Hillard smiled secretly. After some time the conductor came in to examine the tickets. When the examination was over he paused in front of Merrihew, who puffed complacently.

"Signore," the conductor said politely, "*e vietato fumare.*"

Merrihew replied with an uncomprehending stare.

"*Non fumer!*" said the conductor, with his hand at the side of his mouth, as one does to a person who is suddenly discovered to be hard of hearing.

Merrihew smiled weakly and signified that he did not understand.

"*Nicht rauchen!*" cried the official in desperation.

Merrihew extended his hands hopelessly. He had nothing belonging to the conductor. Hillard had the tickets.

"*Niet rooken! Niet rooken!*"

"I say, Jack, what the deuce does he want, anyhow?"

"*Cigare, cigare!*" The conductor gesticulated toward the window.

"Oh!" Merrihew took the cigar from his teeth and went through the pantomime of tossing it out of the window.

"*Si, si!*" assented the conductor, delighted that he was finally understood.

"You might have given me the tip," Merrihew grumbled across to Hillard. He viewed the halfburnt perfecto ruefully and filliped it through the window. "How should I know smoking was prohibited?"

"You had your joke; this is mine. Besides, I remained silent to the advantage of your future education. The conductor has spoken to you in four languages—Italian, French, German and Dutch." Hillard then spoke to the conductor. "May not my friend smoke so long as ladies do not enter?"

"Certainly, since it does not annoy you." Then the conductor bowed and disappeared into the next compartment.

Merrihew inscribed on the back of an envelope, for future reference, the four phrases, and in ten minutes had, with the assistance of his preceptor, mastered their pronunciations.

"I wish I had been born a hotel concierge," he said mournfully. "They speak all languages, and the Lord knows where they find the time to learn them."

"The Englishman, the Parisian and the American are the poorest linguists," said Hillard. "They are altogether too well satisfied with themselves and their environments to bother learning any language but their own, and most Americans do not take the trouble to do that."

"Hear, hear!"

"It is because I am a good patriot that I complain," said Hillard. "I love my country, big, healthy and strong as it is; but I wish my people would brush up their learning, so that these foreigners would have less right to make sport of us."

"There's some truth in what you say. But we are young, and going ahead all the time."

Soon the train began to lift into the mountains, the beautiful Apennines, and Merrihew counted so many tunnels he concluded that this was where the inventor of the cinematograph got his idea. Just as some magnificent valley began to unfold, with a roar the train dashed into a dank, sooty tunnel. One could neither read nor enjoy the scenery; nothing to do but sit tight and wait, let the window down when they passed a tunnel, lift it when they entered one. By the time they arrived in Genoa, late at night, both compared favorably with the coalers in the harbor of Naples.

The English and American tourists have done much toward making Italy a soap-and-water tolerating country (loving would be misapplied). But in Italy the State owns the railroads. There is water (of a kind), but never soap or towels.

Early the next morning the adventurers set out for Monte Carlo, taking only their hand-luggage. More tunnels. A compartment filled with women and children. And hot besides. But the incomparable beauty of the Riviera was a compensation. Ventimiglia, or Vintimille, has a sinister sound in the ears of the traveler, if perchance he be a man fond of his tobacco. A turbulent stream cuts the town in two. On the east side stands a gloomy barn of a station; on the other side one of the most picturesque walled towns in Europe, and of Roman antiquity. The train drew in. A dozen steps more, and one was virtually in France. But there is generally a slight hitch before one takes the aforesaid steps: the French customs. A *facchino* popped his head into the window.

"Eight minutes for examination of luggage!" he cried.

Re held out his arms, and Hillard piled the luggage upon him.

"Come, Dan; lively, if we want good seats when we come out. We change trains."

The two men followed the porter to the ticket entrance, surrendered their coupons, and passed into the customs. The porter had to go round another way. After a short skirmish they located their belongings, which unfortunately were far down toward the end of the barrier. They would have to be patient. Hillard held in his hands his return coupons to Genoa. Sometimes this helps at the frontier; and if one has a steamer ticket, better still. Inspectors then understand that one is to be but a transient guest.

Among the inspectors at Ventimiglia is a small, wizened Frenchman, with a face as cold and impassive as the sand-blown Sphinx. He possesses among other accomplishments a nose, peculiar less for its shape than for its smell. He can "smell out" tobacco as a witch doctor in Zululand smells out a "devil." Fate directed this individual toward the Americans. Hillard knew him of old; and he never forgets a face, this wizened little man.

"Monsieur has nothing to declare?" he asked.

Hillard made a negative sign and opened his cases. With

scarce a glance at their contents, and waving aside the coupons, the inspector applied the chalk and turned to Merrihew.

"Monsieur has nothing to declare?" he repeated.

Merrihew shook his head airily. "*Niente, niente!*" he said in his best Italian. He did not understand what the inspector said; he merely had suspicions.

"Look!" suddenly exclaimed Hillard.

Passing out of the door which led to liberty and to France, their luggage guaranteed by cabalistic chalk marks, were two women. One of them was veiled, the other was not.

"Kitty Killigrew, as I live!" shouted Merrihew, making a dash for the door.

But the inspector blocked the way, beckoned to a gendarme, who came over, and calmly pointed to Merrihew's unopened cases.

"Open!" said the inspector, all his listlessness gone. He had seen people in a hurry before.

"But—" Merrihew struggled to pass.

"For Heaven's sake!" cried Hillard, "be patient and open the cases at once."

Merrihew handled his keys clumsily. The first key on the ring should have been the last, and the last first. It is ever thus when one is in a hurry. Finally he threw back the lids, feeling that in another moment he must have spouted Italian or French out of pure magic, simply to tell this fool inspector what he thought of him.

"Oho! Monsieur-in-a-hurry!" mocked the inspector. "Nothing, nothing!" He took out the two boxes of cigars.

"Why the devil didn't you tell me you had them?" Hillard demanded wrathfully. To find the women by this stroke of luck, and then to lose them again for two boxes of cigars! It was maddening!

As a matter of fact, Merrihew had forgotten all about them, so far as intentional wrong-doing was concerned.

The inspector went through Merrihew's possessions with premeditated leisure. Everything had to come out. He even opened the shaving sets, the collar box, the pin cases, and the tie bag. Other persons pushed by toward the train, uttering their relief aloud. Still the inspector doddered on. "Will you hasten?" asked Hillard. "We do not wish to miss this train."

"Others follow," said the inspector laconically.

Hillard produced a five-franc piece. The inspector laughed without noise and shook his head. This one inspector is impervious to money or smooth speeches. He is the law personified, inexorable.

"Tell him to keep the cigars, but let us go!" Merrihew begged.

No, that would not do. Monsieur had not declared the cigars. If he persisted, the government would confiscate the cigars, but in place of duty there would be a large fine. Monsieur had better be patient and pay the duty only, retaining his valuable cigars. It was very liberal on his (the inspector's) part.

Hillard strained his eyes, but saw neither Kitty nor the veiled lady again. Doubtless they were already on the train. Had Merrihew been an old traveler he would have left him to get to Monte Carlo the best way he could; but Merrihew was as helpless as a child, and he hadn't the heart to desert him, though he deserved to be deserted.

Ding-ding! went the bell. Toot-toot! went the horn. Whee-whee! went the whistle. The train for Monte Carlo was drawing out, and they were being left behind. Hillard swore and Merrihew went white with impotent anger. If only he could hit something! The inspector smiled and went on with his deadly work. When he was certain that they could not possibly catch the train, he chalked the cases, handed the cigars to their owner, and pointed to a sign the other side of the barricade.

"What shall I do now, Jack?" Merrihew asked.

"I refuse to help you. Find out yourself."

So Merrihew, hopeless and subdued, went into the room designated, saw the cigars taken out and weighed, took the bill and presented it with a hundred-lire note at the little window in the off-room. The official there pushed the money back indifferently.

"*Française, Monsieur, française!*"

Merrihew blinked at him. What *was* the matter now? Was the note bad?

"*Change, cambio!*" said the official testily. Would tourists never learn anything?

Merrihew got it through his head somehow where the difficulty lay. He went out again, remembering the sign *Cambio* hanging in front of the news-stand. He lost half a dollar in the exchange, but for the time being his troubles were over.

Meanwhile Hillard had made inquiries at the door. No, the official there told him, he had not noticed the lady in the veil. So many passed; it was impossible to recollect.

And Merrihew found him sitting disconsolately on the barricade.

"I hope you are perfectly satisfied," said Hillard, with an amiability which wouldn't have passed muster anywhere.

"Oh, I'm satisfied," answered Merrihew. He stuffed his

pockets with cigars, slammed the boxes into the case, and locked them up. He collected his belongings and repacked the other case, keeping up a rumbling monotone as he did so. "Oh, yes; I am damned satisfied."

"I warned you about tobacco."

"I know it."

"You should have told me."

"I know that, too; but I didn't want you to lecture me."

"A lecture would have been better than waiting here in this barn for three hours."

"Three hours?" despondently.

"Oh, there's a restaurant, but it's not much better than this. It's bad; flies and greasy plates."

Conversation died. For the first time in the long run of their friendship there was a coolness between them. However, their native sense of humor was too strong for this coolness to last. Merrihew was first to break the silence.

"Jack, I *am* an ass!" penitently.

"I admit it," said Hillard, smiling.

"Let's hunt up the restaurant; I am hungry and thirsty."

And by the time they had found the Ristorante Tornaghi —miserable and uninviting—they were laughing.

"Only, I wish I knew where they were going," was Hillard's regret.

"They?" said Merrihew.

"Yes. The woman with Kitty is the woman I'm going to find if I stay in Europe ten years. And when I find her, I'm going to marry her."

"Sounds good," said Merrihew, pouring himself a third glass of very indifferent Beaune.

"And they may be going anywhere but to Monte Carlo—Paris, Cherbourg, Calais. In my opinion, Monte Carlo is the last place two such women are likely to go to alone."

"Have a cigar," Merrihew urged drolly. "I paid fifteen cents apiece for them in Rome. They are now four for a dollar. And I suppose that I'll have to smoke them all up in Monte Carlo, or the Italian end of this ruin will sink the harpoon into me for fifty more francs. I'd like to get that blockhead over the line. I'd customs him."

"Don't blame him. He is to be admired. He is one of the rarities of Europe—an honest official."

So they sat in the dingy restaurant, smoking and laughing and grumbling till the next train was announced. At four that afternoon they arrived without further mishap at the most interesting station of its size in Europe—Monte Carlo. And Merrihew saw gold whichever way he looked: in the sunshine on the sea, in the glistening rails, in the reflecting windows of the many-terraced hotels, in the orange trees; gold, gold, beautiful gold napoleons.

And then, into the omnibus adjoining, came the man with the scar.

Chapter 13 KITTY ASKS QUESTIONS

The Riviera, from San Remo on the Italian side to Cannes on the French, possesses a singular beauty. Cities and villages nestle in bays or crown frowning promontories; and sheltered from northern winds by mountains rugged and lofty, the vegetation is tropical and rich. Thousands of splendid villas (architectural madnesses) string out along the rock-bound coast; and princes and grand dukes and kings live in some of these. Often a guide will point out some little palace and dramatically whisper that this will be the villa of a famous ballerina, or Spanish dancer, or opera singer, or some duchess whose husband never had any duchy. And seldom these villas are more than a stone's throw from the villas of the princes and grand dukes and kings. Nobility and royalty are fond of jovial company. Aladdin's lamp is not necessary here, where one may build a villa by the aid of one's toes!

Nature—earthly nature—has nothing to do with the morality of humanity, if it can not uplift. Yet humanity can alter nature, beautify it after a conventional manner, or demolish it, still after a conventional manner. On the Riviera humanity has nature pretty well under hand.

Villefranche stands above Nice, between that white city and Monte Carlo. It is quiet and lovely. For this reason the great army of tourists pass it by; there is no casino, no band, no streets full of tantalizing shops. On the very western limit of Villefranche, on the winding white road which rises out of Nice, a road so frequently passed over by automobiles that a haze of dust always hangs over it, is a modest little villa, so modest that a ballerina would scorn it and a duchess ignore it. It is, in truth, a *pensione*, where only those who come well recommended are accepted as guests. It is on the left of the road as you ride east, and its verandas and window balconies look straight out to sea, the eternally blue Mediterranean. A fine grove of shade trees protects it from the full glare of the sun.

In the balcony La Signorina reposed in a steamer chair, gazing seaward. The awning cast a warm glow as of gold upon her face and hair, a transparent shadow. She was at this moment the most precious thing upon which the eye may look—a wholly beautiful woman. Kitty Killigrew, standing in the casement window, stared at her silently, not without some envy, not without some awe. What was going on behind those dreamy eyes? Only once did the woman in the chair move, but this movement was tense with passion: she clenched her hands and struck them roughly on the arms of the chair. Immediately she relaxed, as if realizing how futile such emotion was. Kitty stirred and came out. She sat in the neighboring chair.

"Hilda?" said Kitty.

"Yes, Kitty."

"Who and what are you?" Kitty asked bravely.

La Signorina's eyes wandered till they met Kitty's. There was neither anger nor surprise in the glance, only deliberation.

"And what good would it do you to know? Would it change our positions any? Would it bring money from home any sooner? You already know, without my telling you, that I am unhappy. The adventuress always is."

"Adventuress?" Kitty laughed scornfully. "The proprietor pretends he does not know you, but I am certain he does. He forgets himself sometimes in the way he bows to you. He has even called you *altezza*, which you tell me is Italian for highness."

"He is in hope of a liberal tip."

"The proprietor? One does not tip him."

"That is true. I can not understand his motive, then."

"If he also applied the title to me, it would be different. He rarely notices me. Won't you tell me what the secret is?"

"How beautiful that white sail looks!"

"You know all about me," went on Kitty stubbornly.

"Because you told me. I never asked you a single question."

"And you have told me nothing."

"Why should I? Come, Kitty, be reasonable. Tell me what you think of that sail. Is it not beautiful in the sunset?"

"Is it—love?"

"Love?" La Signorina shrugged. "Poor Kitty, you are trying in vain to make a romance out of my life. What should I know of love? It is a myth, a fable, only to be found in story-books. You should not read so much."

"It is not curiosity," declared Kitty. "It is because I love you, and because it makes me sad when I hear you laugh, when I see you beat your hands against the chair as you did just now." There was a tremble in Kitty's voice that suggested the nearness of tears.

La Signorina turned again, in a passion which was as fierce as it was sudden.

"There *is* a man," she whispered rather than spoke, the pupils in her eyes dilating so that the blue irises nearly disappeared. "But I loathe him, I hate him, I abhor him! And were it not wicked to kill, he would have been dead long ago. Enough! If you ever ask another question, I will leave you. I like you, but I insist that my secrets shall be my own, since they concern you in no manner."

"I am sorry," said Kitty with contrition. "But I suspected there was a man. I understand. He was false to you and broke your heart," romantically.

"No, Kitty; only my pride."

"It is a strange world," mused Kitty.

"It would be otherwise were it not that the heart and the mind are always at war. But let us turn to our affairs. I received a letter to-day."

"From home?" eagerly.

"I have no home, Kitty. The letter is from a friend in Naples. Mr. Hillard and Mr. Merrihew, friends of yours, are in Italy."

Kitty could scarce believe her ears. "Where are they? Where are they stopping?"

"That I do not know. But listen. They have started out to find us. When I tell you that Mr. Hillard is the gentleman I dined with that night before we sailed, you will understand my reasons for wishing to avoid him. From this time on we must never appear on the streets without our veils. If by chance we meet them, we must give no sign. It will be only for a little while. Your letter will come soon, and you may renew your acquaintance with these two gentlemen when you return home. It may be hard for you; but if you wish to stay with me, my will must be a law unto you."

"Not to speak to them if we meet them?" urged Kitty in dismay.

"No."

"But that is cruel of you. They are both gentlemen," said

Kitty, with fierce pride.

"I do not know Mr. Merrihew, but I can say that Mr. Hillard is a gentleman. I have proved that. As for being cruel, I am not; only selfish."

"Are you not a queen who has run away from a kingdom?" asked Kitty bitterly. "One reads about them every day in the papers."

"My dear, you are free to choose one of two paths. Sometimes I need you, Kitty; and the sight of you and the knowledge of your nearness helps me. I shall not urge you one way or the other, but you must make your final choice at once."

Several minutes passed. Kitty looked out to sea, and La Signorina closed her eyes. In her heart Kitty knew that she could no more leave this woman than she could fly. She was held by curiosity, by sentiment, by the romantic mystery.

"I have chosen," she said at length. "I shall stay with you."

"Thanks, Kitty. And now, the affairs of the company. We have played three days and have lost steadily. To-night will be the last chance. Win or lose, to-morrow we shall return to Venice. I do not like the idea of going to Monte Carlo at night; it is not exactly safe. But since beggars mustn't be choosers, we must go. Again I warn you to speak to no one while I am playing; and under no circumstance raise your veil. They have begun to notice us, but it will end to-night. I was mad to think that I could win. And by the way, Kitty, we shall not go back to the Campo Formosa."

Kitty accepted this news brightly. If there was one place she hated, it was the Campo. She had never been so lonely in all her days as in that evil-smelling tenement in the Campo Santa

Maria Formosa.

"Now run and dress," advised La Signorina. "Let me dream a little more, while the sun sets. I can dream a pleasant dream sometimes."

And indeed the dream was not unpleasant, for her thoughts went back to that night in New York. Did he really think of her, then? Was it possible for a man to forget so bizarre an episode? Rather would it not leave a lasting impression? She liked him. He had a clean, kindly face and handsome eyes. How she had played with him! How she had tempted him! And yet, through it all, a gentleman, a witty, interesting, amiable gentleman, who never approached the innuendo, or uttered a double-meaning. On her part she had taken great risks; but the fun had been merry and harmless.

She recalled his liberal-minded patriotism and his sensible comparisons. Surely he was right: the race of gentlemen had not yet died out in far America. With what mystery had he invested her? With what charms had he endued her? She smiled gently. It was pleasant to be made a heroine even for the small space of two hours. He was an idle young man, after a fashion; that was because he had not been waked up. But under his jest and under his laughter she was sure that there was courage and purpose and high emprise. Take care! she thought. Take care! Might not this little dream carry her too far out to sea?... To have met a man like this one in time! How gracefully, how boyishly, he had kissed her hand! More than this, there had been an artless admiration in his upturned eyes, an expression which a gentleman of the Old World would have lacked. Why had she sent him that mask? Had it been a challenge, an indirect challenge, daring him to follow and seek her? She really could not answer. It had been one of those half-conscious whims which may be assigned to no positive cause. Besides, no sensible man would have accepted such a challenge. She knew men tolerably well: after thirty they cease to follow visions; they seek tangible things... . No, they must never meet again. It would not be wise. Her heart, lonely, disappointed, galled as it were by disillusion, might not withstand much storming. And she had no wish to add this irretrievable folly to the original blunder. Too late, too late! Decidedly they must not meet again. She was afraid.

The red rim of the sun sank quickly now, and the sea turned cold and deeply blue, and the orange-tinted sails grew drab and lonely. And with the sun the brightness of her dream went out. Would she never cast out the life which was false, though colorful and fantastic? Would she never accept real life, dull and sober? Romance? She was always seeking it, knowing right well that it was never to be found. Romance! Had it not led her into this very pit from which only death could release her? This impossible vein was surely the legacy of some far ancestor, some knight of the windmills, not of her father and mother, both so practical, so wise, so ambitious. Ah, she thought in her heart, had they but lived to see the folly of what they believed to be wisdom!

No, they must go their separate ways till the end. When she was old she would re-read his letters. With a sigh she rose and went into the room. Kitty was busy with the finishing touches of her toilet. Kitty was not vain; she was only pretty. The older woman kissed her fondly.

"Pretty Kitty Killigrew!" she said. "It is positively lyrical."

"And do you realize that you are the most beautiful

woman in the world?"

"Little flatterer!"

"And if I were a man—" Kitty paused.

"Well, and if you were a man?"

"I'd fall in love with you and marry you." La Signorina looked into the mirror.

Chapter 14 GREY VEILS

The fascination of Monte Carlo is not to be described; it must be seen. Vice shall be attractive, says the Mother of Satan. At Monte Carlo it is more than attractive; it is compelling. A subtle hypnotism prevails. One scarce realizes that this lovely spot is at the same time the basest. What passions have stormed this cliff! What rage and despair have beaten their hands against these bastions of pleasure! How few who plunge into this maelstrom of chance ever rise again! The lure of gold, there is nothing stronger save death. Fool and rogue, saint and sinner, here they meet and mingle and change. To those who give Monte Carlo but a trifling glance, toss a coin or two on the tables, and leave by the morrow's train, it has no real significance; it is simply one of the sights of Europe.

To this latter class belonged the two young men. They had no fortunes to retrieve, no dishonesty to hide, no restitutions to make, no dancers to clothe and house. It was but a mild flirtation. They saw the silken gown outside rather than the rags beneath; they saw the smile rather than the tortured mind behind it.

They dined sumptuously at the café de Paris. They wandered about the splendid terraces on the sea-front, smoking. They had grown accustomed to the many beautiful women, always alone, always with roving eyes. Frequently Merrihew longed to chat with this one or that; and sometimes he rebelled against his inability to speak the maddening tongue. To-night, though the dinner had been excellent and the chambertin all that could be desired, the two were inclined to be moody. So far fortune had not smiled, she had frowned persistently. They found a vacant bench and sat down.

"Ho-hum!" said Merrihew, dangling his monocle to which he had attached a string.

"Heigh-ho!" replied Hillard.

"Curse those cigars!"

"With all my heart!"

They had searched Nice, and Monaco, and Mentone, but the women they sought were not to be found. They decided, therefore, that the women had gone on to Paris, and that there was now no hope of seeing them this side of the Atlantic. They had not entered the Casino during the day; they had been too busy quizzing hotel porters and concierges along the Riviera.

"My system needs a tonic," said Merrihew.

"We'll hold the funeral after to-night's play. Of all the damfool games, it's roulette."

"And I can prove it," Merrihew replied. "I have just fifty dollars left." He took out the gold and toyed with it. "Can't you hear it?" he asked.

"Hear what?"

"The swan-song of these tender napoleons!"

Merrihew had played the numbers, the dozens, the columns, the colors, odd and even. Sometimes he would win a little, but a moment later the relentless rake would drag it back to the bank. His chance to play the good Samaritan to the derelicts of the American Comic Opera Company was fast approaching the dim horizon of lost opportunities. Presently he screwed the monocle into his eye and squinted at the sea, the palaces on the promontory, the yachts in the harbor, all tranquil in shadowy moonlight.

"Nature has done this very prettily. Quite clever with her

colors, don't you know," he drawled, plucking the down on his upper lip, for he was trying to raise a mustache, convinced that two waxed points of hair at each corner of his mouth would impress the hotel waiters and other *facchini*—baseborn.

"Don't be a jackass!" Hillard was out of sorts.

"You agreed with me that I was one. Why not let me make a finished product?" good-humoredly.

"You will have your joke."

"Yes, even at the expense of being blind in one eye; for I can't see through this glass; positive stove-lid. Every time I focus you, you grow as big as a house. No, I'd never be happy as a lord. Well, let us have our last fling. You might as well let me have my letter of credit now."

"You will not set eyes upon it till we return to Genoa. That's final. I know you, my boy, and I know Monte Carlo. Even with your fifty, a watch and a ring, I'm afraid to trust you out of sight."

"I can see that you will never forgive nor forget—those cigars. Come on. We'll take a look at our Italian friend. He's a bad loser. I have seen him lose his temper, too. It's my opinion that he's a desperate man."

"They usually are when they come to Monte Carlo."

So they walked round to the entrance to the gaming halls, where the lights, the gowns, the jewels, the sparkling eyes, the natural beauty and the beauty of enamel, the vague perfumes, the low murmur of voices, the soft rustle of silks, the music of ringing gold, all combine to produce a picture and ensemble as beautiful as a mirage and as false. Nothing is real in Monte Carlo but the little pieces of gold and the passion to win them. The two renewed their tickets of admission and passed on into the famous atrium, stared a while at the news bulletin, whereon all the important events of the day are briefly set forth, and gazed musingly at the bats darting across the ceiling, real bats, a sinister omen such as one sees in imaginative paintings of the Door of Hades. At nine they joined the never-ending procession which passes in and out of the swinging doors day after day, year after year.

The faces one sees in the Hall of Roulette! Here and there one which will haunt the onlooker through the rest of his days. Packed about the long tables were young faces flushed with hope or grey with despair; middle-aged faces which expressed excitement or indifference; old, old faces, scarred and lined and seamed, where avarice, selfishness, cruelty, dishonesty crossed and recrossed till human semblance was literally blotted out. Light-o'-loves, gay and careless; hideous old crones, who watched the unwary and stole the unwary's bets; old women in black, who figured and figured imaginary winnings and never risked anything but their nerves. And there were beautiful women, beautifully gowned, beautifully gemmed, some of them good, some of them indifferent, and some of them bad. Invariably Hillard found himself speculating on the history of this woman or that; the more gems, the more history. Here the half-world of Europe finds its kingdom and rules it madly. The fortunes these women have poured into this whirligig of chance will never be computed. And there was the gentlemanly blackleg, the ticket-of-leave man, and outcasts and thieves; but all of them were well dressed, and, for the time being, well behaved.

Occasionally Merrihew caught some daring beauty's eye, and usually there followed a conversation, familiar to all ages and to all peoples, confined to the eyebrow, the eyelid, and the merry little wrinkles in the corner. When any spoke to him, however, and many did, for his face was fresh and pleasing, he would reply in English that he spoke no French, regretfully.

"There's the chap with the scar. He is a handsome beggar," Hillard admitted. "I wonder what sort of blackleg he is? He's no ordinary one, I'm certain. I begin to recognize the face of the man with him. He's a distinguished diplomat, and he would not associate with a man who was thoroughly bad, according to law, leaving out the moral side of it. Let us watch them."

The Italian played like an old hand; a number once in a while, but making it a point to stake on the colors. Red began to repeat itself. He doubled and doubled. On the sixth consecutive turn he played the maximum of twelve thousand francs, and won. The diplomat touched him on the arm significantly, but the player shook his head. Ten minutes later he had won forty thousand francs. Again he refused to leave his chair.

"If he stays now," said Hillard, "he will lose it all. His friend is right."

"Forty thousand francs, eight thousand dollars!" murmured Merrihew sadly. Why couldn't he have luck like this?

Hillard was a true prophet. There came a change in the smile of fortune. The game jumped from color to color, seldom repeating, with zero making itself conspicuous. The man with the scar played on, but he began to lose, small sums at first, then larger, till finally he was down to his original stake. The scar grew livid. He waited five turns of the wheel, then placed his stake on the second dozen. He lost. He rose from his chair, scowling. His eye chanced to meet Hillard's, and their glances held for a moment.

"Fool!" said Merrihew in an undertone, as the man strolled leisurely past them. "Eight thousand, and not content to quit!"

"My boy, a man who needs a hundred thousand and wins but eight is seldom content." Hillard followed the Italian with his eyes as he approached one of the lounges. There the loser was joined by his friend, and the two of them fell to gesticulating wildly, after the manner of their race. Hillard understood this pantomime; the diplomat had been a share-holder. "Start your play, Dan. I'll find plenty of amusement at the other tables. My watching your game hasn't brought you any luck up to the present. Go in and give 'em a beating."

Merrihew hastened over to the north table. This was, according to report, the table which had no suicide's chair; and Merrihew had his private superstitions like the rest of us. At eleven o'clock the banks closed, so he had but two hours in which to win a fortune. It was not possible for him to lose one; in this the gods were with him.

Meanwhile the trolleys from Nice and Mentone had poured into Monte Carlo their usual burdens of pleasure seekers. On one of the cars from Nice there had arrived two women, both veiled and simply gowned. The conductor had seen them before, but never at night. They seldom addressed each other, and never spoke to any one else. He picked them up at Villefranche. Doubtless they were some sober married women out for a lark. Upon leaving the car they did not at once go into the Casino, but directed their steps toward the terraces, for the band was playing. They sat in the shadow of the statue of Massenet, and near-by the rasp of a cricket broke in upon the music. When the music stopped they linked arms and sauntered up and down the wide sweep of stone, mutually interested in the crowds, the color, and the lights. Once, as they passed behind a bench, the better to view the palaces of the prince, they heard the voices of two men.

"Ho-hum!"

"Heigh-ho!"

As they went on, the women heard something about cigars. The men were Americans, evidently. It was only an inconsequent incident, and a moment later both had forgotten it. By and by they proceeded to the Casino. Rarely women wear veils at Monte Carlo. On the contrary, they go there (most of them) to be seen, admired and envied. Thus, these two were fully aware of the interest they excited. At frequent intervals royalty—the feminine side of the family—steals into Monte Carlo, often unattended. When one's yacht is in the harbor below, it does not entail much danger. There is a superstition regarding veils; but no attendant requested the women to remove them. They dared not, for fear of affronting royalty. It was a delicate situation, so far as the attendants were concerned.

"At which table shall I make the stake, Kitty?"

"The center; there is always a crush there, and we shall not be noticed."

"I do not agree with you there. However, it shall be the center table. What would you do, Kitty, if I should break the bank?"

"Die of excitement!" truthfully.

"You will live through this event, then." With a light careless laugh, La Signorina pressed her way to the table.

The play here was in full swing, and in some cases very high. She opened her purse and took out a handful of gold. These napoleons were all that remained of the capital intrusted her. She hesitated for some time, then placed a coin on the number twenty-five, her age. The ivory ball spun round and round, till it lost some of its force and slanted, struck one of the little silver obstacles, and bounded into one of the compartments. It was the number twenty-five: thirty-five napoleons for one, a hundred and forty dollars! Kitty uttered an ejaculation of delight. Many looked enviously at the winner as the neat little stack of gold was pushed toward her. She took the gold and placed it on black. Again she won. Then fortune packed up and went elsewhere. She lost steadily, winning but one bet in every ten. She gave no sign, however, that her forces were in full retreat from the enemy. She played on, and the hand which placed the bets was steady. She was a thoroughbred. And when the gold was all gone, she opened her empty hands expressively and shrugged. She was beaten. Behind the chair of the banker, opposite, stood the Italian. The scowl still marred his forehead. When the woman in the veil spread out her hands, he started. There was something familiar to his mind in that gesture. And then the woman saw him. For the briefest moment her form stiffened and the shape of her chin was molded in the veil. Slight as this sign was, the Italian observed it. But he was puzzled.

"Kitty," La Signorina whispered, "let us go out to the atrium. I am tired."

They left the hall leisurely and found a vacant settle in the atrium.

"I have a horror of bats," said La Signorina.

"How cold your hands are!" exclaimed Kitty. "Never mind about the money. They will understand."

"Kitty, I am a fool, a fool! I have unwittingly put my head

in the lion's mouth. If I had not reached this seat in time, I should have fallen. I would willingly give all my rings if, at this moment, I could run across the hall and out into the open!"

"Merciful Heaven! Why, what is the matter? What has happened?" Kitty was all in a flutter.

"I can not explain to you."

"Was it some one you saw in there?"

"Silence; and sit perfectly still!"

The swinging doors opened and closed. A man in evening dress came out into the atrium, lighting a cigarette. At the sight of him both women were startled. Their emotions, however, were varied and unlike.

"It is Mr. Hillard, Mr. Merrihew's friend!" Kitty would have risen, but the other's strong hand restrained her.

"Kitty, remember your promise."

"Is *he* the man?"

"No, no! Only, I have said that we must not meet him. It might do him incalculable harm. Harm!" La Signorina repeated; "do you understand?"

"But—"

"Silence, I command you!"

The tone had the power to subdue Kitty. The indignant protest died on her lips. She sat perfectly still, but she would have liked to cry. To let Mr. Hillard pass by in this manner, without a sign of friendliness or recognition! It was intolerable. And he could tell where Merrihew was (as indeed he could!) and what he was doing. She choked and crushed the ends of her veil.

Hillard blew outward a few pale rings of smoke and circled the atrium with an indolent glance which stopped as it rested upon the two veiled women sitting alone. Besides being bored and wanting amusement, a certain curiosity impelled him toward them, and he sank on the settle beside them, with perhaps half a dozen spans of the hand between. He smoked till the cigarette scorched his fingers, then he dropped it, extinguishing the coal with the toe of his pump. He observed the women frankly. Not a single wisp of hair escaped the veils, not a line of any feature could be traced, and yet the tint of flesh shone dimly behind the silken bands of crape; and the eyes sparkled. He nodded.

"A wonderful scene in there," indicating the swinging doors. "Puck was right. What fools these mortals be! Something for nothing will always lure us."

The veils did not move so much as the breadth of a hair.

"Fortune favors the brave, but rarely the foolish."

There was no response, but the small shoe of the woman nearest began to beat the floor ever so lightly. Hillard was chagrined. To be rebuffed the very first time he spoke to a woman in the Casino!

"Perhaps madame does not understand?" he said in French.

One of the women stirred restlessly; that was all.

He repeated the question in Italian, at the same time feeling like a pedant airing his accomplishments.

Nothing.

"I beg your pardon," he said, getting upon his feet. "I see that you do not wish to talk."

Thereupon he bowed, sought another seat, and lighted a fresh cigarette. But not for a moment did his eye leave these two mysterious women. Their absolute silence confused him. Usually a woman gives some sign of disapproval when addressed by a stranger. These two sat as if they neither saw nor heard him. He shook the ash from his cigarette, and when he looked up again, the women were hurrying across the floor to the lobby. He would have given them no further thought had not the Italian with the scar appeared upon the scene, eyed the retreating figures doubtfully, and then started after them. That he did not know them Hillard was reasonably certain. He assumed that the Italian saw a possible flirtation. He rose quickly and followed. If these two women desired to be left alone, he might be of assistance.

The four departed from the Casino and crossed toward the Hotel de Paris, the women in the lead. As yet they had not observed that they were being followed. The car stops at this turn. As the women came to a stand, one of them saw the approaching men. Instantly she fled up the street, swift as a hare. The other hesitated for a second, then pursued her companion frantically. Whatever doubts the Italian might have entertained, this unexpected flight dissipated them. He knew now; he knew, he knew! With a sharp cry of exultation he broke into a run. So did Hillard. He was no longer bored. This promised to be interesting. People turned and stared, but none sought to intercept any of the runners. In Monte Carlo there are many strange scenes, and the knight-errant often finds that his bump of caution has suddenly developed. In other words, it is none of his affair. To look was one thing, to follow, to precipitate one's head into the unknown, was another. And there were no police about; they were on the Casino terraces, or strolling through the gardens, or patrolling the railway station.

Past the park the quartet ran, and took the first turn to the left for a block or more. Then came a stretch of darkness, between one electric lamp and another. And then, as if whisked away by magic, the foremost woman disappeared. The other halted, breathless and wondering. She started again, but a moment too late. The Italian caught her roughly by the arm and with a quick movement tore aside the veil.

"Kitty Killigrew!" Hillard cried.

He sprang forward, grasped the Italian by the shoulders and whirled him round in no gentle manner. The Italian struck out savagely and fearlessly, but Hillard seized his arm and held it firmly. There was a short tableau. Each man could hear the breathing of the other, quick and deep. The devil gleamed in the Italian's eyes, but there was a menace Hillard's equally strong.

"You meddling figure of a dog!"

"Take care lest the dog bite, signore."

"Release my arm and stand aside!"

"Presently. Now, that way is yours," said Hillard, pointing in the direction of the way they had come.

"Are you certain?" The Italian regulated his breathing, forcing down the beat of his heart.

"So certain that if you do not obey me, I shall call the police and let you explain to them."

"I should like nothing better," replied the Italian, with a coolness which dumfounded Hillard.

"Do you know these ladies?"

"Do you?" insolently.

"My knowing them does not matter. But it is any gentleman's concern when a man gives pursuit to a lady who does not wish to meet him, even in Monte Carlo."

"A lady? Grace of Mary, that is droll!"

Hillard released the imprisoned arm, consciously chilled by the tone. There was a patent raillery, a quizzical insolence, which convinced Hillard that the Italian had not given chase out of an idle purpose. While this idea was forming in his mind, the Italian inspected his cuff, brushed his sleeve, and then recalled that he was bareheaded. He laughed shortly.

"We shall meet again," he said softly.

"I hope not," replied Hillard frankly, at the same time placing himself so as to block any sudden attempt to take up the chase. "However, you may find me at the Hotel de Londres."

The Italian laughed again. "You understand the language well," debatingly.

"And the people, too." Hillard had no desire to pass the time of day with his opponent.

"Well, I have said that we shall meet again, and it must be so."

"And your hat, as well as mine, is still in the Casino. The night is cold."

The Italian tugged impatiently at his mustache and permitted his glance to wander over Hillard critically. No, a struggle, much as he longed for it, would not be wise. He swung round on his heel and walked rapidly down the street, much to Hillard's relief. Presently the Italian took the corner, and Hillard turned to reassure Kitty.

But Kitty had vanished!

Chapter 15 *MANY NAPOLEONS*

Having yawned luxuriously, Merrihew sighed with perfect content. The pretty woman sitting opposite smiled at him tenderly, and he smiled back, abstractedly, as a man sometimes will when his mind tries to gather in comprehensively a thought and a picture which are totally different. Before him, in neat little lustrous stacks, stood seven thousand francs in gold, three hundred and fifty effigies of Napoleon the Little. And this was the thought which divided the smile with the picture. Seven thousand francs, fourteen hundred dollars, more than half the sum of his letter of credit! And all this prodigious fortune for a little gold put here, and a little gold put there, wisely, scientifically; for he would have strenuously denied that it was due to bald, blind luck. If only the boys at the club could see him now! He wet his lips suggestively, but the lust for gold was stronger than the call of tobacco. Tobacco could wait; fortune might not. Still, he took out a cigar, bit off the end, and put it back in his pocket. And where the deuce had Hillard gone? Twenty minutes to eleven, and no sign of him since the play began.

He counted off ten coins and placed them on the second dozen. The ball rolled into number twenty-three. He leaned back again with a second sigh, and the pretty woman smiled a second smile, and the wooden rake pushed the beautiful gold over to him. He was playing a system, one bet in every three turns of the wheel, in stakes of forty and eighty dollars. To be sure he lost now and then, but the next play he doubled and retrieved. Oh, the American Comic Opera Company should be well taken care of. He could play the good Samaritan after the manner of a prince, if, indeed, princes ever elected to play that role. Two more bets, and then he would pocket his winnings and go. He laid forty francs on number twenty-six and four hundred on black, leaned upon his elbows and studied the pretty woman, who smiled. If she spoke English… . He scribbled the question on a scrap of paper and pushed it across the table, blushing a little as he did so. She read it, or at least she tried to read it, and shook her head with the air of one deeply puzzled. He sighed again, reflecting that there might have been a pleasant adventure had he only understood French. Hang the legend of the Tower of Babel! it was always confronting him in this part of the world.

Twenty-six, black and even!

Merrihew slid back his chair and rose. He swept up the gold by the handful and poured it into his pockets, casually and unconcernedly, as if this was an every-day affair and of minor importance. But as a matter of fact, his heart was beating fast, and there was a wild desire in his throat to yell with delight. Eighteen hundred dollars, nine thousand francs! A merry music they made in his pockets. Jingle, jingle, jingle! Not only the good Samaritan, but the accursed thousand, that baneful thousand, that Nemesis of every New Year, might now be overtaken and annihilated. O happy thought! His pockets sagged, he could walk but stiffly, and in weight he seemed to have gained a ton. And then he saw Hillard coming across the hall. Instantly he forced the joy from his face and eyes and dropped his chin in his collar. He became in that moment the picture of desolation.

"Is it all over?" asked Hillard gravely.

"All over!" monotonously.

"Come over to the café, then. I've something important to tell you."

"Found them?" with rousing interest.

"I shall tell you only when we get out of this place. Come."

Merrihew followed him into the cloak-room; and as they came out into the night, Hillard put out a friendly hand.

"I am sorry, boy; I wanted you to win something. Cheer up; we'll shake the dust of this place in the morning."

Merrihew took off his hat and tossed it into the air hilariously. As it came down he tried to catch it on the toe of his pump, but active as he was he missed, and it rolled along the pavement. He recovered it quickly.

"Oh, for a vacant lot and a good old whooper-up! Feel!" he said, touching his side pockets. Hillard felt. "Feel again!" commanded Merrihew, touching his trousers pockets. Hillard, with increasing wonder, felt again.

"What is it?" he asked.

"What is it? It is four hundred and fifty napoleons!"

"What?" sharply, even doubtfully.

"That's what! Eighteen hundred dollars, more than three hundred and sixty pounds, nearly a million centesimi, and Heaven only knows what it would be in Portuguese. My system will have no funeral to-night. Pretty fair returns for two hours' work, by George! Now, come on."

He caught Millard by the sleeve and fairly ran him over to the café. Here lie pushed him into a chair and ordered the finest vintage he could find on the card. Then he offered one of the fatal cigars and lighted one for himself.

"Nearly two thousand!" murmured Hillard. "Well, of all the luck!"

"It does seem too good to be true. And what's more, I'm

going to hang on to it. No more for me; I'm through. For the first time in my life I've won something, and I am going to keep it.... I say, what's the matter with your cravat?"

Hillard looked down at the fluttering end and reknotted it carelessly.

"I saw Kitty to-night," he said.

To Merrihew it seemed that all the clatter about him had died away suddenly. He lowered his cigar and breathed deeply. "Where is she?" He rose. "Sit down. I don't know where she is. I'll explain what has happened. And this is it."

Merrihew listened eagerly, twisting his cigar from one corner of his mouth to the other. Once he made a gesture; it was reproachful.

"And why did you bother about him? Why didn't you hold on to Kitty?"

"I confess it was stupid of me. But the gentleman with the scar was an unknown quantity. Besides, why should Kitty, in an episode like this, run away from me, of all persons? That's what is troubling me. And why, when I spoke to them in the Casino, did they ignore me completely?"

"It's your confounded prima donna; she's at the bottom of all this, take my word for it. Something's desperately wrong. Persons do not wear masks and hide in this manner just for a lark. And we have lost them again! Why didn't you knock him down?" hotly.

"I wanted to, but it wasn't the psychological moment. He recovered himself too quickly. You can't knock a man down when he practically surrenders."

"You're too particular. But what's the matter with Kitty? I don't understand. To see you was to know that I was round somewhere. She ran away from me as well as from you. What shall we do?"

"Start the hunt again, or give it up entirely. There are some villages between here and Nice. It must be in that direction; they were about to board the car for Nice. If you hadn't been gambling, if you had been sensible and stayed with me—"

"Come, now, that won't wash. You know very well that you urged me to play."

"You would have played without any urging."

The wine came, but the joy of drinking it was gone; and they emptied the bottle perfunctorily. To Merrihew everything was out of tune now. Why, Kitty Killigrew was worth all the napoleons in or out of France. And Kitty had run away! What was the meaning of it?

"And who is this Italian, anyhow? And why did he run after your prima donna?"

"That is precisely what I wish to find out," answered Hillard. "The lady whom you call my prima donna knew him and he knew her, and she must have had mighty good reasons for running."

"I'm afraid that Kitty has fallen among a bad lot. I'll wager it is some anarchist business. They are always plotting the assassination of kings over here, and this mysterious woman is just the sort to rope in a confiding girl like Kitty. One thing, if I come across our friend with the scar—"

"You will wisely cross to the opposite side of the street. To find out what this tangle is, it is not necessary to jump head first into it."

"A bad lot."

"That may be, but no anarchists, my boy."

Hillard was a bit sore at heart. That phrase recurred and recurred: "A lady? Grace of Mary, that is droll!" As he turned it over it had a bitter taste. The shadow of disillusion crept into his bright dream and clouded it. To build so beautiful a castle, and to see it tumble at a word! The Italian had spoken with a contempt which was based on something more tangible than suspicion. What was she to him, or, rather, what had she been? If she was innocent of any wrong, why all this mystery? Persecution? That did not necessitate masks and veils and sudden flights. Well, he was a man: even as he watched this cloud of smoke, he would watch the dream rise and vanish into the night.

Merrihew solemnly spun his wine-glass, but made no effort to refill it.

"I'm thinking hard," he said, "but I can't make out Kitty."

"No more can I. But if she ran away from me, she had a definite purpose, and some day we'll find out just what it was. I am more than half inclined to give up the chase entirely. You will see Kitty in New York again, and the whys and wherefores will be illumined. But if I keep on thinking of this masquerading lady, I shall get into a mental trouble which will not be at all agreeable. I would to Heaven that she had sung under any window but mine."

"All right. Kitty doesn't wish to meet us. So we'll light out for Venice in the morning. I'm not going to be made a fool of for the best woman alive."

"There is still the Campo Formosa. If they return to Venice, and doubtless they will, for I believe they came here to replenish their purses, we'll hunt up the Campo and make inquiries. It is not anarchism. Anarchists always need money, and they wouldn't let me slip through their fingers, once having taken hold of my curiosity in this way. You may be sure it is something deeper than that. Anarchism wouldn't interest a sensible little woman like Kitty."

"You never can tell what will interest a woman," said Merrihew owlishly.

"There's truth in that. But Kitty isn't romantic; she has her bump of caution."

"I agree to that. She refused me."

They both laughed quietly.

"Well, if nothing happens in Venice, we'll go to Verona, buy a pair of good saddle-horses, and take the road to Florence. That will be something worth while. And it will clear this romantic fog out of our heads."

"That's the most sensible thing you've said in a long time," said Merrihew, brightening considerably. "A leg up and a couple of hundred miles of these great roads! You've hit it squarely, by George! And out of my winnings we can buy ripping hunters. The American Comic Opera Company be hanged! But I'd give half of my winnings if I knew what was at the bottom of it all. Seems as if fate were moving us round for a pastime. We have probably passed and repassed the two women a dozen times."

"And but for those cigars — "

"Will you kindly forget that?"

"If you insist upon it."

"Thanks. We came over to see Italy; let's see it. Now, I'm for turning in. A bit headachey; infernally hot in the roulette room."

In truth, all the enthusiasm was gone from Merrihew's

heart. Since Kitty evinced a desire to avoid him, the world grew charmless; and the fortune of Midas, cast at his feet, would not have warmed him. On the way over to the hotel, however, he whistled bravely and jingled the golden largess in his pockets. He bade good night to Hillard and sought his room. Here he emptied his pockets on the table and built a shelving house of gold. He sat down and began to count. Clink-clink! Clink-clink! What a pleasant sound it was, to be sure. It was sweeter than woman's laughter. And what symphony of Beethoven's could compare with this? Clink-clink! Three hundred and ninety, four hundred, four hundred and ten; clink-clink! And Hillard, turning restlessly on his pillow, heard this harsh music away into the small hours of the morning.

In the meantime the lamps in and about the Casino had been extinguished, and the marble house of the whirligig and the terraces lay in the pale light of the moon. Only the cafés remained open, and none but stragglers loitered there. The great rush of the night was done with, and the curious had gone away, richer or poorer, but never a whit the wiser. In the harbor the yachts stood out white and spectral, and afar the sea ruffled her night-caps. The tram for Nice shrieked down the incline toward the promontory, now a vast frowning shadow. At the foot of the road which winds up to the palaces the car was signaled, and two women boarded. Both were veiled and exhibited signs of recent agitation. They maintained a singular silence. At Villefranche they got out, and the car went on glowingly through the night. The women stopped before the gates of a villa and rang the porter's bell. Presently he came down the path and admitted them, grumbling. Once in the room above, the silence between the two women came to an end.

"Safe! I am so tired. What a night!" the elder of the two women sighed.

"What a night, truly! I should like to know what it has all been about. To run through dark streets and alleys, to hide for hours, as if I were a thief or a fugitive from justice, is neither to my taste nor to my liking."

"Kitty!" brokenly.

"I know! In a moment I shall be on my knees to you, but first I must speak out my mind. Why did you lose your head? Why did you not stand perfectly still when you saw that we were followed from the Casino? He would not have dared to molest us in the open. No, you had to run!"

"He would have entered the car with us, he would have known where we were going, he would have had the patience to wait till he saw beneath our veils. I know that man!" with a hopeless anger.

"It was your flight. It told him plainly that you recognized him."

"I was afraid, Kitty. It was instinct which caused me to fly, blindly."

"And there you left me, standing like a fool, wondering whether to run or not." Kitty was angry for half a dozen reasons. "And why should you run from any man?"

La Signorina did not reply, preferring to hold her tongue, lest it overthrow her. She unwound the thick veil and unpinned her hat. Her hands trembled, and in her eyes and about her mouth there was the weariness of ages. Yet, not all this weariness, not all these transitory lines of pain, took away one jot of her beauty.

"Kitty," she began sadly, "in this world no one trusts us

wholly. We must know why, why; loyalty must have reasons, chivalry must have facts. You have vowed your love and loyalty a hundred times, and still, when a great crisis confronts me, you question, you grow angry, you complain, because my reasons are unknown to you. Because I am lonely, because I feel the need of even your half-hearted loyalty, I shall tell you why, why. Do you know what terror is? No. Well, it was blind terror which made me run. I counted not the consequences; my one thought was of instant flight. I shall tell you why I am lonely, why the world, bright to you, is dark. I am proud, but I shall bend my pride." With a quick movement she lifted her head high and her eyes burned into Kitty's very heart. "I am—"

"Stop! No, no! I forbid you!" Kitty put her hands over her ears. She might gain the secret, but she knew that she would lose the heart of the woman it concerned. "I am wrong, wrong. I have promised to follow you loyally, without question. I will keep that promise. I am only angry because you would not let me speak to Mr. Hillard. And when he called me by name, it was doubly hard. Had I not seen your hand waving from the doorway, I should have spoken. Who this Italian is I do not care. It is sufficient that you fear him. And I myself harbor no kind feelings toward him," rubbing her bruised wrist. "And if he comes down one side of the street I shall take to the other, to say nothing of dodging round the nearest corner. But he is very handsome," Kitty added thoughtfully.

"Are vipers handsome?"

"He is strong, too."

"Strong and cruel as a tiger. How I hate him! But thank you, Kitty, thank you. Sooner or later, if we stay together, I must tell you. The confidence will do me good. Look into my eyes."

Kitty approached, and La Signorina drew her close. "Look in them. They will tell you that I have neither conspired nor plotted, save for my own happiness; that I have wrought harm to no one. But on my side they will tell you that I have been terribly wronged. And all I wish is to be left alone, alone. It was cruel of me to forbid you to speak to Mr. Hillard. But I do not want him tangled up in this miserable, hopeless labyrinth. I wish him to recollect me pleasantly, as a whimsical being who came into his life one night and vanished out of it in two hours."

"But supposing the memory cuts deeply?" ventured Kitty. "Men fall in love with less excuse than this."

"He does not even know what I look like; he knows absolutely nothing except the sound of my voice."

"It is all a blind man needs—a voice."

"Nonsense!" La Signorina opened the window to air the room. She lingered, musing. "You are very good to me, Kitty."

"I can't help being good to you, you strange, lovely woman! For your sake as well as for mine, I hope my letter from home will be in Venice when we arrive. Now I am going to write a letter."

La Signorina still lingered by the window.

Merrihew was pocketing currency in exchange for his gold, when Hillard passed an opened letter to him. It was early in the morning; the sky was as yellow as brass; patches of dew still dampened the sidewalks, and the air was still with the promise of heat in the later day. Merrihew stuffed the last bill into his wallet and gave his attention to the letter. He was not long indifferent, for the letter was from no less a person than Kitty. It was, however, addressed to Hillard.

My dear Mr. Hillard—Do not seek us. It will be useless. This sounds terribly ungrateful, but it must be so. If Mr. Merrihew is with you, and I suspect he is, tell him that some day I will explain away the mystery. At present I know no more than you do. But this please make plain to him: If he insists upon searching for me, he will only double my unhappiness.

Kitty Killigrew.

Merrihew soberly tucked the letter away. "I knew it," he said simply. "She is in some trouble or other, some tangle, and fears to drag us into it. Who left a letter here this morning?" he asked of the concierge.

"A small boy from Villefranche."

"Just my luck," said Merrihew, his hands speaking eloquently. "I said that it would be of no use to hunt in the smaller towns. Well, we had better take the luggage back to the rooms."

"Why?" asked Hillard.

"I am going to Villefranche."

"You will be wasting time. After what happened last night, I am certain that they will be gone. Let us not change our plans, and let us respect theirs, hard as it may seem to you."

"But you?"

"Oh, don't bother about me. I have relegated my little romance to the garret of no-account things, at least for the present," said Hillard, with an enigmatical smile. He sought his watch. "Make up your mind at once; we have only twenty minutes."

"Oh, divine afflatus! And you lay down the chase so

readily as this?" Merrihew was scornfully indignant.

"I would travel the breadth of the continent were I sure of meeting this woman. But she has become a will-o'-the-wisp, and I am too old and like comfort too well to pursue impossibilities."

"But why did she leave you that mask?" demanded Merrihew. "She must have meant something by that."

"True, but for the life of me I can't figure out what, unless she wished to leave with me the last page of the adventure."

"But I don't like the idea of leaving Kitty this way, without a final effort to rescue her from the clutches of this fascinating adventuress. For you must admit that she is naught else."

"I admit nothing, my boy, save that the keenness of the chase is gone." Hillard balanced his watch idly. "As for Kitty, she's a worldly little woman, and can take good care of herself. She is not likely to blunder into any serious conspiracy. Her letter should be sufficient."

"But it isn't. A woman's 'don't' often means 'do.' If Kitty really expects me to search for her and I do not, she will never believe in me again."

"Perhaps your knowledge of women is more extensive than mine," said Hillard, without the least irony.

But this flattery did not appeal to Merrihew. "Bosh! There's something you haven't told me about that makes you so indifferent."

This was a shrewd guess, but Hillard had his reasons for not letting his friend see how close he had shot. "A lady? Grace of Mary, that is droll!" He could not cast this out of his thought. He floated between this phrase and Mrs. Sandford's frank defense of her girlhood friend. Perhaps he was lacking in some particle of chivalry; perhaps he was not in love at all. And of what use to offer faith to one who refused it?

"Time flies," he warned. "Which is it to be?"

"We'll go on to Venice. It would be folly for me to continue the hunt alone. And if you went with me, your half-heartedness would be a damper. We'll go on to Venice."

"Have you any cigars left?" smiling.

"I have thrown away the boxes and filled my pockets."

"That's better. But the Italians are not so severe as the French. We shan't have any trouble recrossing into Italy. All aboard, then."

Merrihew solemnly directed the porter to paste the scarlet labels on his cases. He was beginning to take a certain blasé pride in his luggage. Already it had the appearance of having traveled widely. It would look well on week-end trips at home.

At seven that evening they stepped out of the station in Venice. The blue twilight of Venice, that curves down from the hollow heavens, softening a bit of ugliness here, accentuating a bit of loveliness there; that mysterious, incomparable blue which is without match or equivalent, and which flattens all perspective and gives to each scene the look of a separate canvas! Here Merrihew found one of his dreams come true, and his first vision of the Grand Canal, with its gondolas and barges and queer little bobtailed skiffs, was never to leave him. What impressed him most was the sense of peace and quiet. No one seemed in a hurry, for hurry carries with it the suggestion of noise and turmoil. Hillard hunted for his old gondolier, but could not find him. So he chose one Achille whose ferrule was bright and who carried the number 154. With their trunks, which they had picked up at

Genoa, and small luggage in the hotel barge, they had the gondola all to themselves.

Instead of following the Grand Canal, Achille took the short cut through the Ruga di San Giovanni and the Rio di San Polo. It was early moonlight, and as they glided silently past the ancient marble church in the Campo San Polo the fairy-like beauty of it caught Merrihew by the throat.

"This is the happy hunting grounds," he said. "This beats all the cab-riding I ever heard of. And this is Venice!" He patted Hillard on the shoulder. "I am grateful to you, Jack. If you hadn't positively dragged me into it, I should have gone on grubbing, gone on thinking that I knew something about beauty. Venice!" He extended his arms as a Muezzin does when he calls to prayer. "Venice! The shade of Napoleon, of Othello, of Portia, of Petrarch!"

Hillard smiled indulgently. "I love your enthusiasm, Dan. So long as a man has that, the rest doesn't matter."

Out into the Grand Canal again, and another short cut by the way of the Rio del Baccaroli. As they swept under the last bridge before coming out into the hotel district, Hillard espied a beggar leaning over the parapet. The faint light of the moon shone full in his face.

"Stop!" cried Hillard to Achille, who swung down powerfully on his blade. Hillard stood up excitedly.

The beggar took to his heels, and when Hillard stepped out of the gondola and gained the bridge, the beggar had disappeared.

"Who was it?" asked Merrihew indifferently.

"Giovanni!"

Chapter 16 O'MALLY SUGGESTS

In a bedroom in one of the cheap little *pensiones* which shoulder one another along the Riva degli Schiavoni, from the ducal palace to the public gardens, sat three men. All three were smoking execrable tobacco in ancient pipes. Now and then this one or that consulted his watch (grateful that he still possessed it), as if expecting some visitor. The castaways of the American Comic Opera troupe were on the anxious seat this morning.

"Well, what do you think?" asked Smith.

"Think? Why, she'll be here this morning, or I know nothing about women. That ring was worth a cool thousand." O'Mally shook the nicotine from his pipe. "She'll be here, never you worry. But," with a comic grimace, "it's dollars to doughnuts that both of 'em will be stone-broke. I know something about that innocent little game called roulette."

"But if she's broke, what the devil shall we do?" Smith put this question in no calm frame of mind.

"Forty dollars; it's a heap just now."

"She said she had another plan," said Worth.

"If it's a plan which needs no investments, all well and good. But, on my word, I wouldn't dare advance another cent." Smith's brow wore many wrinkles.

"Nor I," said O'Mally.

"Positively, no," added Worth.

O'Mally mused. "A bill from your tailor will reach you here in eight days, but money! Looks as if they had sent it via Japan."

"The one thing I'm sore about is the way she buncoed us into giving up our return tickets to the chorus."

"Shame on you!" cried the generous O'Mally. "What chance had any of them on this side? Ten to one, nobody home could have sent them money. We men can get along somehow. But I wish I could get some good plug-cut. This English shoe-string tobacco burns like hot lead."

"O'Mally, what's your opinion?"

"On what?"

"La Signorina," said Worth.

"What about her?"

"What do you think of her? She's not one of us; she belongs to another class, and the stage is only an incident."

"Well, I don't know what to think. I've pumped Killigrew, but she seems to be in the dark with the rest of us. That ring and the careless way she offered it as security convinces me that she doesn't belong. But what a voice! It lifts you out of your very boots."

"Even when she talks," said Smith. "Honestly, I'm glad she always wears that veil. I might make a jackass of myself."

"It would be excusable," rejoined Worth, pressing the coal in his pipe and blowing the strong, biting smoke above his head. "She is, without exception, one of the most beautiful women I ever saw or care to see." He rose and walked over to the window and gazed down upon the quay, bright with morning sunshine and colorful with two human currents.

Smith and O'Mally exchanged a swift, comprehensive look. There was one thing upon which they agreed fully, but they had not yet put it into words. When Worth returned to his chair his two companions were inspecting the faded designs in the carpet.

"In Rome there was a grand duke," Worth remarked.

"And how she played him!" laughed Smith.

"And there you are! Imagine an American comic opera star refusing to dine with a real duke! If anything convinces me, it is that. Think of the advertisement it would have been in New York! Think of the fat part for the press agent! No," continued O'Mally, "she doesn't belong."

"The thing that sticks in my mind is the alternative which she has promised to offer." Worth eyed the ceiling. "She said that if she failed at Monte Carlo she had another plan. What? Pawning her jewels? I think not. But whatever it is, I expect to be counted in."

"I, too," agreed Smith.

O'Mally took the small brilliant from his necktie and contemplated it sadly. "The outsiders make fun of us for toting round these sparklers; but often it's board and car-fare home. I paid seventy-five for this; I might be able to raise thirty on it. Of course, she's backed us finely with the hotel man; but if she shouldn't return, it's strapped the three of us will be. And no letters at Cook's this morning."

"Oh, if worst comes to worst, the American consul will forward us to New York. I'm not going to borrow any trouble." And Worth in his turn found employment in the carpet patterns. Presently he got up briskly. "I'm going down to the office."

"Bureau," corrected O'Mally.

"Bureau. There might be a note or something." Worth smiled.

When he was out of the way O'Mally nodded wisely to his friend Smith.

"I hope he won't make a fool of himself over her."

"He has the symptoms. I've seen 'em before," replied

Smith jocularly. "But he's an odd duffer, and there's no knowing what he'll do before the round-up. It's a fine go, anyhow. Here we are, handsomely stranded thousands of miles from home. The only chance I have of finding money in a letter is to sign for next season and draw down enough to pay for a steamer ticket. As for a bank account, Lord! I never had one. I have made two offers for my versatile talents, but no line yet."

O'Mally laughed. "Same boat. I've written to my brother, who has always held that I'm a good-for-nothing. And he may see in this predicament of mine a good chance to be rid of me permanently. But I believe Worth has a bank account at home. He is close-mouthed about his affairs. He received some letters yesterday, but when I quizzed him he made out he didn't hear me. I didn't crowd him. Hope he won't make a fool of himself over La Signorina. Sh! he's coming back."

The door opened and Worth beckoned. "They are in the parlor, waiting. I don't know what news they bring."

There was a brightness in his eyes that meant unmistakable things to his two companions. They laid aside their pipes, tidied up a bit, and went down to the stuffy salon. The two women rose as the men entered. There was good cheer and handshaking. O'Mally's heart sank, however, as he touched the hand of La Signorina. There was no joy in the pressure, nothing but sympathy and subtle encouragement.

"Come," he said cheerfully, "put us out of our misery. Confess that you are both broke, and that Monte Carlo is still on the map."

As a preamble La Signorina raised the inevitable veil to the rim of her hat. Worth sat down in the darkest corner whence he could without inconvenience feast his eyes upon her beauty.

Her tale was short and lightly told, with an interpolation now and then by Kitty.

"I was very foolish," said the erstwhile prima donna. "I might have known that when one is unlucky one may become still more unlucky. The superlative of bad luck has been my portion. But I did so wish to win. I wanted to bring back enough gold to send you all to America."

"But what was to become of you?" asked Worth from behind his fortress of shadow.

"I?" She paused with indecision. The question was not expected. "Oh, Italy is my home. I shall find a way somehow. Put me out of your thoughts entirely. But I am sorry to bring you this bitter disappointment, for it must be bitter. You have all been so good and patient in your misfortune."

"Forget it," said O'Mally. "Sure, we're no worse off than we were before. And here we've had a whole week of hope and fine air-castles. I've seen 'em tumble down so often that I've a shell like a turtle's now. Forget it."

"But there is one thing I wish to understand thoroughly," put in Worth slowly.

"And that?" La Signorina was never sure of this man. He was deeper than the others; he had more polish, more knowledge of the world at large; he was a gentleman by birth. He was a puzzle, and at this period she was not overfond of shifting puzzles into answers.

"You have guaranteed our credit at this hotel. By what means?" Worth held her eye with courage.

"My word," she answered, finding that she could not beat down his eye.

"I know something of these foreign hotel managers.

Words are all right, but they must be backed by concrete values." Worth's eye was still steady and unwavering. "If, as I believe, you have guaranteed our credit here by means of jewels, we must know."

She appealed silently to O'Mally, but he shook his head determinedly.

"It's only right that we should know," he said, wondering why this thing had never entered his thick skull before.

"Let us not indulge in fine sentiment. I have guaranteed your credit here; how I have done so, ought not to matter much."

"But it does," countered Worth. "If by more than word, we insist upon knowing." Worth spoke with feeling. "Do not for a moment doubt my attitude. I understand and appreciate your great generosity. We are absolutely nothing to you, and you are not responsible for our misfortunes. But we men have some pride left. A man might do for us what you have done and we should accept it without comment; but a woman, no. That alters the case entirely."

"Is it from a sense—a misguided sense—of chivalry?" she asked, her lips suggesting a smile.

"That's probably it," O'Mally answered.

And Smith inclined his head in approval.

"You are evading us," went on Worth, not having moved from his stand.

"You insist, then?" coldly.

"Positively insist. If you do not tell us, we shall be forced to pay our bill and take our chances elsewhere." Worth pressed the button in the wall. A servant appeared directly. "The manager, at once."

La Signorina dropped her veil and sat stiffly in her chair. Kitty moved uneasily. Was the man crazy to cross La Signorina like this? The manager appeared. He bowed.

"Madame here," began Worth, indicating La Signorina, "has guaranteed our credit at your hotel."

"Yes. Is not everything satisfactory?" asked the manager eagerly.

"By what means has she established our credit? And do you know her?"

"I never saw madame before till she came here with you gentlemen. What is the trouble?" His brow wrinkled worriedly.

"What security did madame advance?"

"Security?" The manager looked at La Signorina, but she rendered him not the least assistance. "I have given my word to madame not to tell."

"In that case we three gentlemen shall leave this afternoon. You will make out our bill at once."

This time the manager appealed to the lady eloquently.

"You are three foolish men," spoke La Signorina impatiently. "If the manager wishes to tell you he may do so. I give him permission."

The careless way she assigned the third person to the manager more than ever convinced Worth that somewhere and at some time La Signorina had commanded.

"The security I have, gentlemen, is quite sufficient," said the manager.

"Produce it," said Worth. He realized that he had angered La Signorina, and he now regretted his scruples, which in this instance had their foundation on mere curiosity. He would not retreat now.

The manager brought forth a fat wallet and opened it. Out of this he took a flat object wrapped in tissue-paper. Very tenderly he unfolded it. The treasure was a diamond pendant, worth at least a thousand dollars.

"I was to keep this, simply till madame chose to reclaim it. Nothing has been advanced against it." A new thought came into the manager's mind, and he turned slightly pale. "If it is not madame's—?"

"It is mine," said La Signorina. She was very angry, but her sense of justice admitted that Worth was perfectly right. "Once more I ask you not to make me miserable by forcing this trinket back upon me. Will you do me the honor to wait till to-morrow morning?"

The three men involved exchanged questioning looks.

"Till to-morrow morning, then," said Worth. "That will be all," he added, to the manager, who was willing enough to make his escape.

"You will forgive us, won't you?" asked O'Mally. "It could not be. We men have some ideas in our heads that you can't knock out with a club. It was fine of you. You've a heart as big as all outdoors. We'll keep the thought behind the deed. Eh, boys? Do not be angry with us."

"I am only angry to have been found out," she answered, not ungraciously. Then she laughed. "You are the strangest people! One would think, to hear you talk, that I was giving you all this, when I merely advanced security till your remittances come. Well, well, we shall say no more about it. I have a plan to lay before you that is a vastly more interesting matter. It will be something of an adventure to us all."

"Adventure?" O'Mally ran his tongue across his lips like

a thirsty man coming unexpectedly upon a pool of spring-water.

"Adventure? Let us be gone upon it at once," said Worth, anxious to return into the graces of this singular woman.

"Any place, so long as there's board and keep in it," Smith declared.

Kitty tried to read La Signorina's eyes. What madness this time?

La Signorina again raised her veil. From her girdle-bag she took a letter, which she unfolded across her knees. "As I have said, I have friends in Italy, and some of them are rich and powerful. This letter is from a friend I have always known. Has any one of you ever heard of the Principessa di Monte Bianca?"

A thoughtful frown passed from one face to another; and each strove to recall this name among half-forgotten memories. Finally, one by one they shook their heads. The name had a familiar echo, but that was all. It was quite possible that they had seen it in the Paris edition of the *Herald*.

"Let me read this letter to you. She addresses me as Capricciosa, my stage name."

Her audience leaned forward attentively.

My Dear—I was very glad indeed to hear from you, and I shall be only too happy to offer you the temporary assistance you desire. You will recollect that I possess a villa just outside of Florence, a mile or so north of Fiesole. I have never been inside of it but once, in my childhood. The villa is furnished and kept in repair by an ancient gardener and his wife. You and your friends are welcome to occupy the Villa Ariadne as long as you please. You will find one annoyance: in the ravine below the Eighth Corps has a shooting range, and it is noisy when the wind is in the east. Of course you will find all the chests, bureaus, sideboards and closets under seal; for I have not been there since the death of my father. None of the seals may be removed till I occupy the villa legally. However, the gardener and his wife have silver and linen and china, and with these you will be able to get along nicely. The fruits and roses and garden truck will be wholly yours, and if you are vegetarians you can live without expense for weeks. Take the villa, then, and enjoy yourselves. It is rather out of the beaten track, though at times it is invaded by tourists. Besides this letter I am giving you one of official authority, for there is always some formality. If you should need any financial aid, do not hesitate to call upon me.

La Principessa di Monte Bianca.

"A villa!" exclaimed Kitty rapturously. So many villas had she seen, guarded by Lombardy poplars or cypresses, that her mind hungered to live in one, if never so shortly.

"And the villa of a princess!" sighed O'Mally. "Fudge! I'm a patriot, all right, but may I be hanged if I shouldn't like to meet a princess, the real article, just once. What do you say, Smith?"

"Sure! It would be something to brag about. 'When I was in Florence my friend, the Princess di Whadeyuhcallit, said to me,' and so forth. Sounds good. But it's an idle dream, Tom, an idle dream."

"Will you permit me to read the letter?" asked Worth.

La Signorina consented. Worth had an idea; it was as yet nebulous; still, it was a shrewd idea, and needed only a small space to stand. The moment he saw the letter the nebulous idea became opaque. The page was neatly typewritten in Italian, and only the signature was in ink. It was a small, slanting, aristocratic signature.

"Do you read Italian?" she asked with pardonable malice.

"Very little, and nothing on this page." Worth felt embarrassed under her glance. Still he continued to stare at the letter. The crest on the paper, the postmark on the envelope, convinced him of its authenticity. The date was quite recent, and did not correspond with their unhappy sojourn in the Imperial City.

"The question is, shall we accept this offer?" She refolded the letter. "This was the plan I had in mind when we went to Monte Carlo, and a much better plan, too."

"Of course, we shall accept it," said Worth, confident that the mystery was still there, but that for the present he had been fooled.

"But what's the matter with your playing the princess to the neighbors?" suggested O'Mally, his eyes laughing. "I'll be the concierge, Smith the steward, and Kitty your maid."

"And I?" asked Worth.

"Oh, you can be her Highness' private secretary and attend to the correspondence."

The laughter which followed this was light-hearted and careless. Once more worry had taken to wing and they were without burdens. Only La Signorina did not join the merriment. The sparks in her eyes, the silver points of light, the flash of excitement, portended something. She rose with a determined air.

"Mr. O'Mally makes a very good suggestion. It will be an adventure worth recounting. I shall go as the princess. What sport with the country gentlemen! This will be an adventure after one's own heart. Her Highness commands! Will it not be delightful?"

Worth looked at O'Mally, who looked at Smith, who looked at Kitty; then all four looked at La Signorina.

"Are you not lightening our trials by joking?" asked Worth dubiously.

"I am positively serious."

"Impossible! It would be nothing less than madness to fly in the face of this stroke of luck."

"Call it madness, if you like. I shall go as the princess."

"But the authorities! It will be prison."

"I am sufficiently armed for any event. It all depends upon your courage," with a veiled insolence calculated to make any man commit any kind of folly.

"It is not a question of courage," replied O'Mally; "it's prudence."

"Prudence in an Irishman?" more insolent than ever.

"Oh, if you take that tone," said O'Mally, coloring, "why, the thing is done. Henceforth I am your major-domo. No one can call me a coward."

"O'Mally!"

"That's all right, Worth," said O'Mally. "I wouldn't turn back now for sixty-seven jails. You need not join."

"I shan't desert you in a strait like this," remarked Worth quietly. "Only, I think La Signorina rather cruel to force such a situation upon us, when it was entirely unnecessary. Put me against the correspondence."

"If I wasn't flat broke," said Smith, "I'd bow out politely. But where the grub-stake goes I must go. But I don't like this business a little bit. Signorina, do tell us that it's a joke."

"Yes," cried Kitty, still in doubt.

"I repeat, I am perfectly serious."

"But the consequences!" protested Kitty, now terrified.

"Consequences? I shall find a way to avoid them."

"But supposing some one who knows the real princess happens along?" said Worth, putting in his final argument.

"If I get into trouble of that sort, her Highness will help me out. I thank Mr. O'Mally for his suggestion."

"Don't mention it," returned O'Mally dryly. Inwardly he was cursing his impulsive Irish blood.

"It is agreed, then, that to-morrow we depart for Florence as the Principessa di Monte Bianca and suite?"

Tears began to fill Kitty's eyes. To have everything spoiled like this! La Signorina would land them all in prison.

"There's a legal side to it," Smith advanced cautiously. "The law may not see the jest from your point of view."

"I believe I am clever enough to meet any contingency of that order."

"I give up," said Worth despondently. "But your princess must be a very dear friend for you to take such liberties with her name."

"She appreciates a jest as thoroughly as I do; moreover, she will stand by me in anything I may do. To-morrow morning, then. We shall go direct to Florence and engage carriages to take us out to the Villa Ariadne. We are all capable enough actors to carry out the venture successfully. And now, to relieve Mr. Worth's chivalrous mind, I shall reclaim my pendant. You will doubtless have enough money to forward yourselves to Florence. Once you arrive there, you will leave the further burdens upon my shoulders. Come, Kitty, we must be going. I know that I can rely upon you gentlemen to enter with full spirit into the adventure."

"We are all crazy, but who cares?" O'Mally cried. But he trembled in his boots, and thought vainly of a certain comfortable chop-house on old Broadway.

The three men bowed ceremoniously. Worth opened the door for the women, and when it closed after them he turned savagely toward O'Mally.

"You—*ass*!"

"There are others!" retorted O'Mally, afire. "You agreed; so drop it. But what the devil are we going to do?"

"That's the question!" Smith got out his pipe.

"We are all going to the Villa Ariadne, and from there to jail!" And Worth flung out of the salon.

"Jail," mused O'Mally. "Blame me, if I don't believe he's right!"

Chapter 17 GIOVANNI

It is in early morning that one should discover the Piazza San Marco. Few travelers, always excepting the Teutonic pilgrims, are up and about; and there is room for one's elbows in the great quadrangle. The doves are hungry then; and they alight on your hands, your arms, your shoulders, and even your hat. They are greedy and wise besides. Hidden among the statues above the arcades and in the cornices of the cathedral, they watch you approach the vender of corn. In a moment they are fluttering about you like an autumn storm of leaves, subsiding quickly; blue-grey doves with white under-wings and coral feet. During the season the Venetian photographers are kept busy printing from amateur films. For who is so indifferent as not to wish to be snapped a few times with the doves forming a heavenly halo above one's head, one's body in a sentimental pose, and one's eyes looking straight into the camera? Well, well; this is as near saintliness as most of us will ever get.

How the warm sunshine brightens the worn marbles, or flashes from the many windows, or sparkles from the oriental domes! And the colored marbles of the ducal palace fairly palpitate. In the bronze fountain at the left of the cathedral will be more doves taking their morning ablutions.

It was such a picture Merrihew and Hillard, his guide, came upon the morning following their arrival. They had not visited it during the night. They had, with the usual impatience of men, gone directly to the Campo Santa Maria Formosa for the great reward. They had watched and waited till near midnight, but in vain. For once Hillard's usual keenness had been at fault. He had forgotten that the Campo was to be entered from two ways, by gondola and by foot. He and Merrihew had simply guarded the bridge.

"I wonder why Giovanni ran away last night," said Merrihew, balancing a dove on his hand.

"I wonder, too," replied Hillard. "It is possible that he did not recognize me. I find that each day means a new wonder of some sort. Giovanni knows that I would do anything in my power to help him. But he runs away at the sight of me. In fact, they *all* run away from me. I must have the evil eye." He was shaking the cornucopia free of the last kernel of corn when he saw something which caused him to stifle an exclamation. "Dan," he said, "keep on feeding the doves. If I'm not back inside of ten minutes, return to the hotel and wait for me. No questions; I'll tell you everything later."

Merrihew's eyes widened. What now? His tongue longed to wag, but by this time he was readily obeying Hillard in all things.

A neat little woman was buying corn. Hillard stepped over to her and touched her arm. As she faced him, he raised his hat, smiling.

"Oh!" The corn spilled in a golden shower, and the doves, fickle as all flighty things are, deserted Merrihew for the moment.

"And where may I find your distinguished mistress?" Hillard asked pleasantly.

"She is not in the Campo Formosa, signore." Bettina, recovering her scattered wits, laughed.

"But you were—last night."

"Yes. I watched you and your friend for some time." Bettina's eyes were merry. She would play with him. Everything was so tedious now.

"Your mistress is in Venice."

"Perhaps. At least her maid is."

"I should not dare suggest a bribe," he said slyly.

"You might make the attempt, just to see what I should do."

Merrihew stood watching them, having lost interest in the doves.

"Supposing I should drop a hundred-lire note, accidentally, and walk away?" Hillard twisted the ends of his mustache.

"But first I should have to tell you, accidentally, where my mistress is?"

"That, of course."

"A hundred-lire note!" To Bettina this was an enormous sum in these unfortunate days. Her resolution wavered. "A hundred-lire note!" She felt that she could make no strong defense against such an assault.

Hillard drew the note from his pocket and crinkled it. "A new dress and bits of lace."

Bettina saw duty one way and avarice the other. Her mistress would never know. Still, if she should find out that she, Bettina, had betrayed her! Was a hundred-lire note worth the risk of losing her mistress? She began to think deeply. At length she shook her head sorrowfully.

"No, signore. I dare not."

"But a hundred lire!"

"Ah, no, no!" Bettina put her hands over her ears.

"Then I shall follow you step by step, all the day long."

She searched for the jest in his eyes, but there was none.

Yes, he would do it. How was she to escape him? Her glance traveled here and there. By the glass-shop on the corner she espied two *carabinieri*. There lay the way.

"Do you see them?" she asked.

"The *carabinieri*? Yes." But he swore under his breath, as he understood the drift of her inquiry.

"I shall ask them to hold you."

"But I have done nothing."

"Not yet, but you will attempt to follow me."

"Begin," he said, with a banter.

"What's the row, Jack?" Merrihew called out impatiently. Why didn't they talk in a language a fellow could understand?

"Stay where you are, Dan." To Bettina, Hillard repeated: "Begin."

She dusted her hands of the corn and walked resolutely toward the *carabinieri*. Hillard, equally resolute, followed, but with a roving eye which took in all things ostensibly save Bettina. He had a plan by which he proposed to circumvent any interference by the guardians. And Bettina aided him, for she never turned her head till she stood at the side of the *carabinieri*.

"Signori, this man is following me," she said. Hillard came on and would have passed, but they stopped him.

"You are following the signorina," said one.

"I? What put such a preposterous idea into the lady's head?" Hillard demanded indignantly.

For a moment the *carabinieri* entertained some doubt.

"He is following me, I tell you," Bettina reiterated. "I do not wish him ill. Simply detain him till I am out of sight."

This was not unreasonable. "It shall be as the little signorina wishes;" and the *carabinieri* laughed. It was some jest, and they would take their part in it willingly.

Hillard resigned, and Bettina took to her heels. Her victory was a permanent one, for the *carabinieri* released Hillard only when they knew it would be impossible for him to take up the pursuit. So, taking his defeat philosophically, Hillard returned to Merrihew.

"Well, what was it?" asked Merrihew, scattering the doves.

"Did I ever tell you about Bettina?"

"Bettina? No."

"Well, she is the maid. The women we are looking for are here in Venice. Now, what's on the program for the rest of the morning?"

Merrihew jammed his hands into his pockets. "Oh, let's go and take a look at the saints. I'm in the mood for it."

So the two set out at the heels of the German tourists. They went through the cathedral and the ducal palace, and when the bronze clock beat out the noon hour Merrihew was bursting with information such as would have filled any ordinary guide-book. He never dreamed that the world held so many different kinds of stone or half so many saints. As they started off for the hotel he declared that he would be willing to give ten dollars for a good twenty-round fight, as a counter-irritant.

"You ought to be ashamed of yourself!" cried Hillard.

"I know it. It's like caviar; the taste has to grow. I'm capable of only a limited artistic education, Jack; so feed me slowly."

"You're in love."

"That's better than growing maudlin over a raft of saints who never did me any good. Your Titians and your Veroneses are splendid; there's color and life there. But these cross-eyed mosaics!" Merrihew threw up his hands in protest.

Hillard let go his laughter. Merrihew was amusing, and his frankness in regard to his lack of artistic temperament in nowise detracted from his considerable accomplishments.

As they passed out of the quadrangle a man accosted them. It was Giovanni, with a week's growth of beard on his face, his clothes ragged and his shoes out at the toes. Swiftly he enjoined silence.

"Follow me," he said softly.

He led them through tortuous streets, over canal after canal, toward the Campo San Angelo. He came to a stop before a dilapidated tenement and signified that the journey was at an end. The three mounted the dusty worn stairs of stone to the third landing; and from all sides they were assailed by the odor of fish and garlic. Giovanni opened a door and bade them enter.

"Why did you run away from me last night, Giovanni?"

"I was afraid. When I returned for you, you were gone. But last night I was a fugitive, in hiding. To-day I am free," with an exultant note.

"Free?" said Hillard, astonished.

"I shall explain. I have been to Paris. Come."

Seated by the window which overlooked the little canal was a young woman. Her hands lay passively in her lap, and her head was lowered. The pose was resignation. She did not stir as they entered.

"You have found her?" whispered Hillard, a great pity swelling his heart. What, after all, were his own petty troubles in the face of this tragedy?

"*Carissime?*" called the father, his voice thrilling with

boundless love.

At the sound she turned her head. Her face, thin and waxen, was still beautiful, ethereally beautiful, but without life. She was, perhaps, three and twenty.

"I have brought an old friend to see you," said Giovanni. "Do you remember the Signore Hillard?"

"Oh, yes! I am glad." She stood up.

Hillard offered his hand awkwardly, and hers touched it with the chill dampness of snow.

"We are going back to the Sabine Hills, Enrichetta and I." The old man rubbed his hands joyously. "Eh, *carissime*?"

"Yes, father," with a smile which had neither gladness nor interest in it.

"But dare you?" asked Hillard in an undertone.

"Yes. A great noble has interceded for me. The news of his success came this early morning. I am free; I may walk with men again."

Merrihew leaned against the wall, uneasy and wishing himself anywhere but here. Tender and generous, he hated the sight of pain. They were talking in Italian, but intuitively he translated. What a devil of a world it was!

Giovanni made his daughter sit down again, patted her cheeks, then pushed his friends into another room, closing the door.

"I found her," he said in English, the chords in his throat standing out. "And Mother of Christ, how I have suffered! She was dancing. She had to sit at tables and drink with the men. That, or the Seine. When she saw me she gave a great cry and fell. She has not been like herself, but that will pass away in time. Now she sits in silence and broods. I went to the Italian ambassador. He heard my story in full. He wrote personally to the king. To-day I am free. I have had to walk from Milan, almost. I had little money. That letter of credit—so you call it?—is with my cousin in Sorrento."

"How much will you need to get to Rome?"

"Hold on, Jack," interposed Merrihew. "I'll take care of the financial end. I won money at Monte Carlo, Giovanni; so it will hurt nobody if you take five hundred francs."

Giovanni scorned to hide his tears. Ah, these Americans! Who could match them for impulsive generosity? "I will pay it back," he said.

"No, I give it to you, Giovanni. It will ease my conscience of the sin of gambling."

"Both of you will live to a good old age," said Giovanni prophetically. "Good men are needed in the world, and God doesn't take all of them young."

"And the man?" Hillard could not refrain from putting this question.

Giovanni looked down. "The signore told me never to speak of that again."

"So I did," replied Hillard. "But all is changed now."

"Do you think so?" Giovanni did not smile.

"Go back to your hills with your daughter and leave vengeance in the hands of God. Forget this man who has wronged you. You are free now; and with care and love you may bring happiness back to her. Forget."

"If he does not cross my path; and if she lives. I have suffered too greatly to forgive and forget. I promise not to seek him."

This was a great victory, and Hillard thrust out his hand.

Giovanni did not take it.

"No, signore, I have only promised not to seek him."

Merrihew, to divert the trend of conversation, counted out five hundred francs. "Here's your money, Giovanni."

"Thank you!" Giovanni put the bills away. In the best of times he was not voluble. "I shall now leave Venice at once. I have friends in Fiesole, near Florence."

"Good-by, then, Giovanni. Take good care of yourself," said Hillard.

"And you will visit me when you come to Rome?" asked Giovanni earnestly.

"Surely."

The old man went down to the street with them. They were so kind. He hated the thought of losing them. But let them come to the Sabines; there would be wine in plenty, and tobacco, and cherries. He remained standing in the door till they took the turn for the bridge. They waved their hands cheerily and vanished from sight. They never saw Giovanni again; yet his hand was to work out the great epoch in Hillard's destiny.

"Poor devil!" said Merrihew. "You remember, Jack, that I once went in for medicine?"

"Yes."

"Well, I have some part of the gift yet. That little girl will not live three months; heart. There is such a thing as a broken heart, and the girl has it."

"Then Heaven help Giovanni and the man who caused this!"

Chapter 18 THE ARIA FROM IL TROVATORE

"Shall we take a look into the Campo Formosa again to-night?" asked Merrihew, stepping into the gondola.

"It will be a waste of time. Bettina will have warned them. What's the Italian coming to, anyhow? She refused a hundred francs. But I can see that Mrs. Sandford had a hand in this latest event. She has probably written that we might look for them in the Campo." Hillard spoke in a discontented tone. "Oh, bother the both of them! Let us loaf round the barges of the serenaders and hear the singing. I want to be amused to-night."

"All right; we'll listen to the music," grumbled Merrihew. He wanted to find Kitty right away. He would gladly have started out and explored every Campo in Venice that night. Hillard's indifference annoyed him.

"To the barges of the troupes!" said Hillard to Achille, who pushed off with a series of short strokes.

In the great canal of San Marco the scene was like a water-carnival. Hundreds of gondolas, with bobbing lights, swam slowly round the barges of the serenaders, who, for the most part, were fallen operatic stars or those who had failed to attain those dizzy heights. Many of them had good voices, but few of them last long in the damp Venetian night air. To-night there were three of these belanterned barges, taking their stands about three hundred yards apart. The glowing coals of cigarettes and cigars of the men in the gondolas were like low-lying stars, and the cold, bright flash of jewels woke here and there among the many beautifully gowned women. From one barge to another the gondolas drifted, finally clustering round the middle barge of the Troupe San Marco, which offered the best voices. Between songs a man of acrobatic accomplishments would jump nimbly from the prow of one gondola to another, stepping lightly here, balancing neatly there, and always with the upturned tambourine extended for silver and copper largess.

Merrihew sat in the bottom of the gondola, while Hillard lay sprawled across the cushions on the seat. The prima donna was singing the jewel-song from Faust, and not badly. Sometimes the low hum of voices floated across the cadence of the song. Merrihew scanned the faces of all those near him, but never a face took on familiar lines. An Adriatic liner loomed up gray and shadowy behind them, and some of the crew were leaning idly over the rail. The song stopped. The man with the tambourine sallied forth. Out of the momentary silence came the indistinct tinkle of the piano in the barge beyond; some one over there was bellowing the toreador's song. This died away amid a faint patter of applause. How clear all the sounds were! thought Merrihew. The tenor of the San Marco troupe rose with the prima donna. It was *Il Trovatore* this time; a bit noisy.

What was that? Hillard was no longer lethargic. He stumbled over the recumbent Merrihew.

"Why don't you walk all over me?" growled Merrihew. "Sit down!"

"Be still!" said Hillard roughly.

From a gondola on the far side of the barge, standing out of the press and just beyond the radiance of the lanterns, never powerful at best, came another voice, a voice which had a soul in it, a voice which broke into song for the pure joy of it, spontaneously. Clear, thrilling, a voice before which the world bows down. The prima donna in the barge was clever; she stopped. The tenor went on, however, recognizing that he was playing opposite, as they say, to a great singer. Hillard's heart beat fast. That voice! There could not be another like it. And she was here in Venice!

"Achille," he said, "do you hear that voice over there in the dark?"

"Yes, signore."

"Push round to it. See, the singer is standing up now. Hurry!"

This sounded important, and Merrihew scrambled to his feet. Yes, he, too, could see this unexpected cantatrice. In fact, everybody was beginning to stand up. All interest was centered in this new voice. Then, as if conscious of this interest, the singer sat down, but still kept to the melody. Achille backed out of the jam, stole round the barge, and craftily approached the outstanding gondola. The two men still remained on their feet.

"Quick, Achille!" For the far gondola was heading for the Grand Canal.

Merrihew understood now. He grasped Hillard's arm excitedly.

"Follow!" commanded Hillard. "Ten lire if you can come up alongside that gondola. Can you see the number?"

"It is 152, signore; Pompeo. It will be a race," doubtfully.

"No matter; follow. It will be worth your while."

And a race it became. Both gondoliers were long past their youth, but each knew the exact weight and effort to be put upon the oar; no useless energy, no hurried work, no spurting, but long, deep swinging strokes. Up the Grand Canal, past the brilliant hotels. The runaway gondola had perhaps a hundred yards the best of it. Achille hung on, neither losing nor gaining a foot.

"Sit down, signori!" said Achille.

Hillard and Merrihew tumbled back upon the cushions.

"We shall not lose them this time, Dan."

"Are we gaining?"

"Not yet. But wait till they turn into some small canal."

The first loop of the Grand Canal was turned; still Pompeo made no effort to seek the smaller canals. Not till he passed under the Rialto, which afforded him a deep shadow, did he turn. Swiftly he bore into the canal which was filled with the postal-gondolas. But not so soon that Achille did not perceive and follow. On and on, soundless; now the pursuer had the advantage over the pursued. It was Pompeo who had to watch, to call; Achille had only to hang on. And he was gaining. A moment later less than ten yards intervened. O for some clumsy barge to bar the way! Round past the Teatro Malibran, into the Rio di San Marina, into a smaller canal again. Hillard now knew whither they were bound: the Campo Formosa.

At each stroke Merrihew swung forward his body. The end of the race came sooner than any one expected. A police barge nosed round an ell; by the time Pompeo was off again, the ferrule of the pursuing gondola scraped past Pompeo's blade. Pompeo called and Achille answered. There was a war of words, figure of a dog, name of a pig. Achille was in the wrong, but ten lire were ten lire. And he knew that his gentlemen meant no harm.

Hillard caught the gondola by the rail and clung. The canal, lined with a dozen lime barges, became so narrow that Achille could scarce paddle, and Pompeo's oar was useless, being partly under the opposing gondola. The race was over.

"Signorina," said Pompeo, boiling with rage, "shall I call

the police?"

"No, Pompeo," said his solitary passenger.

When Merrihew saw that she was alone, his heart became heavy, and the joy of the chase was gone. But not so with Hillard. At last!

"To the Campo, Pompeo. Mr. Hillard, will you kindly follow? I would speak to you alone, since there is no escape."

Her tone chilled Hillard's ardor somewhat. But to speak to her again, and mayhap see her face!

"Doesn't want the police," whispered Merrihew. "I told you so. Look out for yourself."

The gondolas became free presently, and the way to the Campo Formosa was made without further incident.

"She wishes to see me alone, Dan. You stay in the boat, I'll find out where Kitty is."

The gondolas became moored. Hillard jumped out and went to assist La Signorina, but she ignored his outstretched hand. This was not a promising beginning.

"To the church steps, Mr. Hillard," she said.

He followed her meekly. Merrihew sulked among the cushions.

The solitary electric lamp in the Campo made light enough; and when the two arrived at the steps the woman turned.

"What is it you wish?" she asked. There was not the slightest agitation in her voice; there was not even curiosity.

"One look at your face," he answered simply.

She slowly removed the veil. Then, for the first time, he looked upon the face of this woman who had burdened his dreams. The face was not like any he had conjured. It seemed to him that Vecchio's—Paola Vecchio's—Barbara had stepped down from her frame: beauty, tranquil, flawless beauty. A minute passed; he was incapable of speech, he could only look.

"Well?" she said, in the same expressionless tone.

"Let us begin at the beginning," he replied, with an effort to imitate the evenness of her tone.

"Since this is to be the end."

"Why did you answer my personal in the first place? Why did you not ignore it? I should have been left in peace."

"An impulse of the moment, which I shall always regret."

"Why did you let it go so far as to permit me to dine with you that memorable night?"

"A second impulse, equally regrettable."

"And why, after all had come to an apparent end, why did you send me that mask?"

She did not answer at once.

"Why?" he repeated.

"It is unanswerable. Truthfully, I do not know."

"Have you thought what all this might mean to me?" with warmth.

Again she was silent, but her eyes did not waver.

"When I heard your voice to-night I knew that doubt was no longer in my heart."

"Doubt?"

"Yes, doubt. I knew then that the inexplicable had happened."

"I do not understand."

"The inexplicable. For who will believe that it is possible for a sane man to fall in love with a voice? Had your face been scarred, as I once suspected; had you committed some crime, as I once believed, it would not matter. I am mad." He laughed angrily. "Yes, I love you, knowing not what you are nor caring. I have been mad for weeks, only I did not see my madness in true colors till this moment."

The light seemed to bother her eyes, for she turned her head aside, giving this mad lover the exquisite profile of her face.

"You are indeed mad, or, rather, your jest is."

"Would to Heaven I were jesting! And why did you avoid me in Monte Carlo?"

She realized that there was some justice in his questions and that she was not altogether innocent of the cause of his madness, if it were that.

"I did not speak to you because I wished to avoid this very moment. But since it was destined to be, let us have done. What other questions would you ask, Mr. Hillard?"

"Who is that man—the Italian with the scar—who ran after you that night?"

"I will not answer that."

"'A lady? Grace of Mary, that is droll!'"

"Why do you say that?"

"I am only quoting the man with the scar. Those were the words he used in regard to you."

"Perhaps he is right; perhaps I am not a lady, according to his lights." But she laughed.

"Do not laugh like that! What you are or have been, or might have been to him, is nothing to me. Only one fact remains clear, and that is, I love you."

"No, Mr. Hillard, you are only excited. You have been letting your imagination run away with you. Be sensible. Listen. You know nothing of me; you have neither my name nor my past—nothing. I may in truth be everything undesirable."

"Not to me!"

"I may be a fugitive from the law."

"I do not believe it."

"There may be scars which do not show—in the heart, in the mind. I am sorry, terribly sorry. Heaven knows that I meant no harm. But it seems that fate is determined that every move I make shall become a folly, the ghost of which shall pursue me. I told you to forget me, that I had entered your life only to pass out of it immediately. Forget me!" Her voice was no longer without expression.

"Forget you? I would it were as easy as the asking! I say that I love you, that I shall always love you. But," he added gently, lowering his voice, "I have asked nothing in return."

"Nothing in return?" she murmured.

"No. I offer my love only that it may serve you without reward. Do you need in your trouble a man's arm, a man's heart and mind?"

"I need nothing;" but her voice was now strangely sweet. So, she was loved by one who asked for nothing? This was not like the men she had known. "Do not misjudge me, Mr. Hillard. If indeed you believe that you love me—incredible as it seems to me—I am proud of the honor. But fatality forbids that I accept not only your love but your friendship."

"Not even my friendship?" bewildered. "And why not?"

"To answer that would only be adding to your hurt."

"You are a strange woman. You make it very hard."

"I have no alternative. The harder I make it, the better for your peace of mind. Once you are angry with me, once you are convinced that I am a hopeless puzzle, this fancy you call love will evaporate."

"Do not believe that."

"I never intended that you should see me again, and yet, against my better judgment, I have bared my face to you upon a simple request. I am not without some vanity. Men have called me beautiful. But, oh! it is a sinister beauty; it has brought good to no one, least of all to its owner. You met Mrs. Sandford in Naples. Tell me what she said."

He sought refuge in silence.

"Did she not earnestly warn you against me?"

"Yes," reluctantly.

"And yet you would not heed her warning?" sadly.

"I have told you that I am mad."

"I am coming to believe it. There are two of us. That dinner! And out of an innocent prank comes this! Folly, always folly!" And as she remembered the piece of folly she was about to start out upon, she laughed. "Mad? Yes. Only, to your madness there is some reason; to mine, none."

"So you sometimes recollect that night? You have not forgotten?"

"No. The pleasure I derived has frequently returned to my mind."

"Ah, if only you would tell me what prevents friendship between us."

"You say you love me; is that not answer enough? Love and friendship are as separate as the two poles; and you are man enough of the world to know that. I have no wish to wreck your life nor to make mine more miserable. Well, I will tell you this: there is a barrier between us—a barrier which only death can tear down or break asunder. Give up all idea, all thought of me. You will only waste your time. Come; is your love strong enough to offer a single sacrifice?"

"Not if it is to give you up."

"Very well. I see, then, that I must submit to this added persecution. I can not force you."

"So long as I live I shall go on dreaming of you. So long as you keep me in darkness as to your trouble I shall pursue you. Oh, do not worry about persecution. I shall only seek to be near you."

"Good night," she said, "and good-by!" She wound the veil round her face, took half a dozen steps, halted and turned, then went on, beyond the light, into the dark.

How long Hillard stood by the steps of the church, watching that part of the darkness through which she had disappeared, he never knew. Merrihew tapped him on the arm.

"Wake up, Jack, my boy!" said Merrihew lightly. "I thought, by the way you mooned here, that you had fallen asleep on your feet. Where's Kitty?"

"Kitty? I forgot to ask, Dan," said Hillard dully.

Chapter 19 *TWO GENTLEMEN FROM VERONA*

It was May in the Tuscany Hills; blue distances; a rolling horizon; a sky rimmed like a broken cup; a shallow, winding river, gleaming fitfully in the sun; a compact city in a valley, a city of red-tiled roofs, of domes and towers and palaces, of ruined ivy-grown walls and battlements; shades of Michelangelo and Dante and Machiavelli, the Borgias and the Medicis: Florence, the city of flowers.

Upon a hill, perhaps three miles to the northeast of the city, stood the ancient Etruscan town of Fiesole. The flat white road which passes through the heart of the village leads into the mountains beyond. Here one sees an occasional villa, surrounded by high walls of stone, plastered in white or pink, half hidden in roses, great, bloomy, sweet-scented roses, which of their quality and abundance rule the kingdom of flowers, as Florence once ruled the kingdom of art and learning.

The Villa Ariadne rested upon a small knoll half a mile or more north of and above Fiesole, from which the panoramic beauty of Florence was to be seen at all times, glistening in the sun, glowing in the rain, sparkling in the night. A terrace reached to the very frontal walls, which were twelve feet above the road. On the other side of the road swept down abruptly a precipitous ravine, dangerous to careless riders. A small stream dashed north, twisted, and joined the Mugnone, which in turn emptied into the drab waters of the Arno.

The villa was white and cool in the shade of dark cypresses and beeches and pink-blossomed horse-chestnuts. There were beds and gardens of flowers, and behind the villa a forest spread out and upward to the very top of the overshadowing mountain. The gates and the porter's lodge were at that end of the confines nearest Fiesole. The old gardener and his wife lived in the lodge, earning an extra lira now and then by escorting tourists through the park and exhibiting the Della Robias, the Hadrian mosaic, the fountain by Donatello, and some antique marbles, supposed to have been restored by Michelangelo. He never permitted any one to touch these glories. Periodically the agents of the government paid a visit to ascertain that none of these treasures had been sold or removed. The old gardener spoke some English.

Life ran smoothly enough at the Villa Ariadne. La Signorina, at the very last moment, surrendered to the entreaties of Kitty. She agreed not to pass herself off as the princess. So they occupied the villa pleasurably and in safety. The police, as prescribed by law, made two visits and had gone away satisfied that, however odd they might be, the temporary tenants were proper persons. Among themselves each played the role originally assigned. It was innocent fun now, and La Signorina seemed to enjoy the farce as much as any one. It was a great temptation not to prowl round the forbidden rooms, not to steal a look into the marvelous chests and sideboards, bulging as they knew with priceless glass and silver and linen and laces. But La Signorina each day inspected the seals and uttered solemn warnings.

There was only one in this strange medley of persons who was not contented with his lot, who cared not if the letter from home never came at all, and this person was Worth. To set down the trouble briefly, he was desperately in love with La Signorina; and the knowledge of how hopeless this passion was, together with the frequent efforts he had put forth to repress the ardent declaration, were making him taciturn and solitary. La Signorina never went down to Florence, not even to Fiesole; so Worth never joined his companions when they took, pleasant excursions into the city.

As one fences in the dark, instinctively, so she kept him a foil's length away. Yet she would have been glad had he spoken; she could have silenced him effectually then. It was rather nerve-racking to wait for this unwelcome declaration day by day. They had now lived in the Villa Ariadne for two weeks, a careless, thoughtless, happy-go-lucky family. The gossip might have looked askance at them; but La Signorina would not have cared and the others would not have thought.

Every afternoon at two o'clock O'Mally and the ancient gardener would get together and give each other lessons, the one in English and the other in Italian. When this was done, a small flask of Chianti was forthcoming, and the old man enjoyed himself as he hadn't done since his youth: a pipe of good tobacco and two glasses of Chianti. It was enough for any reasonable man. He never inquired where the wine came from; sufficient it was to him that it came at all. And O'Mally saw no reason for discovering its source; in fact, he admired Pietro's reticence. For, like Planchet in the immortal *Three Musketeers*, O'Mally had done some neat fishing through one of the cellar windows. Through the broken pane of glass he could see bin upon bin of dust-covered bottles, Burgundy, claret, Sauterne, champagne, and no end of cordials, prime vintages every one of them. And here they were, useless to any one, turning into jelly from old age. It was sad. It was more than that—it was a blessed shame. All these bottles were, unfortunately, on the far side of the cellar, out of reach, and he dared not break another window. Under this which served him lay the bin of Chianti. This was better than nothing; and the princess would never miss the few bottles he purloined. Sometimes he shared a bottle with Smith, who was equally incurious.

To-day was warm and mellow. On the stone bench by the porter's lodge, hard by the gate, sat the old Florentine and O'Mally. From some unknown source O'Mally had produced a concierge's hat and coat, a little moth-eaten, a little tarnished, but serviceable. Both were smoking red-clay pipes with long bamboo stems.

"Pietro," said O'Mally, teetering, "have you ever waited for money from home?"

Pietro puffed studiously, separating each word with all the care of a naturalist opening the wings of some new butterfly. He made a negative sign.

"Well, don't you ever wait. There's nothing to it. But I've got an idea."

Pietro expressed some surprise.

"Yes, and a good idea, too. If any tourists come to-day, I propose to show them round the place." O'Mally was quite in earnest.

Pietro's eyes flashed angrily. "No, no! Mine, all mine!"

"Oh, I'm not going to rob you. I'll give you the tips, *amico*. What I want is the fun of the thing. *Comprendery?*"

Pietro understood; that was different. If his Excellency would pay over to him the receipts, he could conduct the tourists as often as he pleased. Yes. To him it was tiresome. Most people were fools.

"Let's begin the lesson, then."

"*Come sta?*" said Pietro, shifting his pipe.

"That's howdy do," said O'Mally. "How is your wife?"

"That ees *Come sta vostra!*"

Pause.

"*Che tempo fa?*" said Pietro suddenly.

O'Mally frowned and jammed down the coal in his pipe. "Who—no, how!—is the weather. Who can say? *Che lo sa?*"

"*Bene!*"

Solemnly they went over the same ground. To be sure, O'Mally always failed to get the right twist to the final vowels, but he could make himself understood, and that was the main thing. It was a rare moment to him at night to strike Smith dumb by asking in Italian for a match, a cigar, or a book. Smith wondered how he did it; but when asked to join the primary class at the porter's lodge, he always excused himself by saying that he was deep in the writing of a comedy, which was true. If there was a play in one's system, the Villa Ariadne was sure to bring it out.

Having finished the lesson for that day, they shared the flask of wine.

"It is old, Pietro," said O'Mally.

"*Vecchio, anticato,*" responded Pietro with grave satisfaction.

"Hold on, now; this is no lesson. You talk English. Now about this guide business. You will let me be guide if I turn over the profits; that is agreed?"

"Yes." Pietro wished the flask had been twice as large.

"All right; that's fixed. By the way, Pietro, did you ever see the princess?"

Pietro looked into the bowl of his pipe. "No; she not come here; never."

"Hum! I should, if I owned a place like this."

"Trouble."

"Trouble? How?"

"I not know. But trouble she come bime-by."

"Rats!" There was not a cloud in the sky, so far as O'Mally could see. And what trouble could possibly befall them?

"Sh!" said Pietro.

The porter's bell rang loudly.

"Tourists!" whispered O'Mally, sliding off the bench and buttoning up his coat. "Remember I am the guide; you get the lire."

Surely Pietro understood, but he was nervous, doubting the ability of this novice to demand the right sum for his labor.

O'Mally settled his cap on straight and went to the gates and opened them. A party of five Americans stood outside—two men, two women, and a girl of twelve or fourteen. The whole party wore that eager look, now familiar to O'Mally, of persons who intended to see everything if they eventually died for it.

"This is the Villa Ariadne?" asked one of the women. She wore eyeglasses and had a bitter expression.

"It is," said O'Mally, touching his cap.

"He speaks English!" cried the woman, turning joyfully to the others. "We wish to see the villa and the park."

"The villa is now occupied, signora," replied O'Mally; "but you are permitted to see the park and gardens."

"How much?" asked one of the men.

"*Cinquanty*," said O'Mally; then correcting himself, "for each person."

"Ten cents? Two lire fifty? Why, this is downright

extortion!" declared the woman with the eyeglasses. She was vehement, too.

O'Mally gave vent to a perfect Italian shrug, and put a hand out suggestively toward the gates.

"Oh, come, dear," protested one of the men wearily; "you've dragged us up here from Fiesole and I'm not going back without seeing what's to be seen."

"That's like you men; always willing to be robbed rather than stand upon your rights. But I vow that you weak men will ruin travel by giving in all the time."

The man at whom this brief jeremiad was hurled painfully counted out two lire fifty, which was immediately transferred to the palm of the guide, who ushered the wayfarers in.

Solemnly Pietro watched them pass, wondering what the terms were. O'Mally led the party to the fountain.

"What's this?" asked the woman.

"This," O'Mally began, with a careless wave of the hand, "is the famed fountain by Donatello. It was originally owned by Catherine d'Medissy. The Borgias stole it from her, and Italy and France nearly came to war over it."

"The Borgias?" doubtfully. "Were these two families contemporaneous?"

"They were," scornfully. "These Borgias were not the head of the family, however. Finally it fell into the hands of the first Prince d' Monty Bianchy, and it has stood where you see it for three hundred years. It is considered the finest specimen of its kind. The Italian government has offered fabulous sums for it."

"I thought the government could force the sale of these things?"

"There has been some litigation over this property,

consequently the government can do nothing till the courts have settled the matter," recited O'Mally glibly.

"Oh."

The quintet consulted their guide-books, but before they had located the paragraph referring to this work, O'Mally was cunningly leading them on to the Della Robbias which hung in the ruined pavilion. With a grand yet familiar air he declaimed over the marvelous beauties of this peculiar clay with an eloquence which was little short of masterful. He passed on to the antique marbles, touching them lightly and explaining how this one was Nero's, that one Caligula's, that one Tiberius'. He lied so easily and gracefully that, wherever it rested, the tomb of Ananias must have rocked. And whenever his victims tried to compare his statements with those in the guide-books, he was extolling some other treasure. They finally put the guide-books under their arms and trusted in the kindness of Providence.

"Do you know," said the woman who had not yet spoken, "you speak English remarkably well? There is an accent I do not quite understand."

O'Mally shivered for a moment. Was she going to spring Dago on him? "I am Italian," he said easily. "I was born, however, in County Clare. My father and mother were immigrants to Ireland." His face was as solemn as an owl's.

"That explains it."

O'Mally took a new lease of life. "Now let me show you the Hadrian mosaic, from the Villa Hadrian in Tivoli, out of Rome." He swept back the sand. "Is it not magnificent?"

"Looks like a linoleum pattern," was the comment of one of the men.

"You are not far from right," said O'Mally. "It was from

this very mosaic that the American linoleums were originally designed."

"Indeed!" said the woman with the glasses.

"Yes, Signora."

"Ma," whispered the girl, "ask him for one of those buttons."

The stage-whisper was overheard by O'Mally. "These buttons," he explained, "cost a lira each; but if the signorina really wishes one—" And thus another lira swelled the profits of the day. O'Mally wondered if he ought not to keep this one lira since it was off his own coat and not Pietro's.

On the balcony of the villa appeared two women. The woman with the glasses at once discovered them.

"Who is that handsome woman?" she demanded.

O'Mally paled slightly. "That," touching his cap respectfully, "is her Highness, La Principessy d' Monty Bianchy, the owner of the Villa Ariadne." Ha! He had them here.

The tourists stared at the balcony. A real live princess! They no longer regretted the two lire fifty. This was something worth while.

"We did not know that the princess lived here."

"It is but a temporary visit. She is here incognito. You must not repeat what I have told you," was O'Mally's added warning.

On the balcony the two women were talking quietly.

"What in the world is that man O'Mally up to now?" said La Signorina curiously.

"Can't you see?" replied Kitty. "He is acting as guide in Pietro's place."

"Merciful heavens!" La Signorina retired, stifling her

laughter.

At the gates O'Mally received his *pourboire* of twenty centesimi, saw his charge outside, closed and locked the gates, and returned to Pietro, who was in a greatly agitated state of mind.

"*Quando!*" he cried.

O'Mally handed him the exact amount, minus the lira for the button.

"*Santa Maria!* All thees? How? No more I take dem; you!"

O'Mally sat down on the bench and laughed. It was as good a part as he had ever had.

Early evening. La Signorina leaned over the terrace wall, her hand idly trailing over the soft cool roses. Afar down the valley shimmered the lights of Florence. There were no outlines; no towers, no domes, no roofs were visible; nothing but the dim haze upon which the lights serenely floated. It might have been a harbor in the peace of night. To the south, crowning the hills with a faint halo, the moon, yet hidden, was rising across the heavens. Stretched out on either hand, white and shadowy, lay the great road. She was dreaming. Presently upon the silence came the echo of galloping horses. She listened. The sound came from the north. It died away, only to return again sharply, and this time without echo. Two horsemen came cantering toward the Villa Ariadne. They drew down to a walk, and she watched them carelessly. It was not long before they passed under her. She heard their voices.

"Jack, this has been the trip of my life. Verona, Padua, Bologna, and now Florence! This is life; nothing like it."

"I am glad, Dan. It has been enjoyable. I only hope our luggage will be at the hotel for us. Twelve days in riding-breeches are quite enough for a single stretch."

La Signorina's hand closed convulsively over a rose, and crushed it. The vine, as she did so, gave forth a rustling sound. The men turned and glanced up. They saw a woman dimly. That was all.

"A last canter to Fiesole!"

"Off she goes!"

The two went clattering down the road.

La Signorina released the imprisoned rose, and, unmindful of the prick of the thorn, walked slowly back to the villa. It was fatality that this man should again cross her path.

Chapter 20 *KITTY DROPS A BANDBOX*

"What's the matter, Jack? Whenever you smoke, your cigar goes out; you read a newspaper by staring over the top of it; you bump into people on the streets, when there is plenty of room for you to pass; you leave your watch under the pillow and have to hike back for it; you forget, you are absent-minded. Now, what's the matter?"

"I don't know, Dan," said Hillard, relighting his cigar.

"Or you won't tell."

"Perhaps that's more like it."

"It's that woman, though you will not acknowledge it. By George, I'd like to meet her face to face; I'd give her a piece of my mind."

"Or a piece of your heart!"

"Bah!" cried Merrihew, flipping his cigar-ash to the walk below, careless whether it struck any of the leisurely-going pedestrians or not.

"You have not seen her face, Dan; I have."

"Oh, she may be a queen and all that; but she has an evil influence over all the people she meets. Here's Kitty, following her round, and the Lord knows in what kind of trouble. She has hooked you, and presently you'll be leaving me to get back home the best way I can."

"It is quite possible, my boy." And Hillard did not smile.

"Come, Jack, have you really got it? If you have, why, we'll pack up and leave by the next steamer. I don't care to wander about Italy with a sick man on my hands."

"Don't be hard on me, Dan," pleaded Hillard, smiling now. "Think of all the Kitty Killigrews you've poured into my uncomplaining ears!"

"I got over it each time." But Merrihew felt a warmth in his cheeks.

"Happy man! And, once you see the face of this adventuress, as you call her, Kitty Killigrew will pass with all the other lasses."

"I?" indignantly. "Rot! She won't hold a candle to Kitty."

"No, not a candle, but the most powerful light known to the human eye—perfect beauty." Hillard sighed unconsciously.

"There you go again!" laughed Merrihew. "You tack that sigh to everything you say; and that's what I've been complaining about."

Hillard was human; he might be deeply in love, but this had not destroyed his healthy sense of humor. So he laughed at himself.

Then they mused silently for a while. On either side, from their window-balcony, the lights of Lungarno spread out in a brilliant half-circle, repeating themselves, after the fashion of women, in the mirror of the Arno. On the hill across the river the statue of David was visible above the Piazza Michelangelo.

"You never told me what she was like," said Merrihew finally.

"Haven't I? Perhaps you never asked. We went through the Pitti Palace to-day. I couldn't drag you from Raphael's *Madonna of the Chair*. She is as beautiful as that."

"Imagination is a wonderful thing," was Merrihew's solitary comment.

"Mine has not been unduly worked in this instance," Hillard declared with emphasis. "Beauty in women has always been to me something in the abstract, but it is so no longer.

There is one thing which I wish to impress upon you, Dan. She is not an adventuress. She has made no effort to trap me. On the contrary, she has done all she could to keep out of my way."

"It's a curious business; the dinner, the mask, the veil, the mystery. I tell you frankly, Jack, something's wrong, and we shall both live to find it out."

"But what? Heaven on earth, what? Haven't I tried to figure it out till my brain aches? I haven't gone forward a single inch. On the steps of the Formosa I told her that I loved her. There, you have it! I was in doubt till I looked at her face, and then I knew that I had met the one woman, and that there was a barrier between us that was not self-imposed. Not even friendship, Dan; not even an ordinary thing like that. I have spoken to this woman on only two occasions, and only once have I seen her face. I am not a disciple of the theory of love at first sight. I never shall be. An educated, rational man must have something besides physical beauty; there must be wit, intellect, accomplishments. Usually we recognize the beauty first, and then the other attributes, one by one, as the acquaintance ripens. With me the things have been switched round. The accomplishments came first; I became fascinated by a voice and a mind. But when I saw her face… . Oh, well! Mrs. Sandford warned me against her; the woman herself has warned me; the primal instinct of self-preservation has warned me; yet, here I am! I had not intended to bother you, Dan."

"It doesn't bother me, it worries me. If I have hurt you with any of my careless jests, forgive me." Merrihew now realized that his friend was in a bad way. Still, there was a hidden gladness in his heart that Hillard, always railing at his (Merrihew's) affairs, was in the same boat now, and rudderless at that.

"You haven't hurt me, Dan. As a matter of fact, your gibes have been a tonic. They have made me face the fact that I was on the highroad to imbecility."

"What shall you do?"

"Nothing. When we have seen Florence we'll drop down to Perugia and Rome, then up to the Italian lakes; after that, home, if you say. The bass season will be on then, and we've had some good sport on Lake Ontario."

"Bass!" Merrihew went through the pleasant foolery of casting a line, of drawing the bait, of lifting the hook, and of reeling in. "Four pounds, Jack. He fit hard, as old Joe used to say. Remember?"

And so naturally they fell to recounting the splendid catches of the gamiest fish in water. When the interest in this waned, Hillard looked at his watch.

"Only nine," he said. "Let's go over to Gambrinus' and hear the music."

"And drink a boot of beer. Better than moping here."

The Hotel Italie was but a few blocks from the Piazza Vittorio Emanuele. They found the *Halle* crowded, noisy and interesting. The music was good, as it always is in Italy, and the beer had the true German flavor, München. Handsome uniforms brightened the scene; and there was flirting and laughter, in which Merrihew found opportunity to join.

"If Kitty should see you!"

"Well, what if she did? When I'm married to her it will be mutually understood that so long as I do not speak to them I may look at pretty women."

"You seem very sure of marrying her."

"It's only a matter of time. The man who hangs on wins finally." Merrihew had lost none of his confidence.

"I see; they marry you to get rid of you," said Hillard. "Yes, the man who hangs on finally wins, in love or war or fortune. But I haven't anything to hang on to."

"Who knows?" said Merrihew, wagging his head.

From the *Halle* they went down-stairs to the billiard-room. The pockets in the table bothered Merrihew; he did not care particularly for the English game; and the American table was occupied by a quartet of young Americans who were drinking champagne like Pittsburg millionaires. The ventilation was so bad that the two friends were forced to give up the game. Under the arcade they found a small table. It was cool and delightful here, and there was a second boot of Munich beer.

Officers passed to and fro, in pairs or with women. Presently two officers, one in the resplendent uniform of a colonel, went past. Merrihew touched Hillard with his foot excitedly. Hillard nodded, but his pulse was tuned to a quicker stroke.

"I hope he doesn't see us," he said, tipping his panama over his eyes.

Merrihew curled the ends of his juvenile mustache and scowled fiercely.

"This is his post evidently," he said. "What a smacking uniform! He must have had a long furlough, to be wandering over Europe and America. If I get a chance I'm going to ask a waiter who he is."

"So long as he doesn't observe us," said Hillard, "I have no interest in his affairs." Had he none? he wondered. "A lady? Grace of Mary, that is droll!" The muscles in his jaws hardened.

"But you twisted his cuffs for him that night in Monte Carlo. Monte Carlo!" reminiscently. "Eighteen hundred dollars, my boy, and a good fourteen still in my inside pocket. Wasn't I lucky? But I'll never forgive Kitty for running away from us. That's got to be explained fully some day."

"He is coming this way again, Dan," Hillard observed quietly.

"Ah!"

They waited. Hillard changed his mind; he pushed back his hat and held up his chin. If the man with the scar saw him and spoke he would reply. The colonel, glancing at the pair casually, halted. At first he was not certain, but as he met the steady eyes of Hillard he no longer doubted. It was true. He turned and spoke to his brother officer. Merrihew's throat grew full, but not from fear. The man with the scar stepped over to the table and leaned with his hands upon it. There was a savage humor in his dark eyes.

"Did I not tell you that we should meet again?" he said to Hillard. "This is a pleasant moment." He stood back again.

"Are you speaking to me?" asked Hillard, not the least perturbed. He had not stirred in his chair, though every muscle in his body was alert and ready at a moment's call.

"Certainly I am speaking to you. You understand Italian sufficiently well. This is the fellow," speaking to his companion, at the same time drawing off his gloves, "this is the fellow I spoke to you about."

"I object to the word fellow," said Hillard, smiling grimly. "Besides, I do not know you."

"Ah, discreet!" sneered the man with the scar.

"Be careful, Enrico," warned the brother officer. "There

are many about, and a scene is not wise. Ask the American to take a walk. You could arrange with more ease."

"Thank you," said Hillard, "but I am perfectly comfortable where I am. If this gentleman has anything to say, he must say it here and now."

"Colonel!" cried the subaltern, as his senior smoothed the gloves and placed them carefully in his left hand, closing his fingers over them.

"Oh, I am calm. But I have been dreaming of this moment. Now!" The colonel readdressed Hillard. "You meddled with an affair that night in which you had no concern," he began truculently.

"Are you quite sure?"

Merrihew eyed Hillard nervously. He did not understand the words, worse luck, but the tone conveyed volumes. It was crisp and angry. Hillard possessed a temper which was backed by considerable strength, and only on rare occasions did this temper slip from his control. Thoroughly angry, Hillard was not a happy man to antagonize.

"Yes, I am sure. And yet, as I think it over, as I recollect the woman," went on the colonel, with a smile which was evil and insinuating... . "Well, I shall not question you. The main thing is, you annoyed me. In Monte Carlo I was practically alone. Here the scene is different; it is Florence. Doubtless you will understand." He struck out with the gloves.

But they never touched Hillard's face. His hand, expectant of this very movement, caught the assailant's wrist, and, with a quick jerk, brought him half-way across the table. He bore down on the wrist so fiercely that the Italian cried faintly. Hillard, with his face but a span from the other's, spoke tensely, but in an undertone.

"Listen carefully to what I have to say, signore. I understand perfectly, but I shall fight no duel. It is an obsolete fashion, and proves nothing but mechanical skill. I do not know what kind of blackguard you are, but blackguard I know you to be. If you ever address me again I promise on the word of a gentleman to give you a whipping which will have a more lasting effect upon your future actions than a dozen sermons. If that will not serve, I shall appeal to the police."

"Poltroon!"

"As often as you please!" Hillard flung him off roughly.

A small but interested crowd had gathered by now, and Merrihew saw visions of Italian jails. Through the crowd the ever-present *carabinieri* shouldered their way.

"It is nothing," said the colonel, motioning them to stand back, which they did with a sign of respect. This sign gave Hillard some food for thought. His antagonist was evidently a personage of some importance.

"Figure of an American pig!"

Hillard laughed. "I might have broken your wrist, but did not. You are not grateful."

The *carabinieri* moved forward again.

"The affair is over," said Hillard amiably. "This officer has mistaken me for some one he knows."

The scar was livid on the Italian's cheek. He stood undecided for a space. His companion laid a restraining hand on his arm. He nodded, and the two made off. What might in former days have been a tragedy was nothing more than a farce. But it spoiled the night for Merrihew, and he was for going back to the hotel. Hillard agreed.

"At first I wanted you to give him a good stiff punch," said Merrihew, "but I am glad you didn't."

"We should have slept in the lockup over night if I had. The *carabinieri* would not have understood my excuses. If our friend is left-handed, he'll be inconvenienced for a day or two. I put some force into that grip. You see, Dan, the Italian still fights his duels. Dueling is not extinct in the army here. An officer who refuses to accept a challenge for a good or bad cause is practically hounded out of the service. It would have been a fine joke if I had been fool enough to accept his challenge. He would have put daylight through me at the first stroke."

"I don't know about that," replied Merrihew loyally. "You are the crack fencer in New York."

"But New York isn't Florence, my boy. I'll show you some fencing to-morrow. If my old fencing master, Foresti Paoli, is yet in Florence, I'll have him arrange some matches. New York affairs will look tame to you then."

"But what has he to do with your vanishing lady?"

"I should like to know."

"I wish I had thought to ask a waiter who the duffer is. Did you notice how respectful the *carabinieri* were?"

"It set me thinking. Oh, I've a premonition that we haven't seen the last of this distinguished gentleman. Perhaps we'll find out who he is sooner than we care to."

"When the time comes," said Merrihew with a laugh, "be sure you soak it to him, and an extra one for me."

Early on the morrow they rode out to the Cascine, formerly a dairy-farm, but now a splendid park. The bridle-paths are the finest in the world, not excepting those in the Bois de Bologne in Paris. They are not so long, perhaps, but they are infinitely more beautiful. Take, for instance, the long path under a tunnel of enormous trees, a bridle-path where ten men may ride abreast with room to spare, and nearly half a mile in length; there is nothing like it.

"I tell you what it is, Jack; Italy may put a tax on salt and sea-water, but always gives something in return; she puts up a picture-gallery or a museum, or a park like this. What do we get back in America? *Niente!*"

For two hours they romped through the park, running races, hurdling, and playing rough pranks upon each other, such as only expert riders dare attempt. They were both hardened by the long ride down to Florence, a pair of animals as healthy as their mounts. They had determined not to sell the horses till the last moment. A riding-master in the Via Lorenzo ii Magnifico agreed to board them against the time of sale.

In the three days in Florence they had been through the galleries and the museums; and Merrihew, to his great delight, began to find that he could tell a Botticelli from a Lippi at first glance. He was beginning to understand why people raved over this style or that. There was something so gentle, so peaceful in a Botticelli that he really preferred it to some of the famed colorists, always excepting Veronese, to whom he had given his first admiration.

For luncheon this day Hillard took him to Paoli's in the Via dei Tavolini—the way of the little tables. Here Merrihew saw a tavern such as he had often conjured up while reading his Dumas; sausages and hams and bacons and garlic and cheeses and dried vegetables hanging from the ceiling, abrupt passages, rough tables and common chairs and strange dishes; oil, oil, oil, even on the top of his coffee-cup, and magnums of red and white Chianti.

Hillard informed him that this was the most famous Bohemian place in the city, the rendezvous of artists, sculptors, writers, physicians, and civil authorities. The military seldom patronized it, because it was not showy enough. Merrihew enjoyed the scene, with its jabber-jabber and its clatter-clatter. And he was still hungry when he left, but he would not admit it to Hillard, who adapted himself to the over-abundance of oil with all the zest of an expatriated Tuscan.

At three o'clock they went to the fencing academy of Foresti Paoli, near the post-office. Foresti was a fine example of the military Italian of former days. He was past sixty, but was as agile as any of his celebrated pupils. As Hillard had written him the night before, he was expected. He had been a pupil of Foresti's, and the veteran was glad to see him. Merrihew saw some interesting bouts, and at length Foresti prevailed upon Hillard to don the mask against an old pupil, a physician who had formerly been amateur champion of Italy. Hillard, having been in the saddle and the open air for two weeks, was in prime condition; and he gave the ex-champion a pretty handful. But constant practice told in the end, and Hillard was beaten. It was fine sport to Merrihew; the quick pad-pad of the feet on the mat, the short triumphant cries as the foil bent almost double, and the flash of the whites of their eyes behind the mask. Merrihew knew that he should love Florence all the rest of his days.

They were entering the Via Tornabuoni, toward the Havana cigar-store, when a young woman came out of the little millinery shop a few doors from the tobacconist's. Immediately Hillard stepped to one side of her and Merrihew to the other.

"You can not run away this time, Kitty Killigrew!" cried Merrihew joyously.

Kitty closed her eyes for a second, and the neat little bandbox slipped to the sidewalk.

Chapter 21 *AN INVITATION TO A BALL*

In the Villa Ariadne the wonderful fountain by Donatello was encircled by a deep basin in which many generations of goldfish swam about. Only the old gardener knew the secret of how these fish lived through the chill Florentine winters. Yet, every spring, about the time when the tourists began to prowl round, the little goldfish were to be seen again, ready for bread-crumbs and bugs of suicidal tendencies. Forming a kind of triangle about the basin were three ancient marble benches, such as the amiable old Roman senators were wont to lounge upon during the heat of the afternoon, or such as Catullus reclined upon while reading his latest lyric to his latest affinity. At any rate, they were very old, earth-stained and time-stained and full of unutterable history, and with the eternal cold touch of stone which never wholly warms even under warmest sun. The kind of bench which Alma-Tadema usually fills with diaphanous maidens.

At this particular time a maiden, not at all diaphanous, but mentally and physically material, sat on one of these benches, her arms thrown out on either side of the crumbling back, her chin lowered, and her eyes thoughtfully directed toward the little circle of disturbed water where the goldfish were urging for the next crumb. Now, as Phoebus was somewhere near four in the afternoon, he was growing ruddy with effort in the final spurt for the western horizon. So the marbles and the fountain and the water and the maiden all melted into a harmonious golden tone.

Merrihew was not so poetical as to permit this picture to go on indefinitely; so he stole up from behind with all the care of a practised hunter till he stood directly behind the maiden. She still dreamed. Then he put his hands over her eyes. She struggled for a brief moment, then desisted.

"It is no puzzle at all," she declared. "I can smell horse, horse, and again horse. Mr. Merrihew—"

"Yes, I know all about it. I should have fetched along a sachet-powder. I never remember anything but one thing, Kitty, and that's you." He came round and sat down beside her. "There's no doubt that I reek of the animal. But the real question is," bluntly, "how much longer are you going to keep me dangling on the string? I've been coming up here for ten days, now, every afternoon."

"Ten days," Kitty murmured. She was more than pretty to-day, and there was malice aforethought in all the little ribbons and trinkets and furbelows. She had dressed expressly for this moment, but Merrihew was not going to be told so. "Ten days," she repeated; and mentally she recounted the pleasant little journeys into the hills and the cherry-pickings.

"And dangling, dangling. I've been hanging in mid-air for nearly a year now. When are you going to put me out of my misery?" His tone was chiding and moody.

"But am I to be blamed if, after having refused twice to marry you, you still persist?" Kitty assumed a judicial air.

"All you have to do," sadly, "is to tell me to clear out."

"That's just it," cried Kitty wrathfully. "If I tell you to go it will be for good; and I don't want you to go that way. I like you; you are cheerful and amusing, and I find pleasure in your company. But every day in the year, breakfast and dinner!" She appealed to the god in the fountain. What unreasonable beings men were!

"But you haven't refused me this time."

"Because I wish to make it as easy as possible for you." Which of the two meanings she offered him was lost upon Merrihew; he saw but one, nor the covert glance, roguish and mischievous withal. "Come, let us be sensible for ten minutes."

Merrihew laid his watch on the bench beside him. Kitty dimpled.

"Don't you love it in Florence?" she asked.

"Oh, yes," scraping the gravel with his crop. "Hillard says I'm finishing my bally education at a canter. I can tell a saint from a gentleman in a night-gown, a halo from a barrel-hoop, and I can drink Chianti without making a face."

Kitty laughed rollickingly. For beneath her furbelows and ribbons and trinkets she was inordinately happy and light of heart. Her letter had come; she was only waiting for the day of sailing; and she was to take back with her the memory of the rarest adventure which ever befell a person, always excepting those of the peripatetic sailor from Bagdad.

"I want to go home," said Merrihew, when her laughter died away in a soft mutter.

"What! leave this beautiful world for the sordid one yonder?"

"Sordid it may be, but it's home. I can speak to and understand every man I meet on the streets there; there are the theaters and the club and the hunting and fishing and all that. Here it's nothing but pictures and concierges and lying cabbies. If I could collect all my friends and plant 'em over here, why, I could stand it. But I'm lonesome. Did you ever try to spread frozen butter on hot biscuits? Well, that's the way I feel."

This metaphor brought tears of merriment to Kitty's eyes. She would have laughed at anything this day.

"Daniel, you are hopeless."

"I admit it."

"How beautiful the cypresses are in the sunshine!" she exclaimed, standing.

He reached out and caught her hand, gently pulling her down to the bench.

"The ten minutes are up," he said.

"Oh, I said let us be sensible for ten minutes," she demurred.

"I've been telling you the truth; that's sensible enough. Kitty, will you marry me?"

"Could you take care of me?"

"I have these two hands. I'll work."

"That would be terrible! Oh, if you were only rich!"

"You don't mean that, Kitty."

"No," relenting, "I don't. But you bother me."

"All right. This will be the last time. Will you marry me? I will do all a man can to make you happy. I love you with all my heart. I know. You're afraid; you've an idea that I am fickle. But not this time, Kitty, not this time. Will you?"

"I can not give up the stage." She knew very well that she could, but she had an idea.

"I don't ask even that. I'll travel with you and make myself useful."

"You would soon tire of that." But Kitty eyed him with a kindly look. He *was* good to look at. Kitty was like the timid bather; she knew that she was going to take the plunge, but she must put one foot into the water, withdraw it, shudder, and try it again.

"Tire?" said Merrihew. "If I did I shouldn't let you know

it. I'm a homeless beggar, anyhow; I've always been living in boarding-houses and clubs and hotels; it won't matter so long as you are with me."

Kitty threw a crust to the goldfish and watched them swirl about it greedily. Merrihew had no eyes but for her. Impulsively he held out his hand. Kitty looked at it with thought; this would be the final plunge. Then, without further hesitance, indifferent to the future or the past, conscious only of the vast happiness of the present, Kitty laid her hand in his. He would have drawn her into his arms had not they both seen O'Mally pushing through the box-hedge, followed by some belated tourists. Merrihew swore softly and Kitty laughed.

On the terrace the tea-table dazzled the eye with its spotless linen, its blue Canton, and its bundle of pink roses. Hillard extended his cup for a second filling, vaguely wondering where Merrihew was. They had threshed continental politics, engineering, art and the relative crafts, precious stones, astronomy and the applied sciences, music, horses, and geology, with long pauses in between. Both knew instinctively that this learned discourse was but a makeshift, a circuitous route past danger-points. "Have you ever heard of telling fortunes in tea-grounds?" he asked.

"Yes. It is a pleasant fallacy, and nothing ever comes true." And La Signorina vaguely wondered where Kitty was. She needed Kitty at this moment, she who had never needed anybody.

The tramp of feet beyond the wall diverted them for a space. A troop of marksmen from the range were returning cityward. They were dirty and tired, yet none seemed discontented with his lot. They passed in a haze of dust.

The man and woman resumed their chairs, and Hillard bent his head over the cup and stared at the circling tea-grounds in the bottom. The movement gave her the opportunity she desired: to look freely and without let at his shapely head. Day after day, serene and cloudless Florentine days, this same scene or its like had been enacted. It took all her verbal skill to play this game safely; a hundred times she saw something in his eyes that warned her and armed her. When he passed that evening on horseback she knew that these things were to be. She had two battles where he had only one; for she had herself to war against. Each night after he had gone she fought with innocent desire; argument after argument she offered in defense. But these were all useless; she must send him away. And yet, when he came, as she knew he would, she offered him tea! And in rebellion she asked, Why not? What harm, what evil? Was it absolutely necessary that she should let all pleasure pass, thrust it aside? The suffering she had known, would not that be sufficient penance for this little sin? But on his side, was this being fair to him? This man loved her, and she knew it. Up to this time he had met her but twice, and yet he loved her, incredible as it seemed. And though he never spoke of this love with his lips, he was always speaking it with his eyes; and she was always looking into his eyes.

She never looked into her own heart; wisely she never gave rein to self-analysis; she dared not. And so she drifted on, as in some sunny dream of remote end.

How inexplicable were the currents and cross-currents of life! She had met a thousand men, handsomer, more brilliant; they had not awakened more than normal interest. And yet this man, quiet, humorous, ordinarily good-looking, aroused in her heart discord and penetrated the barriers to the guarded sentiment. Why? Always this query. Perhaps, after all, it was simply the initial romance which made the impression so lasting. Ah, well; to-morrow or the next day the end would come; so it did not matter.

There was one bit of light in this labyrinth: Worth had spoken; that disagreeable incident was closed. And this present dream, upon what reef would it carry her? She shrugged. This action brought Hillard back to earth, for he, too, had been dreaming. He raised his head.

"Why did you do that?" he asked.

"Do what?"

"Shrug."

"Did I shrug? I did so unconsciously. Perhaps I was thinking of O'Mally and his flock of tourists."

"Doesn't it annoy you?"

"Not in the least. It has been a fine comedy. I believe he is the most accomplished prevaricator I ever met. He remembers the lie of yesterday and keeps adding to it. I don't see how he manages to do it. He is better than Pietro. Pietro used to bring them into the house." She gathered up a handful of the roses and pressed them against her face, breathing deeply.

Hillard trembled. She was so beautiful; the glow of the roses on her cheeks and throat, the sun in her hair, and the shadows in her eyes. To smother the rush of words which were gathering at his lips, he raised his cup and drank. Ten days! It was something. But the battle was wearing; the ceaseless struggle not to speak from his full heart was weakening him. Yet he knew that to speak was to banish the dream, himself to be banished with it.

"If I were a poet, which I am not—" He paused irresolutely.

"You would extemporize on the beauty of the perspective," she supplemented. "How the Duomo shines! And the towers, and the Arno—"

"I was thinking of your hair," he interrupted. "I have never seen anything quite like it. It isn't a wig, is it?" jestingly.

"No, it is my own," with an answering smile.

"Ah, that night! It is true, as you said; it is impossible to forget the charm of it."

She had recourse to the roses again. Dangerous ground.

"You have not told me the real reason why you sang under my window that night."

"Have I not? Well, then, there can be no harm in telling you that. I had just signed the contract to sing with the American Comic Opera Company in Europe. I saw the world at my feet, for it would be false modesty to deny that I have a voice. More disillusions! The world is *not* at my feet," lightly.

"But I am," he replied quietly.

She passed this declaration. "I might have more successfully applied to the grand opera in New York; but my ambition was to sing here first."

"But in comic opera?"

"Another blunder, common of its kind to me. Have I not told you that I am always making missteps such as have no retracing?"

"Will you answer a single question?"

She stroked the roses.

"Will you?"

"I can make no promise. Rather ask the question. If I see

the wisdom of answering it, I shall do so."

"Is there another man?" He did not look at her but rather at her fingers embedded in the roses. Silence, which grew and lengthened.

"What do you mean?" she asked evenly, when she realized that the silence was becoming too long.

"In Venice you told me that there was a barrier. I ask now if this barrier be a man."

"Yes."

A wrinkle of pain passed over his heart. "If you love him —"

"Love him? No, no!... I had hoped you would not speak like this; I relied upon your honor."

"Is it dishonorable for me to love you?"

"No, but it is for me—to permit you to say so!"

He could hear the birds twittering in the boughs of the oak. A lizard paused on the damp stone near-by. A bee hovered over the roses, twirled a leaf impatiently, and buzzed its flight over the old wall. He was conscious of recognizing these sounds and these objects, but with the consciousness of a man suddenly put down in an unknown country, in an unknown age, far away from all familiar things.

"I deplore the misfortune which crossed your path and mine again," she went on relentlessly, as much to herself as to him. "But I am something of a fatalist. We can not avoid what is to be."

He was pale, but not paler than she.

"I offer you nothing, Mr. Hillard, nothing; no promise, no hope, nothing. A few days longer, and we shall separate finally."

She was about to rise and ask him to excuse her and retire, when Merrihew and Kitty came into view. There was nothing now to do but wait. She sought ease from the tenseness of the moment in sorting the roses. Hillard stirred the cold dregs in his tea-cup. Cold dregs, indeed! The light of the world was gone out.

Merrihew's face was as broad and shining as the harvest moon. He came swinging down the path, Kitty's arm locked in his. And Kitty's face was rosy. Upon reaching the table Merrihew imitated the bow of an old-time courtier.

"It is all over," he said, swallowing. "Kitty has promised to marry me as soon as we land in America. I'm a lucky beggar!"

"Yes, you are," said Hillard. "Congratulations to both of you."

La Signorina took hold of Kitty's hands. This was a much-needed diversion.

"Is it true, Kitty?"

"Yes, ma'am," Kitty answered, with a stage courtesy. "I have promised to marry him, for there seemed no other way of getting rid of him."

Hillard forced a smile. "It's a shame to change such a pretty name as yours, Miss Killigrew."

"I realize that," replied Kitty with affected sadness.

"Go to!" laughed the happy groom-elect. "Merrihew and Killigrew; there's not enough difference to matter. And this very night I shall cable to America."

"Cable to America?" echoed a tri-chorus.

"Yes; to have a parson in the custom-shed when we land. I know Kitty, and I am not going to take any chances."

This caused real laughter. La Signorina relighted the tea-lamp, and presently they were all talking together, jesting and offering suggestions. No matter how great the ache in the heart may be, there is always some temporary surcease. Hillard was a man.

They laughed quietly as they saw O'Mally gravely conducting his charge to the gates. He returned with Smith. Both were solemn-visaged.

"Well, noble concierge?" inquired La Signorina. "Why, you look as if you were the bearer of ill-tidings."

"Perhaps I am," said O'Mally. He tossed his cap on the stones and sat down with Smith on the iron bench. "No, no tea, thank you. What I need is a glass, a whole glass, of good Irish whisky. This thing has been on my mind since noon, but I concluded to wait rather than spoil the whole day. I should have known nothing about it if it hadn't been for old Pietro."

"What has happened?" asked Merrihew.

"Enough," said O'Mally laconically. He directed his next words to La Signorina. "You are sure of this friend of yours, the princess?"

"Certainly," answered La Signorina, her astonishment increasing.

"She gave you the right authority?"

"Absolutely," more and more astonished.

"Agreed that we could remain here as long as we pleased?"

"Yes, yes!" impatiently.

"Well, before I swing the thunder, let me tell you something," said O'Mally. "I was in Florence a few days ago. I made some inquiries."

"About my friend the princess?"

"Yes. It was impertinent, I know. I interviewed four or five hotel concierges. Only one of them ever heard of the name; and then it was an old prince, not a woman. This concierge directed me to another, but as he spoke only Italian, we could not make things fit. But when I mentioned the princess' name, he shrugged and laughed, as if something highly amusing had hit him."

"Go on, Mr. O'Mally; go on. This is interesting. Your doubt is not at all complimentary to me. The police have recognized my authority."

"And that's what feazes me. But the main thing is this: your princess has played us all rather a shabby trick. In the letter you read to us in Venice she said that she had never visited this villa."

"Only in her youth," replied La Signorina, her brows drawing together in a frown. "But I know her so well; she is not in the habit of making misstatements. To the point at once. What has happened to bring about all this pother?"

"It is simply this: our little jig is up," responded O'Mally. "Read these and see for yourself." He gave to her a broad white envelope and a clipping from *La Nazione* of the day before.

She seized the clipping eagerly, but the eagerness died from her face quickly, leaving it pale and stony. The clipping fluttered unheeded from her fingers to the ground. Her gaze passed from one face to another, all the while a horror growing in her eyes. Slowly she picked up the envelope and drew out the card. Her eyes filled, but with tears of rage and despair.

"Tell me, what is it?" cried Hillard, troubled, for his keen lover's eyes saw these changes.

In answer she gave him the card. He read it. It *was* rather a knock. Now, why should the Principessa di Monte Bianca take it into her head to give a ball in the Villa Ariadne, Wednesday week, when she had loaned the villa indefinitely to her friend, La Signorina?

Chapter 22 TANGLES

Hillard passed the card to Merrihew, who presented it to Kitty. Smith had already seen it. He waved it aside moodily. La Signorina's eyes roved, as in an effort to find some way out. Afar she discovered Worth, his chin in his collar, his hands behind his back, his shoulders studiously inclined, slowly pacing the graveled path which skirted the conservatory. From time to time he kicked a pebble, followed it and kicked it again, without purpose. Whether he saw them or not she could not tell. Presently he turned the corner and was gone from sight. During the past few days he had lived by himself; and for all that she did not like him, she was sorry for him.

"It's a pretty kettle of fish," said O'Mally, rather pleased secretly in having created so dramatic a moment. "She might have been kind enough, however, to notify us in advance of her intentions. I am still broke," disheartened; "and the Lord knows what I'll do if I'm shunted back into the hands of the tender hotel managers and porters. There is nothing for us to do but to clear out, bag and baggage. It's a blamed hard world. I wish I had kept some of old Pietro's tips." He spoke with full dejection. Up to this time he had been playing the most enjoyable part in all his career, plenty to eat and to drink and no worry. And here the affair was ended with the suddenness of a thunder-clap.

"I'm even worse off than you are, Tom," said Smith. "You've got a diamond. The sooner we light out the better. In a day or two the princess will be piling in upon us with her trunks and lackeys and poodles."

"Poodles!" La Signorina was white with anger.

"Why, yes," said Smith innocently. "Nearly all Italian

ladies carry one or more of those woozy-eyed pups. Good-by to your sparkler, Tom, this trip, if we ever expect to see the lights of old Broadway again."

O'Mally sighed deeply. The blow had finally fallen.

Then La Signorina rose to her feet. She took the card from Kitty's fingers, tore it into many pieces and flung them over the wall.

"We have been betrayed!" she cried, a storm in her eyes.

"Betrayed?"

O'Mally looked at Smith; Hillard stared at Merrihew; Kitty regarded La Signorina with wonder.

"Betrayed? In what manner?" asked Hillard.

"Her Highness has had no hand in this. I know. Some one with malice has done this petty thing." To La Signorina everything had gone wrong to-day. "I shall telegraph her Highness at once. I say that we have been made the victims of some practical joke."

"Joke or not, we can't stay here now," Smith declared. "All the high muckamucks in and roundabout Florence will be getting out their jewels and gowns. If we send a denial to the paper, and we really have no authority to do that, there'll be a whole raft of 'em who will not see it. And since nobody knows how many invitations have been sent out or to whom they have been sent—oh, what's the use of all this arguing? The thing's done. No matter how we figure it, we're all railroaded. Third-class to Naples and twelve days in the steerage. Whew!"

"I guess Hillard and I can help you," said Merrihew. "We'll see that you get home all right."

"To be sure," assented Hillard. Poor devils!

"We'll make good, once we strike Broadway," replied

O'Mally gratefully.

La Signorina, her arms folded, her lips compressed into a thin line of scarlet, the anger in her eyes unabated, began to walk back and forth, and there was something tigerish in the light step and the quick turn. The others, knowing her to be a woman of fertile invention, patiently and in silence waited for her to speak.

But the silence was broken unexpectedly by O'Mally. He gripped Smith by the arm and pointed toward the path leading to the gates.

"Look!" he whispered.

All turned, and what they saw in nowise relieved the tenseness of the situation. Two *carabinieri* and an inspector of seals, dusty but stern of countenance, came up the path. O'Mally, recollecting the vast prison at Naples, saw all sorts of dungeons, ankle-deep in sea-water, and iron bars, shackles and balls. Every one stood up and waited for this new development to unfold itself. La Signorina alone seemed indifferent to this official cortège. The inspector signed to the *carabinieri*, who stopped. He came on. Without touching his cap—a bad sign—he laid upon the tea-table a card and a newspaper, familiar now to them all.

"Signora," he said politely but coldly to the whilom prima donna, "will you do me the honor to explain this? We have some doubts as to the authority upon which this invitation was issued." He spoke fluent English, for the benefit of all concerned.

Hillard waited for her answer, dreading he knew not what.

She spoke evenly, almost insolently. "The invitation is perfectly regular."

Everybody experienced a chill.

This time the inspector bowed. "Then her Highness will occupy her villa?"

"She is already in possession. I am the Principessa di Monte Bianca," calmly.

Had an earthquake shattered the surrounding hills, and gulfs opened at their feet, it could not have spread terror more quickly among the transient guests at the Villa Ariadne than this declaration. They were appalled; they stood like images, without the power to take their eyes off this woman. This transcendental folly simply paralyzed them. They knew that she was not the princess; and here, calmly and negligently, she was jeoparding their liberty as well as her own. Mad, mad! For imposture of this caliber was a crime, punishable by long imprisonment; and Italy always contrived to rake in a dozen or so accomplices. They were all lost indeed, unless they could escape and leave La Signorina alone to bear the brunt of her folly.

The keen-eyed inspector took mental note of these variant expressions.

"Your Highness," he said, his cap setting the dust on the stones flying, "a thousand pardons for this disagreeable intrusion. It was not officially known that your Highness was here."

"It is nothing," replied the pseudo princess. "Only I desired to remain incognito for the present."

"And the seals?" purred the official.

"We shall go through that formality the morning after the ball. At present I do not wish to be disturbed with the turning of the villa upside down, as would be the case were the seals removed."

"That will require the permission of the crown, your Highness."

"Then you will set about at once to secure this permission."

The air with which she delivered this command was noble enough for any one. The inspector was overcome. "But as your Highness has never before occupied the villa, some definite assurance—"

"You will telegraph to Cranford and Baring, in the Corso Umberto Primo, Rome. They will supply you with the necessary details and information."

The inspector inscribed the address in his notebook, bowed, backed away and bowed again. The crunch of the gravel under his feet was as a sinister thunder, and it was the only sound. He spoke to the *carabinieri*. They saluted, and the trio marched toward the gates.

There remained a tableau, picturesque but tense. Then Kitty began to cry softly.

"Are you mad?" cried Hillard, his voice harsh and dry.

La Signorina laughed recklessly. "If you call this madness."

"Smith, my boy," said O'Mally, moistening his lips, "you and I this night will pack up our little suit-cases and—*movimento, moto, viaggio*, or whatever the Dago word is for move on. I'm out of the game; the stakes are too high. I pass, signorina."

"How could you do it?" sobbed Kitty.

Merrihew patted her hand and scowled.

"What an ado!" said La Signorina, shrugging. "So you all desert me?"

"Desert you?" O'Mally resumed his seat and carefully loosened the topmost buttons of his coat. "Of course we shall desert you. We are sane individuals, at any rate. I have no desire to see the inside of an Italian jail, not knowing how to get out. What under the sun possessed you? What excuse have you to offer for pushing us all into the lion's mouth? You could have easily denied all knowledge of the invitation, referred them to your princess, wherever she may be, and we could have cleared out in the morning, poor but honest. And now you've gone and done it!"

Hillard leaned against a cypress, staring at the stones.

"In Venice," said she, her voice gentle, "you accepted the chance readily enough. What has changed you?"

O'Mally flushed. What she said was true. "I was a fool in Venice," frankly.

"And you, Mr. Smith?" continued La Signorina, as with a lash.

But it was ineffectual. "I was a fool, too," admitted Smith. "In Venice it sounded like a good joke, but it looks different now." He sat down beside O'Mally.

"So much for gallantry! And you, Kitty?"

"I made a promise, and I'll keep it. But I think you are cruel and wicked."

"No nonsense, Kitty," interposed Merrihew. "I've some rights now. You will have this villa to-night."

"I refuse," replied Kitty simply.

Hillard slipped into the pause.

"Did you issue those invitations yourself?" he asked this strange, incomprehensible woman.

"Do you believe that?" La Signorina demanded, with

narrowing eyes.

"I don't know what to believe. But I repeat the question."

"On my word of honor, I know no more about this mystery than you do." And there was truth in her voice and eyes.

"But are you not over-sure of your princess? Being a woman, may she not have changed her plans?"

"Not without consulting me. I am not only sure," she added with a positiveness which brooked no further question, "but to-morrow I shall prove to you that her Highness has not changed her plans. I shall send her a telegram at once, and you shall see the reply. But you, Mr. Hillard, will you, too, desert me?"

"Oh, as for that, I am mad likewise," he said, with a smile on his lips but none in his eyes. "I'll see the farce to the end, even if that end is jail."

"If!" cried O'Mally. "You speak as though you had some doubt regarding that possibility!"

"So I have." Hillard went to the table, selected a rose, and drew it through the lapel of his coat.

"I say, Jack!" Merrihew interposed, greatly perturbed.

"And you will stay also, Dan."

"Are you really in earnest?" dubiously. Why hadn't this impossible woman sung under somebody else's window?

"Earnest as I possibly can be. Listen a moment. La Signorina is not a person recklessly to endanger us. She has, apparently, put her head into the lion's mouth. But perhaps this lion is particularly well trained. I am sure that she knows many things of which we are all ignorant. Trust her to carry out this imposture which now seems so wild. Besides, to tell the truth, I do not wish it said that I was outdone by Miss Killigrew in courage and the spirit of adventure."

"Oh, give me no credit for that," broke in Kitty.

La Signorina, however, rewarded Hillard with a look which set his pulses humming. Into what folly would he not have gone at a sign from this lovely being? In his mind there was not the shadow of a doubt: this comedy would ultimately end at some magistrate's desk. So be it.

Merrihew cast about helplessly, but none held out a hand. He must decide for himself.

"Do you mean it, Kitty?"

"Yes."

O'Mally's face wore several new wrinkles; and both he and Smith were looking at the green mold on the flag-stones as interestedly as if China was but on the other side. Kitty saw nothing, not even the hills she was staring at.

"Since you have made up your mind, Jack," said Merrihew doggedly, "why, there's nothing for me to do but fall in. But it's kings against two-spots."

"Mental reservation?" said the temptress. "Mr. Hillard has none."

"I am not quite certain I have none," replied Hillard, renewing his interest in the rose.

A moment later, when he looked up, her glance plunged into his, but found nothing. Hillard could fence with the eyes as well as with the foils.

"Well," she said, finding that Hillard's mental reservations were not to be voiced, "here are three who will not desert me."

"That's all very well," rejoined O'Mally; "but it is different with those two. Mr. Hillard's a millionaire, or near it, and he could buy his way through all the jails in Italy. Smith here, Worth and Miss Killigrew and myself, we have nothing. More than that, we're jotted down in the police books, even to the mole on the side of my nose. There's no way out for us. We are accomplices."

"You will leave in the morning, then?" asked La Signorina contemptuously.

"I hope to."

"Want of courage?"

"No. Against physical danger I am willing to offer myself at any time to your Highness," with a touch of bitter irony. "But to walk straight into jail, with my eyes open, that's a horse of a different color."

"I like you none the less for your frankness, Mr. O'Mally. And I apologize for doubting your courage. But if to-morrow I should produce a telegram from her Highness that would do away with all your doubts?"

"I'll answer that when I see the telegram." O'Mally made an unsuccessful attempt to roll a cigarette. This honeyed blarney, to his susceptible Irish blood, was far more dangerous than any taunts; but he remembered in time the fable of the fox and the crow. "We have all been together now for many weeks. Yet, who you are none of us knows."

"I am the princess," laughing.

"Oh, yes; of course; I forgot. But I mean your real name."

"My real name? Have you ever before asked me what it is?"

"Perhaps we have been a little afraid of you," put in Smith.

The shadow of a smile lay upon her lips and vanished.

"My name is Sonia Hilda Grosvenor." And her voice was music.

"Pardon me," said O'Mally drolly, "but were any of your ancestors—er—troubled with insanity?"

This query provoked a laughter which gave them all a sense of relief.

"My father had one attack of insanity, since you ask." La Signorina's face sobered. She stepped over to the wall, rested upon it, and searched the deepening eastern horizon. Yes, her father had been insane, and all her present wretchedness was due to this insanity of a rational mind. For a moment she forgot those about her, and her thought journeyed swiftly back to the old happy days. "Yes, there is a species of insanity in my veins." She turned to them again. "But it is the insanity of a sane person, the insanity of impulse and folly, of wilfulness and lack of foresight. As Mr. O'Mally said, I have gone and done it. What possessed me to say that I am the princess is as inexplicable to me as to you, though you may not believe it. But for me there is no withdrawing now; flight would do us no good. We, or I, I should say, have created a suspicion, and if we ran away we should be pursued from one end of Italy to the other, till this suspicion was dissipated. We should become suspects, and in Italy a suspect is liable to immediate arrest. I am sorry that I have tangled you up in this. I release you all from any promise," proudly.

"If you talk like that—" began O'Mally.

"Sh!" Smith elbowed him sharply in the small ribs.

"It's all right, Smith. No one can force me into a scrape of this sort; but when she speaks like that! Signorina, or I should say, Miss Grosvenor, you have the most beautiful voice in the world. Some day, and we are all out of jail, I expect to hear you in the balcony scene with some famous *tenore robusto* as Romeo.

You will be getting three thousand a week. You needn't bother about the telegram; but I'll have to have a new suit," touching the frayed cuffs of his coat. "Now, if we go to jail, how'll we get out?"

"Trust me!" La Signorina had recovered her gaiety.

"Well," said Smith, "suppose we go and break the news to Worth?"

Hillard refused to canter, so the two walked their horses all the way into Florence. Merrihew spoke but seldom and Hillard not at all. By now the sun had gone down, and deep purple clouds swarmed across the blue face of heaven, forecasting a storm.... . It was not dishonorable for him to love this woman, but it was not honorable for her to listen. Sonia Hilda Grosvenor; that solved no corner of the puzzle.

"To-morrow," said Merrihew, "I'm going to look up the jail and engage rooms ahead. It might be crowded."

Hillard raised his face and let a few drops of cooling rain patter on his cheeks. "I love her, I love her!" he murmured.

Chapter 23 *THE DÉNOUEMENT*

The morning sun poured over the hills, throwing huge shadows in the gorge below. The stream, swollen by the heavy rains of the past night, foamed and snarled along its ragged bed. The air was fresh and cool, and the stately cypresses took on a deeper shade of green. Lizards scampered over the damp stones about the porter's lodge or sought the patches of golden sunshine, and insects busied themselves with the daily harvest. O'Mally sniffed. As the wind veered intermittently there came to him the perfume of the locust trees, now in full bloom, the flowers of which resembled miniature cascades hanging in mid-air. Pietro rocked, his legs crossed, his face blurred in the drifting tobacco smoke.

"No more tourists, Pietro."

"No." Pietro sighed, a ruminating light in his faded eyes.

"Did you ever see La Signorina before? Do you know anything about her?"

"Never! No!" answered Pietro, with the perfect candor of an accomplished liar.

"Have you ever seen her Highness?"

"When she so," indicating a height about two feet from the ground.

"You said that you had never seen her."

"Meestake."

"How old would she be?"

Pietro wrinkled his brow, "Oh, *quaranta, cinquanta;* fifty-forty. Who knows?"

"Fifty! How old are you?" suspiciously.

"*Settanta;* seventy."

"Well, you look it. But why hasn't the princess ever been here, when it's so beautiful?"

"Woman."

"What woman?"

"La Principessa. Many villas, much money."

O'Mally kicked at one of the lizards. "I thought she might be young."

"No. But La Signorina-bah! they ar-r-r-rest her. *Patienza!*"

"You think so?"

"Wait."

"But her friend the princess will come to her assistance."

Pietro laughed scornfully, which showed that he had some doubts.

"But you won't betray her?"

"Never!" puffing quickly.

"It's a bad business," admitted O'Mally. This old rascal of a gardener was as hard to pump as a frozen well.

Pietro agreed that it was a bad business. "Eenspector, he come to-day, *domani*—to-morrow. He come nex' day; watch, watch!" Pietro elevated his shoulders slowly and dropped them sharply. "All ar-r-r-rest!"

"You think so?"

"*Si.*"

"But you wouldn't betray her for money, Pietro?"

"No!" energetically.

Pietro might be loyal; still, O'Mally had some shadow of doubt.

"La Signorina is very beautiful," irrelevantly. "Ah!" with a gesture toward the heavens. "And if she isn't a princess, she ought to be one," slyly.

"*Zitto!* She come!" Pietro got up with alacrity, pocketing his pipe, careful that the bowl was right side up.

She was as daintily fresh in her pink frock as a spring tulip; a frock, thought O'Mally, that would have passed successfully in any ball-room. She was as beautiful as the moon, and to this bit of Persian O'Mally added, conscious of a deep intake of breath, the stars and the farther worlds and the roses close at hand. Her eyes were shining, but her color was thin. O'Mally, for all his buffoonery, was a keen one to read a face. She was highly strung. Where would they all land finally?

"I have been looking for you, Mr. O'Mally," she said.

"At your Highness' command!"

Pietro, hearing this title, looked from one to the other suspiciously.

"I have just received a telegram from her Highness."

An expression of relief flitted over Pietro's withered countenance.

"It wasn't necessary," said O'Mally gallantly.

"But I wish you to read it. I know that you will cease to dream of dungeons and shackles." There was a bit of a laugh in her voice. It was reassuring.

"All right." O'Mally accepted the yellow sheet which the government folds and pastes economically. There were fifty words or more. "I can make out a word or two," he said; "it's in Italian. Will you read it for me?"

"I forgot," apologetically.

Briefly, La Principessa di Monte Bianca gave Sonia Hilda Grosvenor full authority to act as her proxy in giving the ball; that in case of any difficulty with the civil authorities to wire her at once and she would come. As for the invitation, she knew absolutely nothing about it.

This last statement rather staggered the erstwhile concierge. If the princess hadn't issued the invitation, who the deuce had? "This leaves me confused, but it improves the scenery a whole lot. But who, then, has done this thing?"

"To solve that we must look nearer home."

"Have you any idea who did it?" he inquired anxiously.

"No."

"Have you another invitation?"

"I tore up the only one."

"That's too bad. A stationer's imprint might have helped us."

"I was angry and did not think. To-morrow a dozen temporary servants will be added to the household. We shall be very busy."

"Before and after," said O'Mally dryly. He wondered what she on her part had telegraphed the real princess. It was all very mystifying.

"Listen!" she said.

"Horses," declared O'Mally.

"Two," said Pietro, with a hand to his ear.

La Signorina's color deepened.

"Our friends," laughed O'Mally; "come up to see if we are still out of jail."

The dreamy, pleasurable days at the Villa Ariadne were no more. The spirit of suspicion, of unrest, of doubt now stalked abroad, peering from veiled eyes, hovering on lips. And there was a coming and going of menials, a to-and-froing of extra gardeners and carpenters, and the sound of many hammers. The ball-room and the dining-room were opened and aired, the beautiful floors polished, and the dust and cobwebs of twenty years were vanquished.

In Florence there was a deal of excitement over the coming affair, for the Villa Ariadne had once been the scene of many a splendid entertainment. Men chatted about it in their cafés and the women chattered about it in their boudoirs. And there was here and there a mysterious smile, a knowing look, a shrug. There had always been a mystery regarding the Principessa di Monte Bianca; many doubted her actual existence. But the prince was known all over Europe as a handsome spendthrift. And the fact that at this precise moment he was quartered with the eighth corps in Florence added largely to the zest of speculation. Oh, the nobility and the military, which are one and the same thing, would be present at the ball; they were altogether too inquisitive to decline.

Daily the inspector of seals made his solemn round, poking into the forbidden chambers, into the lofts, into the cellars. He scrutinized every chest and closet with all the provocative slowness of a physiologist viewing under the microscope the corpuscles of some unhappy frog. The information he had received from Rome had evidently quieted his larger doubts; but these people, from the princess down to the impossible concierge, were a new species to him, well worth watching. An American princess; this accounted for much. He had even looked up the two Americans who rode up from Florence every day; but he found that they were outside the pale of his suspicions; one of them was a millionaire, known to the Italian ambassador in the United States; so he dismissed them as negligible quantities. He had some pretty conflicts with Pietro;

but Pietro was also a Tuscan, which explains why the inspector never obtained any usable information from this quarter.

Hillard and Merrihew eyed these noisy preparations broodingly. To the one it was a damper to his rosal romance; to the other it was the beginning of the end: this woman, so brilliant, so charming, so lovely and human, could never be his. Well, indeed, he understood now why Mrs. Sandford had warned him; he understood now what the great mistake was. Had fate sent her under his window only for this? Bitterness charged his heart and often passed his lips. And this other man, who, what, and where was he all this time?

He was always at her heels now, saving her a care here, doing a service there, but speaking no more of his love. She understood and was grateful. Once she plucked a young rose and gave it to him, and he was sure that her hand touched his with pity, though she would not meet his eyes. And so Merrihew found but little difficulty in picking up the thread of his romance.

As for O'Mally, he spent most of his leisure studying time-tables.

At four o'clock on the afternoon of the day before the ball, now that the noise had subsided and the servants were in their quarters, La Signorina went into the gardens alone. An hour earlier she had seen Hillard mount and ride away, the last time but once. There seemed to bear down upon her that oppression which one experiences in a nightmare, of being able to fly so high, to run madly and yet to move slowly, always pursued by terror. Strive as she would, she could not throw off this sense. After all, it was a nightmare, from the day she landed in New York up to this very moment. But how to wake? Verily, she was mad. Would any sane person do what she had done and was yet about to do? She might have lived quietly and peacefully till the end of her days. But no! And all her vows were like dried reeds in a tempest, broken and beaten. Even now there was a single avenue of escape, but she knew that she could not profit by it and leave these unfortunate derelicts to shift for themselves. It was not fair that they should be made to suffer for her mad caprices. She must play it out boldly to the final line, come evil or not.... Love! She laughed brokenly and struck her hands in suppressed fury. A fitting climax, this! All the world was mad and she was the maddest in it.

Some one was coming along the path. She wheeled impatiently. She wanted to be alone. And of all men Worth was not the one she cared to see. But the sight of his pale face and set jaws stayed the words she was inclined to speak. She waited restlessly.

"I realize that my presence may be distasteful to you," he began, not without some minor agitation. It was the first time in days that he had stood so near to her or had spoken while alone with her. "But I have something to say to you upon which your future welfare largely depends."

"I believed that we had settled that."

"I am not making any declaration of love, madame," he said.

"I am listening." This prelude did not strike her favorably.

"There has been a tremendous wonder, as I understand, about this ball."

"In what way?" guardedly.

"In regard to the strange manner in which the invitations were issued."

"Have you found out who did it?" she demanded.

"Yes." The light in his eyes was feverish despite the pallor of his face.

"Who was it?" fiercely. Oh, but she would have revenge for this miserable jest!

"I issued those invitations—with a definite purpose."

"You?" Her eyes grew wide and her lips parted.

"I!" a set defiance in his tone.

"It is you who have done this thing?"

"Yes. I am the guilty man. I did the work well, considering the difficulties. The list was the main obstacle, but I overcame that. I represented myself as secretary to her Highness, which, when all is said, was the very thing agreed upon in Venice. I am the guilty man;" but he spoke like a man who was enjoying a triumph.

"And you have the effrontery to confess your crime to me?" her fury blazing forth.

"Call it what you please, the fact remains."

"What purpose had you in mind when you did this cowardly thing? And I had trusted you and treated you as an equal! And so it was you who perpetrated this forgery, this miserable jest?"

"Forgery, yes; jest, no." Her anger did not alarm him; he had gone too far to be alarmed at anything.

"Why did you do it?"

"I did it as a man who has but a single throw left. One chance in a thousand; I took that chance and won."

"I do not understand you at all." She was tired.

"As I said, I had a definite purpose. An imposture like this is a prison offense. I asked you to marry me. I do so again."

"You are hiding a threat!" The mental chaos cleared and left her thought keen and cold.

"I shall hide it no longer. Marry me, or I shall disclose the imposture to the police."

"Oh!" She shot him a glance, insolent and piercing. Then she laughed, but neither hysterically nor mirthfully. It was the laughter of one in deadly anger. "I had believed you to be a man of some reason, Mr. Worth. Do you suppose, even had I entertained some sentiment toward you, that it would survive a circumstance like this?"

"I am waiting for your answer."

"You shall have it. Why, this is scarcely on the level with cheap melodrama. Threats? How short-sighted you have been! Did you dream that any woman could be won in this absurd fashion? You thought nothing of your companions, either, or the trouble you were bringing about their heads."

"Yes or no?" His voice was not so full of assurance as it had been.

"No!"

"Take care!" advancing.

"I am perfectly capable of taking care. And heed what I have to say to you, Mr. Worth. You will leave this villa at once; and if you do not go quietly, I shall order the servants to put you forth. That is my answer."

"You speak as though you were the princess," he snarled.

"Till Thursday morning I *am*!" La Signorina replied proudly.

"I shall inform the police."

"Do so. Now, as there is nothing more to be said, be gone!"

He saw that he had thrown and lost; and a man who loses his last throw is generally desperate. Regardless of consequences, he seized her roughly in his arms. She struck him across the eyes with full strength, and she was no weakling. He gasped in pain and released her.

"If I were a man," she said quietly, but with lightning in her eyes, "you should die for that!" She left him.

Worth, a hundred varied emotions rocking him, stared after her till she was no longer in sight. There were tears in his eyes and a ringing in his head. Fool! To play this kind of game against that kind of woman! Fool, fool! He had written the end himself. It was all over. He went to his room, got together his things, found a cart, and drove secretly into Florence.

On the night of the ball there was a brilliant moon. Rosy Chinese lanterns stretched from tree to tree. The little god in the fountain gleamed with silver on one side and there was a glow as of life on the other. From the long casement windows, opened to the mild air of the night, came the murmur of music. The orchestra was playing Strauss, the dreamy waltzes from *The Queen's Lace Handkerchief*. Bright uniforms and handsome gowns flashed by the opened windows. Sometimes a vagrant puff of air would find its way in, and suddenly the ball-room dimmed and the dancers moved like phantoms. The flames of the candles would struggle and, with many a flicker, right themselves, and the radiant colors and jewels would renew their luster.

O'Mally, half hidden behind a tree, wondered if he had not fallen asleep over some tale by Scheherazade and was not dreaming this. But here was old Pietro standing close by. It was all real. At odd whiles he had a vision of Kitty in her simple white dress, of Merrihew's flushed face, of Hillard's frowning pallor, of La Signorina wholly in black, a rare necklace round her white throat, a star of emeralds in her hair, her face calm and serene. Where would they all be on the morrow?

"Pietro, she is more than beautiful!" sighed O'Mally.

"But wait," said Pietro. He alone among the men knew the cause of Worth's disappearance. "Trouble."

Leaning against the door which gave entrance to the ball-room from the hall were two officers, negligently interested in the moving picture. "What do you make of it?" asked one.

"Body of Bacchus, you have me there!"

"Shall we go?"

"No, no! The prince himself will be here at eleven. He was, singularly enough, not invited; and knowing the story as I do, I am curious to witness the scene. The women are already picking her to pieces. To give a ball in this hurried manner, without ladies in attendance! These Americans! But she *is* beautiful," with evident reluctance.

Hillard, peering gloomily over their shoulders, overheard. The prince! Oh, this must not be. There could be only one prince in a matter of this kind. He pushed by the Italians without apology for his rudeness, edged around the ball-room till he reached La Signorina's side. He must save her at all hazards.

"A word," he whispered in German.

"What is it?" she asked in the same tongue.

"The prince himself will be here at eleven."

"What prince?"

"Di Monte Bianca. Come, there is no time to lose. I have been holding my carriage ready ever since I came. Come."

"Thank you, but it is too late." She smiled, but it was a

tired and lonely little smile. "Wait near me, but fear nothing." She had long since armed her nerves against this moment.

"But—"

"Enough! Leave everything to me."

"In God's name, who and what are you that you show no alarm when such danger threatens?"

"I have told you to wait," she answered.

He stepped back, beaten, discouraged. He would wait, and woe to any who touched her!

At precisely eleven the music ceased for intermission. There was a lull. Two *carabinieri* pushed their way into the ball-room. Tableau.

"Which among you is called the Principessa di Monte Bianca?" was asked authoritatively.

"I am she," said La Signorina, stepping forth.

The *carabinieri* crossed quickly to her side.

"What do you wish?" she asked distinctly.

"You are under arrest for imposture. You are not the Principessa di Monte Bianca; you are known as La Signorina, a singer."

Hillard, wild with despair, made as though to intervene.

"Remain where you are!" he was warned.

As the *carabinieri* were about to lay hands upon La Signorina, a loud voice from the hall stopped them.

"One moment!" An officer in riding breeches and dusty boots entered and approached the dramatic group. Hillard and Merrihew recognized him instantly. It was the man with the scar. "What is the trouble?"

"This woman," explained one of the *carabinieri*, saluting respectfully, "is posing as your wife, Highness. We are here to arrest her."

"Do not touch her!" said the prince. "She has the most perfect right in the world to do what she has done. She *is* the Principessa di Monte Bianca, my wife!"

Chapter 24 MEASURE FOR MEASURE

Silence invested the Villa Ariadne; yet warm and mellow light illumined many a window or marked short pathways on the blackness of the lawn. Of the hundred lanterns hanging in the gardens, not a dozen still burned, and these offered rather a melancholy reminder of joy and laughter departed. The moon was high in the heavens now, and the shadows cast by the gloomy cypresses put the little god in the fountain in complete darkness. A single marble bench stood out with that vividness which only marble and moonshine can produce. All the carriages, save one, were gone. A solitary saddle-horse rattled his bit, pawed restively, and tossed his head worriedly from side to side, as if prescience had touched him with foretelling.

On the other side of the wall, lurking in the dark niches, was a tall, lean, grey-haired old man who watched and listened and waited. Whenever he ventured into the moonlight the expression on his face was exultant but sinister. He was watching and listening and waiting for the horse. At the first sound of the animal's prancing hoofs on the stones by the porter's lodge, the old man was prepared to steal to the self-appointed place somewhat down the road. What befell there would be wholly in the hands of God. Seven years! It was a long time. He had not hunted for this man; he was breaking no promise; their paths had recrossed; it was destiny. So he waited.

Within the ball-room the candles were sinking in their brass sconces and little waxen stalactites formed about the rims. The leaving of the guests had been hurried and noisy and without any particular formality or directness. In truth, it resembled a disorderly retreat more than anything else. The dénouement was evidently sufficient; they had no desire to witness the anti-climax, however interesting and instructive it might be. *Carabinieri* and tableaux and conjugal reunion; it was too much to be crowded all into one night. Good-by! During this flight his Highness the Principi di Monte Bianca, Enrico by name, had taken the part of an amused spectator; but now that the last of the unwelcome guests was gone, he assumed the role premeditated. He strode up and down the floor, his spurs tinkling and his saber rattling harshly. He stopped before this painting or that, scrutinized the corners to ascertain what artist had signed it; he paused an interval before the marble faun, which he recognized as a genuine antique. These things really interested him, for he had never been inside the Villa Ariadne till this night. And there was an excellent reason. Occasionally he glanced at the group on the opposite side of the room. He laughed silently. They were as lively as so many sticks of wood. Oh, he would enjoy himself to-night; he would extract every drop of pleasure from this rare and unexpected moment. Had she been mad, he wondered, to give him out of hand this longed-for opportunity? A month longer and this scene would have been impossible. At last he came to a stand in front of La Signorma, who was white and weary. The two had not yet exchanged a word.

"So," he said, "after five years I find you, my beautiful wife!" With one hand hipping his saber and the other curling his mustaches, he smiled at her. "What a devil of a time you have given me! Across oceans and continents! A hundred times I have passed you without knowing it till too late. And here, at the very moment when I believed it was all over, you fling yourself into the loving arms of your adoring husband! I do not understand."

"Be brief," she replied, the chill of snows in her voice. Her hate for this man had no empty corners. "I have played foolishly into your hands. Say what you will and be gone."

"What a welcome!"

"Be quick!"

There was danger in her voice now, and he recognized the tense quality of it. "I shall telegraph to the attorneys in Rome to partition the estates, my heart!" mocking her. "The king will not add to his private purse the riches of Colonel Grosvenor and the Principi di Monte Bianca, your father and mine, old fools! To tell the truth, I am badly in need of money, and, head of Bacchus! your appearance here is life to me, my dear Sonia. Life! I am a rich man. But," with a sudden scowl, dropping the mask of banter, "I do not understand these companions of yours." He eyed the group coldly. "What position in my household does this gentleman occupy?" indicating Hillard and smiling evilly.

"Give no heed," said La Signorina, as Hillard took a step forward.

"So it is all true, then?" he asked despairingly. "You are his wife?"

"Yes. Forgive me, but did I not warn you many times? In the eyes of the Italian civil law I am this man's wife, but in the eyes of God and the Church, never, never!"

"What do you mean?"

"In a few days I shall write you; in this letter I promise to explain everything. And you will forgive me, I know."

"Forgive you? For what? There is nothing to forgive on my side; the gift is on yours. For I have been a meddler, an unhappy one."

"Will you and Mr. Merrihew go now? I do not wish you

two to witness this scene."

"Leave you alone with this wretch? No!" said Hillard.

"Well?" cried the prince impatiently. He was not inclined toward these confidences between the American and his wife. "I have asked a question and nobody replies. I inquire again, what position does he hold?"

"This villa is mine," she answered, the sharpness of her tone giving hint to the volcano burning in her heart. "However the estates may be partitioned, this will be mine. I command you to leave it at once, for your presence here is as unwelcome to me as that of all creeping things. I find that I do not hate you; I loathe you."

The prince laughed. That she loathed or hated him touched him not in the quick. Love or hate from this woman who knew him for what he was, a soulless scoundrel, was nothing. She was simply a sack of gold. But this was his hour of triumph, and he proposed to make the most of it.

"I could have let the *carabinieri* take you to prison," he said urbanely. "A night in a damp cell would have chastened your spirit. But I preferred to settle this affair as quickly as possible. But this friend of yours, he annoys me."

"Is it possible?" returned Hillard. "Your Highness has but to say the word and I will undertake the pleasure of relieving you of this man's presence."

"Be still," she said. "Will you go?" to the prince.

"Presently. First, I wish to add that your dear friend is both thick-skulled and cowardly. I offered to slap his face a few nights ago, but he discreetly declined."

Hillard laughed shortly. He desired to get closer to this gentlemanly prince.

"For my sake!" whispered La Signorina.

"I am calm," replied Hillard, gently releasing his arm from her grasp. He approached the prince smiling, but there was murder and despair in his heart. "Had I known you that night, one of us would not be here now."

"It is not too late," suggested the prince. "Come, are you in love with my wife?"

"Yes."

The bluntness of this assertion rather staggered the prince. "You admit it, then?" his throat swelling with rage.

"There is no reason why I should deny it."

"She is your—"

But the word died with a cough. Hillard, a wild joy in his heart, caught the prince by the throat and jammed him back against the rose-satin panel, under a dripping candelabrum. The prince made a violent effort to draw his sword, but Hillard seized his sword-arm and pinned it to the panel above his head. The prince was an athlete, but the man holding him was at this moment made of iron. The struggling man threw out a leg after the manner of French boxers, but his opponent met it with a knee. Again and again the prince made desperate attempts to free himself. He was soon falling in a bad way; he gasped, his lips grew blue and the whites of his eyes bloodshot. This man was killing him! And so he was; for Hillard, realizing that he had lost everything in the world worth living for, was mad for killing.

For a time the others were incapable of action. Merrihew, Kitty, O'Mally and Smith were in the dark as to what had passed verbally; they could only surmise. But here was something they all understood. La Signorina was first to recover. She sprang toward the combatants and grasped Hillard's hand, the one buried in the prince's throat, and pulled. She was not strong enough.

"Merrihew, O'Mally, quick! He is killing him!" she cried wildly.

The two, Merrihew and O'Mally, finally succeeded in separating the men, and none too soon. The prince staggered to a chair and sank heavily into it. A moment more and he had been a dead man. But he was not grateful to any one.

La Signorina turned upon Hillard. "And you would have done this thing before my very eyes!"

"I was mad," he panted, shamed. "I love you better than anything else in God's world, and this man means that I shall lose you."

"And you would have come to me across his blood?" wrathfully.

"I was not thinking of that. The only thought I had was to kill him. God knows I'm sorry enough." And he was.

"Ah, what a night!" She swayed and pressed her hand over her eyes. "No, do not touch me," she said. "I am not the kind of woman who faints."

The prince lurched toward Hillard, but fortunately Merrihew heard the slithering sound of the saber as it left its scabbard. Kitty screamed and O'Mally shouted. Merrihew, with a desperate lunge, stopped the blow. He received a rough cut over the knuckles, but he was not aware of this till the excitement was past. He flung the saber at O'Mally's feet.

"You speak English," said Merrihew, in an ugly temper, half regretting that he had interfered with Hillard. "You may send your orderly to the Hotel Italie to-morrow morning, and your saber will be given to him. You will not carry it back to

Florence to-night. Now, it is time to excuse yourself. We can get along without you nicely."

The prince tore at his mustaches. He would have put them all to the sword gladly. Meddlers! To return to Florence without his saber was dishonor. He cursed them all roundly, after the manner of certain husbands, and turned to La Signorina.

"I am in the way here," he said, controlling his passion with difficulty. "But listen attentively to what I say: you shall remain my wife so long as both of us live. I had intended arranging your freedom, once the estate and moneys were divided, but not now. You shall read my wife till the end of the book; for unless I meet you half-way, the marriage contract can not be broken. In the old days it was your conscience. The still small voice seems no longer to trouble you," turning suggestively to Hillard. "You are stopping at the Hotel Italie?"

"I am. You will find me there," returned Hillard, with good understanding.

"Good! Your Highness, to-morrow night I shall have the extreme pleasure of running your lover through the throat." He picked up his cap, which lay on one of the chairs, put it on cavalierly, and took his princely presence out of their immediate vicinity.

"It will do my soul good to stand before that scoundrel," said Hillard, stretching out his hands and closing them with crushing force. "He has felt the power of my hand to-night. I will kill him."

La Signorina laid a hand on his arm. "No, Mr. Hillard, you will fight no duel."

"And why not? I do not see how it can be avoided."

"You have told me that you love me. As it stands I may

sometimes see you, but if you kill him, never."

"He is far more likely to kill me," said Hillard morosely. "And perhaps it would be a kind service."

"Shame!" she cried. "Have you no courage? Can you not accept the inevitable manfully? Think of me. I can fight no duels; I must live on and on, tied legally to this man. And it is you who will add misery to my unhappiness? You will not fight him," with the assurance of one who has offered a complete argument.

"Very well. To be called a coward by a man like that is nothing. I shall not fight him."

"Thank you." And she gave him her hand impulsively.

"I love you," he murmured as he bent to kiss the hand; "and it is not dishonorable for you to hear me say so."

"I forbid you to say that!" But the longing of the world was in her eyes as she looked down at his head. She released her hand. "My friends, to-morrow our little play comes to an end. This is no longer Eden. We must go."

"This is what comes of American girls marrying these blamed foreigners," growled the tender-hearted O'Mally. "Why did you do it?"

"I am almost Italian, Mr. O'Mally. I had no choice in the matter; the affair was prearranged by our parents, after the continental fashion."

"I'm sorry I spoke like that," O'Mally said contritely.

"No apologies, if you please. It is only just that you should know something of the case, considering the manner in which I imposed upon you all."

"I'll punch Worth's head when I run across him." O'Mally clenched his fists.

"That would change nothing. He was a part of destiny; he

has served his little turn and has gone. Were we not a happy family together for weeks?" La Signorina smiled wanly. "To-morrow I am going to write Mr. Hillard; I am going to tell him the story. From your point of view you may write me down a silly fool, but one's angle of vision is not immutable."

"You're the finest woman in the world," declared O'Mally; "and whatever you have done has been right, I know."

Then Kitty ran up to La Signorina and embraced her; and the eyes of both of them swam in tears.

"You will be happy, at any rate, Kitty."

"Poor girl!" cried Kitty. Princesses were mortal like other people. "How I love you! Come back with us to America."

"I must live out the puzzle over here."

When Hillard and La Signorina were at length alone, he asked: "When shall I see you again?"

"Who knows? Some day, perhaps, when time has softened the sharp edges of this moment, the second bitterest I have ever known. To-morrow I shall write, or very soon. Now, give me your promise that you will no more seek me till I send for you."

"You will send for me?" with eagerness and hope.

"Why not?" proudly. "There is nothing wrong in our friendship, and I prize it. Promise."

"I promise. Good-by! If I remain any longer I shall be making mad, regrettable proposals. For a little while I have lived in paradise. Wherever I may be, at the world's end, you have but to call me; in a month, in a year, a decade, I shall come. Good-by!" Without looking at her again, he rushed away.

She remained standing there as motionless as a statue. It seemed to her that all animation was suspended, and that she could not have moved if she had tried. By and by she gazed round the room, fast dimming; at the guttering candles, at the empty chairs, at the vacant doors and hollow windows... . He had not asked her if she loved him, and that was well. But there was not at that moment in all the length and breadth of Italy a lonelier woman than her Highness the Principessa di Monte Bianca.

Meanwhile the prince, raging and out of joint with the world, mounted his horse. He would have revenge for this empty scabbard, or he would resign his commission. His throat still ached and pointed lights danced before his eyes. Eh, well! This time to-morrow night the American should pay dearly for it. His short laugh had an ugly sound. This American was just the kind of chivalric fool to accept a challenge. But could he handle foils? Could he fight? Could any of these damned American heretics fight, save with their fists? It was the other man's lookout, not his. He put the duel out of his mind as a thing accomplished. Shortly he would have compensation commensurate for all these five years' chagrin. To elude him all this time, to laugh in his face, to defy him, and then to step deliberately into his power! He never could understand this woman. The little prude! But for her fool's conscience he would not have been riding the beggar's horse to-day. She was now too self-reliant, too intelligent, too cunning; she was her father over again, soldier and diplomat. Well, the mystery of her actions remained, but he was no longer the broken noble. So why should he puzzle over the whys and wherefores of her motives? Ah! and would he not dig his hands deep into the dusty sacks of gold and silver? Life again, such as he craved; good cigars and good wine and pretty women who were no ardent followers of Minerva. To jam part of this money down the throats of his yelping creditors, to tear up his paper and fling it into the faces of the greedy Jews! Ha, this would be to live! Paris, or Vienna, or London, where he willed; for what hold had the army now?

He was an expert horseman, but, like all Italians, he was by nature cruel. As he passed the gates the horse slid and stumbled to his knees; he was up instantly, only to receive a hard stroke between the ears. This unexpected treatment caused the animal to rear and waltz. This was not the stolid-going campaign mount, but his best Irish hunter, on which he had won prizes in many a gymkhana. There was a brief struggle, during which the man became master both of himself and the horse. They were just passing the confines of the villa when a man darted out suddenly from the shadows and seized the bridle.

"At last, my prince!"

"Giovanni?"

Instinctively the prince reached for his saber, knowing that he had need of it, but the scabbard was empty. He cursed the folly which had made him lose it. This encounter promised to be a bad one. What mouth of hell had opened to cast this beggar, of all men, in his path? Oddly enough his thought ran swiftly back to the little *casa* in the Sabine Hills... . Bah! Full of courage, knowing that one or the other would not leave this spot alive, he struck his horse with purpose this time, to run his man down. But Giovanni did not lose his hold; hate and the nearness of revenge made him strong.

"No, no!" he laughed. "She is dead, my prince. And I, I was not going to seek *you*; I was going to let hell claim you in its own time. But you rode by me to-night. This is the end."

"Let go, fool!" roared the prince, slashing Giovanni across the face with the heavy crop.

Giovanni laughed again and drew his knife. "I shall not miss you this time!"

The prince, a trained soldier, shifted the reins to his teeth, buried his knees in the barrel of the horse, unhooked his scabbard and swung it aloft, deftly catching the reins again in his left hand. But Giovanni was fully prepared. He released the bridle, his arm went back and the knife spun through the air. Yet in that instant in which Giovanni's arm was poised for the cast, the prince lifted his horse on its haunches. The knife gashed the animal deeply in the neck. Still on its haunches it backed, wild with the unaccustomed pain. The lip of the road, at this spot rotten and unprotected, gave way. The prince saw the danger and tried to urge the horse forward. It was too late. The hind-quarters sank, the horse whinnied in terror, and the prince tried in vain to slip from the saddle. There came a grating crash, a muffled cry, and horse and rider went pounding down the rock-bound gorge.

Giovanni listened. He heard the light, metallic clatter of the empty scabbard as it struck projecting boulders; he heard it strangely above the duller, heavier sound. Then the hush of silence out of which came the faint mutter of the stream. Giovanni trembled and the sweat on his body grew cold: less from reaction than from the thought that actual murder had been snatched from his hands. For several minutes he waited, dreading, but there was no further sound. He searched mechanically for his knife, recovered it, and then crept down the abrupt side of the gorge till he found them. They were both dead. A cloud swept over the benign moon.

"Holy Father, thou hast waited seven years too long!" Giovanni crossed himself.

He gazed up at the ledge where the tragedy had begun. The cloud passed and revealed the shining muskets of two *carabinieri*, doubtless attracted by the untoward sounds. Giovanni, agile and muscular as a wolf, stole over the stream and disappeared into the blackness beyond. But there was an expression of horror on his face which could not have been intensified had Dante and Vergil and all the shades of the Inferno trooped at his heels.

Chapter 25 FREE

It was Merrihew who woke the sleeping cabby, pushed Hillard into a seat, and gave the final orders which were to take them out of the Villa Ariadne for ever. He was genuinely moved over the visible misery of his friend. He readily believed that Hillard's hurt was of the incurable kind, and so long as memory lasted the full stab of the pain would recur. So to get him away from the scene at once was the best possible thing he could do. Merrihew noticed the little group of men collected at the edge of the road, but he was too deeply absorbed in his own affairs to stop and make inquiries. The principal thing was to reach Florence without delay. He smoked two cigars and offered scarcely a dozen words to Hillard. When they arrived at the white hotel in the Borgognissanti and the night watchman drew the great bolts to admit them, Merrihew was glad. And all this to evolve from an unknown woman singing under Hillard's window but six months ago! And a princess! Truly the world was full of surprises.

He went to bed, advising Hillard to do the same. Mental repose was needed before they could sit down and discuss the affair rationally.

At nine in the morning Hillard heard a fist banging on the panels of the door.

"Open, Jack; hurry!" cried Merrihew outside. There was great agitation in his voice.

Hillard opened the door. "What's the trouble, Dan?" he asked.

Merrihew closed the door and whispered: "Dead!" As the light from the window fell upon his face it disclosed pale cheeks and widely opened eyes.

"Who?" Hillard's heart contracted. "In God's name, who?"

"The prince. They found him and his horse at the bottom of the gorge. There was a broken place in the road, and over this they had gone. The concierge says that there has been foul play. Tracks in the dust, a strange cut in the neck of the horse, and a scabbard minus its saber. Now, what the devil shall I do with the blamed sword?"

Dead! Hillard sat down on the edge of the bed. Dead! Then she was free, free.

"What shall I do with it?" demanded Merrihew a second time.

"The sword? You really brought it?"

"Yes. And if they find us with it—"

"Put it in the bottom of the trunk and leave it there till you land in New York. But the prince dead? You are sure?"

"All Florence is ringing with the story of the ball, the wind-up, and the tragedy. He's dead, no doubt of it. Shall we go up to the villa this morning?"

"No, Dan;" but all the weariness went out of Hillard's eyes.

And then Merrihew noticed. Hillard still wore his evening clothes and the bed was untouched.

"That's very foolish."

"Why? I couldn't have closed my eyes," replied Hillard.

"But won't she need you up there?" Merrihew was obviously troubled.

"If she needs me she'll send for me. But I am not needed, and she will not send for me. I shall remain here and wait."

"He's dead. Things work out queerly, don't they?"

"She is free. Thank God!"

"You are not sorry, are you?"

"Sorry? In a way, yes. He was a blackleg, but it isn't pleasant to contemplate the manner of his end."

"Well, I can frankly say that there's no such sentiment on my side. He'd have cut you down if I hadn't stopped him," said Merrihew, rubbing his swollen knuckles.

"It was measure for measure: I should have killed him had not you and O'Mally interfered."

"That's true. But what's back of all this muddle? Why was she masquerading as an opera singer, when fortune and place were under her hand?"

"She has promised to write."

"By George!"

"What now?"

"Didn't Giovanni tell us that he had friends in Fiesole, and that he was going to visit them?"

"Giovanni? I had forgotten. But what had my old valet against the prince?"

"Giovanni had a daughter," said Merrihew. "His knife left a scar on the man. The prince carried a long scar on his cheek. Two and two make four."

"But Giovanni had promised us."

"If this man did not cross his path. It looks as if he did."

Hillard had nothing to offer. He simply began dressing in his day-clothes, stopping at times and frowning at the walls. Merrihew wisely refrained from adding any questions. He was human; he knew that somewhere in Hillard's breast the fires of hope burned anew.

The day passed without additional news. But at night the last of the American Comic Opera Company straggled into the hotel, plus various pieces of luggage. O'Mally, verbose as ever, did all the talking and vending of news.

"You wouldn't know her," he said, referring to La Signorina—for they would always call her that. "When she heard of that duffer's death I swear that she believed you had a hand in it. But when she heard that the accident had occurred before you left the villa, she just collapsed. Oh, there was a devil of a mess; police agents, *carabinieri*, inspectors. It was a good thing that there were plenty of witnesses to prove that the prince had called La Signorina his wife, or she would be in jail this night, and we along with her. The police were hunting for the missing saber. Of course we knew nothing about it," with a wink at Merrihew. "I don't know what would have happened if her lawyer hadn't hurried up from Rome and straightened out things. Queer business. But she's a princess, all right; and she doesn't need any foreign handle, either. Kitty, you stick to America when you think of getting married."

"I shall," said Kitty demurely.

"My opinion," went on O'Mally, "is that the prince beat his nag out of pure deviltry, and the brute jumped into the gorge with him. The *carabinieri* claim that they saw a man in the gorge. They gave chase, but couldn't find hide nor hair of him."

Merrihew looked significantly at Hillard, who signed to him to be silent.

"I am glad that we can sail Saturday," said Kitty. She was very tired.

"So am I," echoed Smith. "All I want is a heart-to-heart talk with old Broadway. Never again for mine!"

"Go on!" said O'Mally. "You'll be talking about this for the next ten years."

"As to that I don't say. But never my name on a foreign contract again, unless it takes me to London. No more *parle Italiano*. Let's go over to the Grand. There's an American barkeep over there, and he'll sympathize with us."

"You're on!" said O'Mally willingly.

When they were gone, Hillard asked Kitty if she had any news.

"She said that she would write you, and for you to remain here till you received the letter."

"Was that all?"

"Yes. Have you seen anything of that wretched man Worth, who is the cause of all this trouble?"

"No, nor do I care to."

"Suppose the three of us take a stroll along the Lungarno?" suggested Merrihew. "It will be the last chance together."

"You two go. I am worn out," said Hillard. "I had no sleep last night."

So Kitty and Merrihew went out together. They climbed the Ponte Vecchio, leaned against the rail back of the bust of Cellini and contemplated the trembling lights on the sluggish waters.

"I hate to leave him alone," said Merrihew.

Kitty nestled snugly against his arm. "Don't worry about him. It is all well with him."

"How do you know?"

"I am a woman."

"Oh!" A bell crashed out across the river; it was nine

o'clock. "Do you love me, Kitty Killigrew?"

"Very much, Mr. Merrihew."

"But why did you keep me waiting so long?"

"That's one of the few secrets I shall never tell you."

Merrihew pursued his investigations no further. "We shall have to live in a flat."

"I should be happy in a hut. What an adventure we have had! I regret none of it."

"Neither do I." And then, sure of the shadow and the propitiousness of the moment, he kissed her. Kitty would never have forgiven him if he hadn't. "I've bought you a cricket to take home."

"A cricket?"

"Yes. These Florentines consider crickets very lucky, that is, the first you find in May. You put him in a little wire cage and feed him lettuce, and if he sings, why, there's no doubt about the good luck. Funny little codger! Looks like a parson in a frockcoat and an old-fashioned stock."

"Good luck always," said Kitty, brushing his hand with her lips.

They were gone, and Hillard was alone. He missed them all sorely, Merrihew with his cheery laugh, Kitty with her bright eyes, and O'Mally with his harmless drolleries. And no letter. It would not be true to say that he waited patiently, that he was resigned; he waited because he must wait. There had been a great shock, and she required time to recover her poise. Was there a woman in all the world like her? No. She was well worth waiting for. And so he would wait. She was free now; but would that really matter? There was no barrier; but could she love him? And might not her letter, when it did come, be a valedictory?

Daily he searched the newspapers for news of Giovanni; but to all appearances Giovanni had vanished, as indeed he had, for ever out of Hillard's sight and knowledge.

The letter came one week after the departure of his friends. It was post-marked Venice. And the riddle was solved.

Chapter 26 *THE LETTER*

Shall I say that I am sorry? No. I am not a hypocrite. Death in all forms is horrible, and I shudder and regret, but I am not sorry. Does it sound cruel and heartless to express my feelings thus frankly? Well, I am human; I do not pose as being better than I am. I have suffered a grievous wrong. At the hands of this man I lost my illusions, I learned the words hate and loathing, shame and despair. Again I say that I regret the violence of his end, but I am not sorry to be free. If we wait long enough the scales of Heaven will balance nicely. Some outraged father or brother, to this alone do I attribute his death.

Let me be as brief as possible; I have no desire to weary you, only the wish to vindicate in part what appeared to you as a species of madness.

My father was Colonel Grosvenor, of the Confederate army, during the Civil War. On General Lee's staff was an Italian named the Principi di Monte Bianca. He was an Arab for wandering. The tumult of battle would bring him round the world. Rich, titled, a real noble, he was at heart an adventurer, a word greatly abused these inglorious days. For does not the word adventurer stand for the pioneer, the explorer, the inventor, the soldier and the sailor? It is wrong to apply the word to the impostor. My father was cut from the same pattern, a wild and reckless spirit in those crowded times. The two became friends such as you and Mr. Merrihew are. Their exploits became famous. My father was also rich and a man of foresight. He knew that the stars and bars was a flag of temporary endurance. All that portion of his wealth which remained in the South he readily sacrificed with his blood. His real wealth was in foreign securities, mines, oils, steel, steamships. When the war terminated, the prince prevailed upon my father to return with him to Italy. Italy was not new to my father; and as he loved the country and spoke the language, he finally consented. He saw the shadow of the reconstruction and dreaded it; and there were no ties of blood to hold him in the States. Italy itself was in turmoil. *Il Re Galantuomo*, that Piedmontese hunter, Vittorio Emanuele, wished to liberate Venice from the grasp of Austria, to wrest temporal power from the Vatican, and to send the French troops back to France. Well, he accomplished all these things, and both my father and the prince were with him up to the time he entered the Quirinal. After victory, peace. My father invested in villas and palaces, added to his fortune through real estate in Rome, lived in Florence a little while, and settled down to end his days in the Venetian palace on the Grand Canal. He and the prince met daily at Florian's and planned futures or dreamed over the noisy past.

Then my father, still young, remember, fell in love with the daughter of a Venetian noble. It was a happy union. Shortly after the prince also married. He was, with the exception of my father, the most lovable man I ever knew. Brave, kindly, impetuous, honorable, witty and wise; it does not seem possible that such a father should have such a son. Though he covered it up with all the rare tact of a man of the world, his marital ties were not happy like my father's.

There came a great day: a young prince was born, and the rough king stood as his god-father. Later I added my feeble protest, at the cost of my mother's life. These domestic histories! how far more vital to the welfare of nations than the flaming pages of war and politics! As I grew up I became my father's constant companion; we were always out of doors. By and by he sent me to America to school; for he still loved his country and was not that fault-finding scold, the expatriate. And I may as well add that your defense of America pleased me as few things have in these later years. I returned from America to enter a convent out of Rome. From there I went to Milan and studied music under the masters. My father believed in letting youth choose what it would. Music! What should I have done without it in the dark hours?

One fatal day the old prince and my father put their heads together and determined that this great friendship of theirs should be perpetuated; the young prince should marry the young signorina. When will parents learn not to meddle with the destinies of their children? So they proceeded to make the alliance an absolute certainty. They drew up the strangest of wills. Both men were in full control of their properties; there was no entailed estate such as one finds in England. They could do as they pleased; and this was before Italy had passed the law requiring that no art treasures should be sold or transported. Fortunately for me, my mother's property was considerable.

The impossible clauses in the joint will read that if we two young people declined the bargain the bulk of the estates should revert to the crown; again, if we married and separated and were not reunited inside of five years, the fortunes should become the crown's; if, having separated from my husband, either for just or unjust reasons, I should secretly or publicly occupy any villa or palace mentioned in the will, it would be a tacit admission that I accepted my husband. Was there ever such an insane tangle kindly meant? We must marry, we must be happy; that our minds and hearts were totally different did not matter at all. Do you understand why I went from city to city, living haphazard? Sometimes I was very poor, for my income from my mother's estate was paid quarterly, and I did not inherit my father's business ability. During the recent days in Venice I had to offer my jewels because I dared not write my attorneys for an advance, for I did not wish them to know where I was.

Time went on. How young I was in those days! What dreams I dreamed! The old prince died suddenly, his wife followed. And then my kind and loving father went the way. I was very, very lonely. But I was taken under the wing of a duchessa who was popular at court. At this period the young prince was one of the handsomest men in Europe. Foolish women set about to turn his head. He was brave, clever and engaging. Dissipation had not yet enmeshed him. My heart fluttered naturally when I saw him, for he was permitted to see me at intervals. Young girls have dreams which in older years appear ordinary enough. He was then to me Prince Charming. I was really glad that I was to marry him.

On completing my education I decided to live in Rome, where the prince was quartered. I went into the world with serene confidence, believing that all men were good like my father and his friend. The old duchessa mothered the rich American girl gladly; for, though I was half Italian, they always considered me as the child of my father. I was presented at court, I was asked to dinners and receptions and balls. I was quite the rage because the dowager queen gave me singular attention. My head was in a whirl. In Europe, as you know, till a woman is married she is a nonentity. I was beginning to live. The older women were so attentive and the men so gallant that I lost sight of the things that counted. As I was a fluent linguist, and as I possessed a natural lightness of heart, my popularity was by no means due to my property. I believe I sang wherever I went, because I loved music, because it was beautiful to send one's voice across space in confidence; it was like liberating the soul for a moment.

The prince by this time seemed changed in some way; but I was blindly young. A girl of twenty in European society knows less than a girl of fifteen in the States. Often I noticed the long scar on his cheek. He had received it, he said, in some cavalry exercise. As the Italians are reckless horsemen, I accepted this explanation without question. I know differently now! But he was as courteous and gallant to me as ever.

Now, there was another clause in this will. It was the one thing which made the present life tolerable and possible to me. We were to be married without pomp, quietly, first at the magistrate's and then at the church.

Have you not often seen the carriage pass you in the streets? The bride in her white dress and veil and the bouquet of roses? The ribbon round the driver's whip? The good-natured smiles of the idlers, the children running out and crying for a rose? They say that a rose given by the bride brings luck. It was thus we passed through the streets to the magistrate's. I did not know then that I was not in love, that I was only young and curious. I threw roses to any who asked. The prince sat beside me in full-dress uniform, looking very handsome and distinguished. We heard many compliments. The prince smiled, but he was nervous and not at ease. I thought nothing of this at the time. I believed his nervousness a part of my own. To be sure there was a fair gathering at the magistrate's, for the name of Monte Bianca was widely known. But there was none of our own class present; they would be at the church.

The magistrate performed his part in the affair. Legally we were man and wife. We were leaving for the church, when at the very doorway a handsome woman, sad-eyed, weary, shabbily dressed, touched me on the arm.

"A rose, Signora!"

I gave it to her, smiling pityingly.

"God pray," she said, "that this man will make you happier than he made me!"

The prince was at my elbow, pushing me toward the carriage. But something had been said that could not be lightly passed. I stood firm.

"Let us be on!" said the prince eagerly.

"Wait!" I turned to the woman. "Signora, what do you mean by those words?"

"His Highness knows." She pointed to the prince, whose face I now saw, strangely enough, for the first time. It was black with rage and ugliness.

"What has he been to you?" I demanded.

She answered with a gesture, pathetic but easily translatable. It was enough for me. I understood. In that moment I became a woman without illusions. Without looking at the prince I entered the carriage and closed the door in his face. He stormed, he pleaded, he lied. I was of stone. There was a scene. He was low enough to turn upon the poor woman and strike her across the face with his gloves. Even had I loved him, that would have been the end of the romance. I ordered the driver to take me home. There would be no wedding at the church that day. There was a great scandal. Every one took up the prince's cause, with the exception of the king. But my determination was not to be moved.

The prince was almost bankrupt. He had squandered the liberal fortune left him independently of the will. He had sold to the Jews half of the fortune he expected to get after marrying me. He had not the slightest affection for me; he was desperate and wanted the money. How old and wise I became during that ride home from the magistrate's! The prince called, but I was not at home to him. He wrote many times, but I replied to none of his letters. He struck but one string; I was foolish to let a little peccadillo of bachelorhood stand in the way; all men were the same; the position I took was absurd. I never answered. I returned to Venice. I have seen him but twice since; once at Monte Carlo and that night at the Villa Ariadne. How he begged, schemed, plotted, and manoeuvered to regain my favor! But I knew now. I vowed he should never have a penny; it should all go to the crown.

When at length he found that I was really serious, he became base in his tactics. *He* was the one who was wronged. He gave life to such rumors among those I knew that soon I found doors closed to me which had always been open. No Italian woman could see the matter from my point of view. I was an American for all that my mother was a Venetian, therefore I was wrong.

So great was this man's vanity that he truly believed that all he had to do was to meet me face to face to overcome my objections! I have already told you that my impulses are as mysterious to me as to others. Why I went to the Villa Ariadne is not to be explained. I do not know.... A comic opera singer! But I shall always love those light-hearted companions, who were cheerful under misfortune, who accepted each new calamity as a jest by the Great Dramatist. Perhaps the truth is, this last calamity was brought about by my desire to aid them without letting them know who I was. I have committed many foolish acts, but innocent and hurtless. To you I have been perfectly frank. From the first I warned you; and many times I have given you hurts which recoiled upon my own head. But all for your good. I wanted you to be clear of the tangle. There! That is all. There is no more mystery concerning Sonia Hilda Grosvenor.

And so the letter ended. There was not a word regarding any future meeting; there was nothing to read between the lines. A great loneliness surged over Hillard. Was this, then, really the end? No! He struck the letter sharply on his palm. No, this should not be the end. He would wait here in Florence till the day of doom. He would waste no time in seeking her, for he knew that if he sought he would not find.

Day after day dragged through the hours, and Florence grew thinned and torrid. Sometimes he rode past the Villa Ariadne, but he never stopped. He could not bring himself to enter those confines again alone.

In the meantime he had received a cable from Merrihew, stating that he and Mrs. Merrihew would be at home after September. He read the line many times. Good old Dan! He was right; it took patience and persistence to win a woman.

It was in the middle of June that, one afternoon, the concierge handed him a telegram. It contained but three words:

"Villa Serbelloni, Bellaggio."

Chapter 27 BELLAGGIO

The narrowness of the imagination of the old masters is generally depicted in their canvases. Heaven to them was a serious business of pearly gates, harps, halos, and aërial flights on ambient pale clouds. Or, was it the imagination of the Church, dominating the imagination of the artist? To paint halos, or to starve? was doubtless the Hamletonian question of the Renaissance. Now Hillard's idea of Heaven—and in all of us it is a singular conception—was Bellaggio in perpetual springtime; Bellaggio, with its cypress, copper-beech, olive, magnolia, bamboo, pines, its gardens, its vineyards, its orchards of mulberry trees, its restful reaches, for there is always a quality of rest in the ability to see far off; Bellaggio, with the emerald Lecco on one side and the blue-green Como on the other, the white villages nestling along the shores, and the great shadowful Italian Alps.

The Villa Serbelloni stands on the wooded promontory, and all day long the warm sunshine floods its walls and terraces and glances from the polished leaves of the tropical plants. The villa remains to-day nearly as it was when Napoleon's forces were in Milan and stabling their horses in the monastery of Santa Maria delle Grazia, under the fading *Last Supper*, by Da Vinci. It is a hotel now, the annex of one of the great hostelries down below in the town. A tortuous path leads up to the villa; and to climb it is to perform the initial step or lesson to proper mountain-climbing. Here and there, in the blue distances, one finds a patch of snow, an exhilarating foretaste of the high Alps north of Domo d' Ossola and south of the icy Rhone.

The six-o'clock boat from Como puffed up noisily and

smokily to the quay, churning her side-paddles. The clouds of sunset lay like crimson gashes on the western mountain peaks. Hillard stepped ashore impatiently. What a long day it had been! How white the Villa Serbelloni seemed up there on the little hill-top. He gave his luggage to the porter from the Grand and followed him on foot to the hotel, which was only a dozen steps from the landing. No, he would not dine at the hotel, all but empty at this time of year. He was dining at the Villa Serbelloni above. He dressed quickly, but with the lover's care and the lover's doubt. Less than an hour after leaving the boat he stepped forth from the gardens and took the path up to the villa. The bloom on the wings of the passing swallow, the clouds on the face of the smooth waters, the incense from the flowers now rising upon the vanished sun, the tinted crests encircling, and the soft wind which murmured drowsily among the overhanging branches, all these made the time and place as perfect as a lover's mind could fancy.

Sonia, Sonia; his step took the rhythm of it as he climbed. Sonia, Sonia; the very silence seemed to voice it. And she was waiting for him up there. How would she greet him, knowing that nothing would have brought him to her side but the hope of love? With buoyant step he turned by the porter's lodge and strode down the broad roadway to the villa, a deepening green arch above him.

Handsome he was not; he was more. With his thin, high-bred face, his fine eyes, his slender, graceful figure, he presented that type of gentleman to whom all women pay unconscious homage, whether low-born or high, and in whom the little child places its trust and confidence.

He arrived shortly. As he entered the glass-inclosed

corridor the concierge rose from his chair and bowed. Hillard inclined his head and went on. There was no one in the dining-room. In the restaurant there was no one but a lonely Russian countess, who had spent part of the year at the villa for more than a decade. He doffed his hat as he passed through the room and gained the picturesque terrace. Afar he saw a table spread under the great oak. A woman sat by it. She was gazing down the winding terraces toward the Lecco. It was still daylight, and he would have known that head of hair among the ten thousand houris of heaven. Softly, softly! he murmured to his heart, now become insurgent.

Whatever may have been the dream she was following, she dismissed it upon hearing his step, strangely familiar. She did not rise, but she extended her hand, a grave inquiry in her slumbrous eyes. With equal gravity he clasped the hand, but held back the impulse to kiss it. He was not quite sure of himself just then. He sat down opposite her and, smiling, whimsically inquired:

"Now, where did we leave off?"

At first she did not understand.

He enlightened her. "I refer to that Arabian Nights entertainment in New York. Where did we leave off that interesting discussion?"

She smiled brightly. "We shall take up the thread of that discourse with the coffee."

"Why not countermand the order for dinner? I am not hungry."

"But I am," she replied. She was wholly herself now. The tact with which he began his address disembarrassed her. For two days, since she despatched the telegram, she had lived in a kind of ecstatic terror; she had even regretted the message, once it was beyond recall. "I am human enough to be hungry, sometimes." She summoned the waiter.

The dinner was excellent, but Hillard scarcely knew what this or that plate was. All his hunger lay in his eyes. Besides, he did not want to discuss generalities during the intermittent invasions of the waiter, who never knew how many times he stood in danger of being hurled over into the flowering beds of lavender which banked the path of the second terrace. And when he brought the coffee and lingered for further orders, it was Hillard who dismissed him, rather curtly.

"Now! Let me see," he said musingly. "We had agreed that it would be best never to meet again, that to keep the memory of that night fresh in our minds, a souvenir for old age, it were wisest to part then. Well, we can keep the memory of it for our old age; it will be a little secret between us, and we shall talk it over on just such nights as this."

"Isn't this oak the most beautiful you have ever seen?" she remarked, looking up at the great leafy arms above her head.

"The most beautiful in all the world;" but he was not looking at the oak.

"Think of it! It's many centuries old. Empires and kingdoms have risen and vanished. It was here when Michelangelo and Raphael and Titian were ragamuffins in the populous streets; it was leafing when Petrarch indited pages to his Laura; when Dante gazed melancholily upon his Beatrice— Oh, what a little time we have!"

"Then let us make the most of it," he said.

He reached for her hand, which lay upon the cover; but, without apparent notice of his movement, she drew back her hand.

"I have waited patiently for weeks."

She faced him with an enigmatical smile, lighted a match, blew it out, and drew a line across the center of the table.

He laughed. "What, again?"

"Observe."

"Why, there is a break in it!" eagerly and joyously.

She leaned over. "So there is;" but there was no surprise in her voice.

"Is it possible for me to come through?"

"There is one way."

"Put the caskets before me, Portia; I shall not be less wise than Bassanio."

She touched her lips with the knuckle of a finger, in a mood reflective. "A camel and the needle's eye."

"That referred to the rich man. All the world loves a lover, even the solemn old prophets."

"Are you sure?" a return of the old malice.

As a rejoinder he smoothed out the telegram she had sent to him. "Why did you send this to me?"

Her lips had no answer ready; and who can read a woman's heart?

"There can be but one reason," he pursued.

"Friendship."

There was a swish of petticoats, and she was standing at the side of her chair. The beginning of the night was cool, but the fire of the world's desire burned in her cheeks, and she was afraid. She stepped to the railing, faced the purpling mountains, lifted her chin, and sang *Die Zauberflöte*. And Hillard dared not touch her till the last note was gone. She felt his nearness, however, as surely as if he had in fact touched her. She tried to sing again, but this time no sound issued from her throat. There was something intangibly hypnotic in his gaze, for presently, without will, she turned and tried to look coldly into his eyes.

"I did not come here because of friendship," he said. "Only one thing brought me—love and the hope of love."

She stared at him, her hand at her throat.

"Love and the hope of love," he repeated. Then he took her in his arms suddenly, hungrily, even roughly. "You are mine, mine; and nothing in the world shall take you from my arms again. Sonia?"

"Don't!" she cried breathlessly. "He is looking."

"It is only a waiter; he doesn't count. Friendship?" He laughed.

"Please!" still struggling.

"Not till you tell me why you sent that telegram."

She pressed her palms against him and stood away. She looked bravely into his eyes now.

"I sent it because I wanted you, because I am tired of lying to my heart, because I have a right to be happy, because—because I love you! Take me, and oh! be good and kind to me, for I have been very lonely and unhappy…. Kiss me!" with a touch of the old imperiousness.

The rim of the early moon shouldered above the frowning death-mask of Napoleon, the huge salmon-tinted mountain on the far side of the Lecco. In the villages the day-sounds had given way to the more peaceful voices of the night. They could hear the occasional light laughter of the gardeners on the second terrace; the bark of a dog in the hills; from the house of the silk-weaver came the tinkle of a guitar. In the houses on the hill opposite and in the villages below the first lights of evening began to glimmer, now here, now there, like fireflies become stationary.

"See Naples and die," she whispered, "but the spirit will come to Bellaggio."

THE END

Lightning Source UK Ltd.
Milton Keynes UK
UKHW021935270519
343408UK00003B/111/P